Tangled Vines of Good Intentions

Tangled Vines of Good Intentions

By Kay Lee

This is a work of fiction. All the characters, organizations, and events portrayed in this novel are either products of the author's imagination or are used fictitiously.

Tangled Vines of Good Intentions © 2019 by Kay Lee.
All rights reserved.

Printed in the United States of America

Published by Author Academy Elite PO Box 43, Powell, OH 43035
www.AuthorAcademyElite.com

All rights reserved. This book contains material protected under International and Federal Copyright Laws and Treaties. Any unauthorized reprint or use of this material is prohibited. No part of this book may be reproduced or transmitted in any form or by any means, electronic or mechanical, including photocopying, recording, or by any information storage and retrieval system, without express written permission from the author.

Identifiers:

Library of Congress Control Number: 2019918570

ISBN: 978-1-64746-024-2 (paperback)

ISBN: 978-1-64746-025-9 (hardcover)

ISBN: 978-1-64746-026-6 (ebook)

Available in paperback, hardcover and e-book

Book design by Jetlaunch. Cover design by GoldenLionDesign.

Dedication

Dedicated to my real-life Gert, Evie, Eddie and Brian. Thanks for bringing me home.
Thanks for loving me.
Thanks for always supporting my creative side.
I am grateful for you, every single day.

Foreword

Author Kay Lee is fearless and bold in her approach as she tells a story of loss, grief, despair, forgiveness, grace, and healing. Her honest and touching approach is non-judgmental and graceful, while at the same time forthright and direct—a rare balance seen in today's world; and she maintains that equilibrium throughout her novel, allowing the reader to question their own judgment upon each character's motives and actions. "Maybe we're not so different after all," she suggests.

And because Kay has found that symmetry and sure footing, she's been able produce a brilliant manuscript that is universal in its message, familiar in its content, and healing in its result. To write and truly understand what it feels like to be adopted will only become whole in its fullest and honest nature if one has been there themselves. Kay understands, having not only been adopted at birth, but also having never been able to locate her biological parents. She's lives it, along with all of the questions, hurts, and emotions of somehow feeling out of place.

We live in a world where topics such as adoption are many times overshadowed by what the world views as more important, more pressing issues. As a result, Kay had two choices: give up, and believe the lie that a story such as this wouldn't make a difference, or revisit her past, feel the pain and desperate emotions, and write it all down—all for the benefit of others who think that no one else understands.

She chose the latter, and Tangled Vines of Good Intentions is the result.

A brilliant novel of family tragedy and pain balanced with colorful characters, honest dialogue, and graceful victory, Tangled Vines of Good Intentions takes the reader along a journey where surprise twists and turns are scattered throughout the pages, and where what you think is real is certainly not what it appears.

I encourage you to come join Kay on this relevant journey and revelation. You might just see a bit of you, or someone you know, within the pages of this incredible novel; and in doing so, you might just take a hold of forgiveness and grace, and finally decide to let go of any judgment or grudges, whether conscience or not, that was festering in your heart.

—Russ Womack, Author of Orange

Cassandra

As she slowly opened her eyes on the morning of January 23, 2010, she looked around and took it all in. There were beautiful flowers on her nightstand; purple roses with large leafy green accents, and she could smell pancakes from the kitchen. This was a great start. The sun was shining, despite the cold, dry, January air. She sat up and peeled back the layers of goose down that lay on top of her. As she took in a deep breath, she smiled, and a little flicker of excitement ran through her. She felt ready, not different than the day before, but still ready. Cassie threw on her robe and headed out to see Gram.

"Happy Birthday, Love!" Gram shouted with glee. There were two mylar purple and silver birthday balloons tied to her chair at the kitchen table. The table was set, and the first batch of pancakes was keeping warm in the oven.

"Thank you. Beautiful flowers, Gram." After giving the chef a big squeeze, Cassie went to the table to take her seat. As she got closer, she saw a letter with her name on it. The envelope

Tangled Vines of Good Intentions

was off-white and looked more like stationery than a regular mailing envelope. Cassie thought it might be another love letter from Gram, until she looked closer. As she approached the table, she could see it was worn-looking; there was no stamp or return address, and it was sealed.

"What's this, Gram?" Cassie asked with excitement in her voice.

"That is a letter for you." Gram was short and didn't turn to face Cassie as she responded.

Cassie looked at it for a second, and then decided to open it up and check it out. The letter was a few pages, handwritten, but she couldn't place the handwriting. It was dated January 26th, but the year was 18 years ago. A little stunned, Cassie sat down and began reading the letter.

To our precious baby girl,

Today we brought you home from the hospital, introduced you to your brother, and welcomed you into our hearts. We have created a room for you with a crib that your grandparents bought you and have plans to paint the walls pink.

Your brother drew you a special picture and we hung it on your bedroom door. Today you completed our family and we couldn't be happier. We are sharing all this with you because it is important that you know how loved you are. All the people in your life are happy that you are here, and truly want good things for you in the future.

We have some news to tell you. Today we made a decision, together as your parents, to write this letter for your 18th birthday. We can only hope that you have had a wonderful time in this life. We want the best for you and hope that you feel our love on your special day.

Cassandra

Cassandra, today we brought you home from the hospital after a closed adoption process. Some friends of ours who worked in the nursery told us just two days ago that you were up for adoption. Your father and I went to see you, and knew that we wanted you in our home, to be our daughter.

The decision not to tell you was a very difficult one for us. Together we decided that we wouldn't want you growing up thinking that you were different, or not as important to us. You are our daughter, no matter who gave birth to you.

When her eyes were too blurry to continue reading, Cassie blinked the overflow onto a puddle on the table. She was not sure if she was breathing. The sound of her throbbing heart filled her head and her ears. She started to go completely numb. Slowly, she picked her head up from the letter. Gram looked at her like she was a poor lost dog but didn't approach her. The seconds felt like hours as her world came crashing down in slow motion.

Why was Gram looking at her? Why was she not curious? How long had she known? And with that, Cassie stood up and stumbled to her room. She slammed the door and threw herself on her bed. Curled in a fetal position, she let the pain and confusion consume her as she shuddered with tears and sobbed into her pillow.

Eddie

It was finally April 1984 and college graduation was only one week away. Eddie and his friends were off to the lake for their last camping weekend. At 22 years old, they were still kids; even so, they couldn't recognize who they were when they started school four short years ago. They threw back beers and sat around the campfire each telling a story more hilarious than the last.

"Remember that weekend we went to the mountain?" Jef was cut off mid-sentence as Kenny picked up on his memory.

"You mean when we got drunk and put a mattress on the floor under the balcony so we could take turns jumping off?" Kenny roared.

"Well, I was gonna say, when we put the mattress in the middle of the floor so we could wrestle like the heavyweights, using aluminum pans as props!" Jef added.

"Don't you remember that good weed we got from Richard's cousin? I swear I was seeing things!" Chuck said

"Pretty sure everyone was seeing things, except you Johnny! What happened?" Richard elbowed his friend to continue the story, knowing full well what happened.

"Sure guys, laugh it up. I was out for the rest of the season after that." Johnny shook his head at the thought.

"We should have put the mattress at the bottom of the stairs apparently!" Richard had the whole group laughing again.

"Richie, I was sleep walking man, I swear. I never even opened my eyes till I was at the bottom." Johnny joined in with the laughter.

"And you're welcome for making you that splint for the ride home," Eddie said with a grin.

Their laughter carried through the darkness and over the calm water. The fire crackled and sizzled brightly, lighting the joy and smiles on their youthful faces. The guys had been escaping to the lake to camp since their freshman year. They were all roommates when they came to school, and best friends by the end of their first semester. Lake trips were for thinking and not thinking, for laughing, and for letting off steam. They were always together, going through this phase of their lives. This was one of the things Eddie would miss the most. He always had camaraderie with his two brothers growing up, and when he moved out of state for college, the bonds with his schoolmates filled that void. Now, as the world was fighting to survive the mid-80s, the guys would be graduating and doing their best to keep up on their own. Some were continuing school, hoping find direction in life after they earned their Masters. Others were returning home to hunt for jobs, trying to make their parents proud, and figuring out how to navigate life on their own. They all felt like the real world was knocking; time to strap in and hang on. They would all be scattering throughout New England. Now Eddie would have just one comrade.

Perhaps the most important of all the people in his world, Eddie would be spending the next phase of his life with his love, Evie. He knew what they had was powerful and was really looking forward to the adventures to come in the story of their life together. She was his support system, his partner, and the person he wanted to wake up to every day for the rest of his forever.

As his friend Chuck nudged him, Eddie shook his head and instantly realized he was lost in thought over Evie.

"Hey, Ed! Come in, Ed!" Chuck laughed.

"I'm here. Sorry. Hey, remember that time we went ice fishing?" Eddie tried to recover but his mind was floating.

The group busted out laughing, but they all knew that he was deeply in love with Evie. The two met sophomore year in an anatomy class. They were partnered together in frog dissection. Eddie looked at the lifeless animal and flashed back to his childhood. He and his brothers running effortlessly around in the heat of the summer, playing ball, tag, and finishing their days at the frog pond. He hesitated, and when Eddie just couldn't make the first cut, Evie was quick to take the lead.

Her beauty caught him off guard. Clear pearlescent skin and enchanting green eyes were draped in golden locks with hints of brilliant red. She had a soft and slightly rounded face that exploded to life when she smiled her big bright smile. Not too tall, or too skinny, her rounded hips were often the culprit for untimely excitement from Eddie. Her beauty was classic and understated. Evie was strong-willed and determined. It was sheer coincidence that they were both from the same state, just an hour away from each other. Eddie always thought she could have lived clear across the country, it wouldn't matter—he was meant to cross paths with this girl. They were meant to be.

They both went home after their first year at college and were inseparable. They met each other's family and shared stories and laughs about their childhood. They spent time talking. Eddie loved to share with her and listen to her point of view on things. Walking the local mountain trail, was usually when Eddie would get a glimpse into Evie's childhood.

"I remember sneaking some of my dad's alcohol and drinking up here with my friends," Evie confessed.

"When was this?" Eddie was surprised.

"During summer break from school, mostly."

"I bet your dad was furious!" Eddie said, actually amazed that she would risk something like that.

"He never knew. I was just that slick!"

"Or lucky! I never got away with anything. There was always one of them that knew something or thought they did and forced us into a confession. They were tough," Eddie said. They found a clearing, and he spread a blanket on the high green grass. "Do you ever want to go back?" Eddie hesitated, not really sure what he was trying to ask.

"What? Back where?" Evie's eyes were big with curiosity.

"Do you ever wish you could go back to when you were a kid?" He clarified.

"Hell no. How about you?"

"Sometimes. I miss being with my brothers and always having them by my side. They would usually take the fall for me, if I was late for curfew, or pulled some stupid prank at school! It just feels like it is all moving so fast. But I love college, don't get me wrong. I just was happy back then too." Eddie closed his eyes and soaked up the warm sunshine.

Evie sat up quickly, breaking their peaceful position to face Eddie full on. "I earned college. Always being forced to do what they wanted me to. Never having anyone who understood me. It was suffocating. I need space, I need air, and I need to think without my parents telling me what to think. I wouldn't go back for anything," Evie said assuredly.

"I hear you! You are woman, hear you roar! Fly like an eagle Evie!" Eddie snickered. He didn't think twice about her need to be independent. They were together and that was it.

He had no intention of treating her like her parents did. He loved her just the way she was.

"Joke all you want, but start smothering me Dodd, and you will see how fast I can run," Evie said.

"Oh, beautiful woman, all I want to do is smother you." With that, Eddie rolled over, pulled her down and covered her body with his. His face was inches above hers, and he ran his fingers through her long waves. Her hair was silky and shined brilliantly in the afternoon sun. He looked deep into her eyes and admired the intricate flecks of green and light brown that created the stunning color of her eyes. He ran his hand down her plump, youthful cheek, and slowly lowered his head for a sweet kiss. As he landed on her soft lips, she spread them a bit and sucked in his lower lip, and then proceeded to bite him.

"Ouch! Oh, that's how it's gonna be, huh?" Still on top of her, he knew he easily had 50 pounds on her and would win this fight. He moved both her hands to the top of her head and pinned them with one of his. Showing no mercy, he launched a full tickle attack on her under-arms and sides of her stomach.

"Aahhh!! Eddie…stop…it…tickles," Evie said through deep laughter that brought tears to her eyes. He listened to her wails and shrieks and hoped the ranger wasn't anywhere in earshot.

Both Eddie and Evie were on track to graduate with a bachelor's degree in nursing and wanted to continue to get their graduate degrees. Their young love was effortless. They were both strong students, had intentions of continuing their education, and enjoyed a variety of outdoor activities in their down time. They even watched baseball together from time to time. This was all they needed; they were living in the moment. There was nothing to worry about or argue over, only fun to be had and time to be spent together.

They moved into off-campus housing together the second semester of their junior year. Both had full class schedules and jobs at the local clinic. Eddie was always very focused on his work and often made more time for work and less for play. He knew full well that his grades would suffer if it were any other way. Evie was a quick learner and played equally as hard as she worked. Many nights she'd stumble back into the apartment to find Eddie up with his nose buried in a textbook. It wasn't until she was standing right in front of him, slowly stripping off each layer of clothing and letting it fall to the floor, that he even noticed she was there. The allure of alcohol on her breath and the sight of her full breasts at his eye level ripped him from his work and shifted his complete focus to caressing her body. It was as if he'd never been studying at all.

    He wrapped his arms around her waist and buried his face in her chest. While gently sucking and biting at her nipples, his free hand caressed her full breast until his woman was moaning with pleasure. Eddie stood over her and kissed a trail up her chest, to her neck, to her cheek, before settling on her perfect earlobe. All the while she clawed at his back in pleasure. She stumbled to remove her shoes, but before she knew it, he swept her off her feet and started toward the bedroom. Without flipping on the light, he gently laid her on the bed and showered her with deep loving kisses. His tongue filled her mouth, which drove Evie crazy.

    "Baby, I am so wet. Stop teasing me. I need it. I need you," she cried out. And with that they made love until they were both too exhausted to continue and fell asleep cradled in each other's arms, clothes on the floor, book open on the desk.

    He couldn't get enough of her. Christmas break of their senior year, Eddie made his way to Evie's house to speak with her father about marriage. The sweat was starting to bead on his forehead as he pulled up to their house, knowing that Evie was out shopping. It was dinner time, and he was certain he would be interrupting. As he rang the bell, he thought for a split second that he should run and hide, but he was not quick enough or perhaps too nervous to move, and the door swung open as he stood there. Evie's mother greeted him with a friendly, but confused expression.

"Good evening, ma'am." Eddie thought he heard himself stutter.

"Why, hello, Ed. You know that Evie is out with friends for the evening?" Sally said.

"Yes, ma'am. I was hoping to speak to Mr. Somers for a moment." Eddie fidgeted with his fingers.

"Um, sure. We just sat down to eat steak and mashed potatoes. Are you hungry?"

Although Eddie was starving, he did not want to get distracted from his mission. "No, thank you. This should only take a minute of your time." Eddie shuffled in to see Bud, Evie's father, already digging into his hot meal. He didn't verbally acknowledge his guest.

"Hello Mr. Somers. Looks delicious." With that Sally had a plate in her hand and started serving Eddie.

"I insist. You are much too skinny, anyhow," Sally said with a stern look in her eye. Evie got her green eyes from her mother. They were a warm color, and Eddie knew better than to argue. The three sat in silence for what felt like an eternity.

The Somers' home always felt tense. It was well decorated throughout, with an opulent chandelier above the dark mahogany eight-person dining table. The kitchen had a new oven and matching goldenrod refrigerator, which looked regal set in the real wood paneled cabinetry. Sally was a woman of taste. The living room, set off from the grand dining room and kitchen, had two chairs and a small couch covered in plastic. Even the couch cushions were covered. There were several antique coffee tables that displayed crystal figurines and candy dishes. But it was more about what he didn't see that struck Eddie as odd. Evie was their only child and Eddie could remember just two pictures of her displayed in their home. Next to one of the chairs was a silver picture frame showing off a young Evie with two tight braids draping behind her shoulders, her smile barely visible. The other was her high school graduation portrait. It was large and hung in the hallway to the bedrooms at the back of the house. Her hair was pinned up and she was decorated with pearl earrings and a matching necklace. She looked miserable and stunning all at the same time. Still, there were no paintings, or drawings, or diplomas on the walls. Eddie never saw any handmade items that looked like they could have been gifts from a child, and if there were any stuffed animals or dolls ever in that home, they were extinct before Eddie arrived. The house had no warmth.

Eddie could only half enjoy Sally's good cooking knowing he still had a job to do. As he sat at the oversized table, sculpting his potatoes, he knew his window of opportunity was closing.

"What can I do you for, Ed?" Bud said. Eddie watched as he rubbed his belly and loosened the clasp on his belt.

The voice in Eddie's head was screaming, now or never! "Well Mr. Somers, as you know, Evie and I will be graduating soon and moving to New York to continue our schooling. We are very much in love and I am completely committed to her happiness."

There was no movement from Bud, no facial expression, as Eddie prattled on, terrified to ask the real question. "I am interested in building a future with Evie, a long and happy future. And I believe our future starts with marriage. I came here this evening to ask you, and Mrs. Somers of course, if you would be ok with…I mean if you would support the union of your daughter and me?" Eddie exhaled, not aware that he was holding his breath. When no one moved, or spoke, he felt a wave of panic. "I mean, I know we have only been together for two years, and we have to stay focused on classes, and we are still pretty young…"

"Ed, stop talking," Bud interrupted. He obliged and was grateful to have someone else do the talking. "Ed, you seem like a fine young man. You have a good head on your shoulders.

Tangled Vines of Good Intentions

You two seem very good together. But let me tell you young man, life gets much harder. There are challenges in your future that you can't even imagine. You and your manhood, and your devotion will be tested and stretched to limits you have not yet seen. And so I ask you, Ed, what will you do when things get hard? Who will you run to for help? Who will you trust to get you out of a jam?" Bud did not seem to be playing around, and the expectant look on his face clued Eddie into the fact that he was awaiting a response.

"Uhhh…I…I will work as hard as I can to provide for your daughter, Sir. I would like to think that if we face challenges as a team, then we can get through them successfully together." Eddie knew it sounded corny, but this was a statement that he believed in. He knew he could and would love her through all of their ups and downs.

"Well if you are sure about that, then I suggest you ask Evie and see if she will have you."

Mrs. Somers let out a little shriek of excitement as she hopped up and stretched her arms out to Eddie. He appreciated the reassuring squeeze, but part of him was coming to realize that this may not have been the hardest part of this process.

On the drive back to his house, Eddie replayed what had just occurred. After dinner he couldn't get out of there fast enough. When Eddie pulled into his parents' driveway it was dark. He could smell the smoke from his father's pipe the second he opened the car door. Eddie made his way to the patio where his father was smoking peacefully in the faint glow of the house lights. "Hey, Dad."

"Son."

Eddie regarded his father as an easy-going man. Raising three boys was a test of patience, and his father always proved to have far more than his mother. Most impressive to Eddie was the way his father seemed to understand how his children's minds worked, and was never mad for very long, no matter what kind of trouble they found themselves in.

Eddie

"Dad, I would like to ask Evie to marry me." Eddie felt it best to cut to the chase. He was still trying to unwind from his anxiety filled meal.

"I assume you mentioned this to Mr. Somers?" Mr. Dodd liked to stick to tradition and was always making sure his boys were gentlemen.

"I was just with them. Both he and Mrs. gave me their blessing." Eddie said proudly, as a smile spread across his face making him look exactly as young as he was. He took a seat on the picnic bench next to his dad. Eddie felt his father's strong hands pat him on the shoulders in a congratulatory fashion. He looked over at him as he puffed his pipe. His dad was looking long and hard at him, too.

"It makes me proud to see my boys turning into men and loving beautiful, good natured women. I know you think you are ready. But there is something about being a husband and loving a wife that you can never be ready for. You think at this moment you will never love another as deeply, and you could never love this one more. Let me tell you, you are wrong. As time goes by you will love her more with each passing second. Sure, you'll fight. You may want to turn your back on her and give up. But you won't, because you love her too much, and because there probably isn't another woman out there that will put up with your crap. And if that woman gives you the gift of a child, then you are forever grateful. When you look into that baby's eyes you will literally feel your heart swelling. And you will know that you love that little person as much as you love your wife, and you will spend the rest of your life protecting them. It is hard. It is beautiful. And I am sure you are not ready, but you have to start sometime. I am thrilled for you, Son." Eddie took his father's hand as he offered him a firm handshake. "Now, let's see what your mother thinks of all this." Mr. Dodd led the way back to the house.

Eddie could see his mother through the kitchen window as they approached. He suspected that she was about to make herself a cup of coffee and settle in to watch her evening program. He saw her skirt flare at the bottom as she turned quickly to face the two coming in from the dark. "Well, don't you two look suspicious," Gert said, turning back to the stove.

Their kitchen was warm. The cabinets were pea green, complemented by the white Formica countertops with streaks of gray and black. His mother's cookie jars decorated the area around the stove, and her mixer sat with a handmade cover in the corner. On the window over the sink his mother proudly hung her stained-glass birds, all gifts from her boys. Piggy banks were housed on top of the fridge, which was adorned with hand painted magnets and assorted Polaroid pictures. This was his mother's space.

"Ma, can I talk to you for a minute?" Eddie was trying to be a bit more tactful with his mother.

"Sure. What's up Eddie?" Gert held her cup to her lips and gave a gentle blow. Eddie and his father parked at the table, making it clear that her program would have to wait.

"I was wondering if you would run a very important errand with me tomorrow," Eddie started.

"With you? Hmmm…I think you are old enough to run just about every errand on your own by now! This ought to be good. Go on."

"Ma, I need you to go down to the jewelers with me. I need your help picking out a ring for Evie. An engagement ring for Evie," Eddie paused. He couldn't read her face.

"Have a little heart, Gerty, say something!" Mr. Dodd attempted to get a reaction from his wife who had been standing silently for minutes.

Eddie eyed her as she cleared her throat and took a sip of her black coffee. "What brought this on?" She asked.

Eddie was completely thrown off guard and took a second to form his own response. "Love. Love brought this on. I want to love her for the rest of my life, and marriage is the next step to doing that. It feels natural and right for us."

Eddie

"Ed, Evie is a fine girl, but are you sure she is ready to be a wife? She seems like she has a little more childish behavior to get out of her system." Gert wasn't sure those were the right words to say, but she knew that she needed to voice her concerns now.

"Childish behavior? What would you know about her behavior? I live with her and have been with her for almost two years. She's going to be a nurse, for crying out loud!"

"Calm down, Ed," Mr. Dodd said. Eddie unknowingly made his father neutral like Switzerland.

"Honestly, I think you two have some big personality differences. I think you keep her grounded. I agree that you know her far better than I do, but I am going to speak now, and forever hold my peace. You deserve a woman who will be there to support you as much as you support her. I only want to be sure that you are both ready to make such a serious commitment right now. There really is no rush. If you both are confident and want to embark on this journey together, I will support you with all of my love. Please just make sure you are *both* ready to settle down. I am thrilled that you love her so much, dear."

"Will you help me pick out a ring?" Eddie was focused on the task at hand.

"Of course." And with that, Gert gave him a big hug. "Now, go turn my program on, would you?" She asked.

The ring shopping trip was a success. Despite his mother's apprehension, Eddie noticed that she was really making an effort. They never saw eye to eye, which caused many blow ups in his teen years; but to him, Gert was a superhero. She kept the family running even in times when they were all running in different directions. She was able to maintain a home, spend time with the garden club, and have a happy marriage—none of which went unnoticed by her youngest, Eddie.

He knew his mother would come around to the marriage idea. He was thrilled that his plan was coming together, and that in mere days Evie and he would be heading back to school, with her engagement ring in hand.

Eddie had no intention of waiting long before proposing, but life did. On the drive back to school that Sunday, Evie had a terrible headache, or hangover, and slept most of the way. The next day they hit the ground running. Between school and work it felt like they never had a moment to slow down. They were both accepted into grad school in New York but had to sign up for the NCLEX exam before starting, which added an additional time commitment with study sessions. The days, weeks, and months flew by. In fact, Evie insisted that Eddie take the camping trip with his friends as a way to get a break from what had become their normal hectic routine. Although he would have preferred to have her by his side, he knew that he needed it.

And so with graduation six days away, Eddie was drunk with his buddies at the lake, preparing for his proposal to the woman he loved.

When they were too drunk to stay awake, they crawled to the nearest tent and passed out, fully clothed, on top of the sleeping bags. One by one the bright rays of sunshine woke the guys and beckoned them to embrace the daylight. And that they did; diving off the dock, floating in inner tubes, fishing from the canoe. Two would tend to the fire pit and forage for wood for the evening, while another duo would make PBJs or fluff sandwiches for lunch. They were totally self-sufficient in the woods.

"Ed, I just have to say, I do not look good in powder blue," Johnny said.

"What? That is a great suggestion, John. I will be sure to tell Evie!" Eddie smirked and gave his friend an elbow.

"Seriously, Eddie, are you ready for marriage?" Chuck was always the one to start the honest conversations.

"I mean, sure man. Was I ready to go to college? Am I ready to leave college? Am I ready to get a job? Who the hell knows? All I know is that I don't want to be without her. And that's enough for me," Eddie grinned.

"You two will be exactly like my parents, in a happy, quiet, sex-free marriage!" Richard snorted. And with that, Eddie hurled himself toward his friend who was just fast enough to evade him and took off running. Both guys sprinted toward the lake, and with a mouth full of sandwich, Richard dove off the dock headfirst. Eddie was in a mid-air cannon ball, timed perfectly to clobber him as he came up for air. The rest of the guys shouted and laughed from the dock, egging them on. Eddie would miss this carefree life.

He decided to do it while the family was in town for graduation. The two families agreed to go to a nice restaurant for a celebration dinner after graduation, and the reservation had been made. He was hoping that the excitement of graduation would distract him from the life-changing moment that would follow. What if she said no? The two had never had a serious conversation about marriage. They had many wine-filled evenings where they giggled about naming their child Alfalfa or Hazelroot. And each time they discussed a case from work involving a child, Eddie would tell Evie what a good mother she would be, and she would reciprocate. He knew those moments alone did not equal a serious conversation, but he still believed in the element of surprise, and even more importantly, he believed in true love.

The graduation ceremony was long, but the room was filled with an exuberance. Everyone was ready for the next phase of life. They were practically running out the door to get into the world. Perhaps because this class of 1984 was still so young, and they had not yet seen all that this world was capable of.

The restaurant had a few grads and families in attendance. Eddie and Evie shot smiles at classmates and waved as people were ushered in and out. They were seated at a round table in a fairly quiet area of the restaurant. The deep red tablecloth sat neatly on the table as it set the stage for the umpteen place settings of salad forks and dinner forks, water glasses, wine glasses, coffee cups, and butter packets.

The group of eight was cordial but did not seem to have an easy conversation at first. However, as the drinks started to flow, so did the banter.

The moms exchanged baking tips and laughed at their picky eaters, referring to their husbands. Gert told Sally about her fruit pies, and they both agreed that the orchard was starting to raise their prices, while the fathers spoke of business, politics, and on how they both thought the VCR was a fad that would never last. Evie started a table conversation about the latest episode of MacGyver that pitted the men against the women, with the men claiming that the women only watched for Richard Dean Anderson. Evie chuckled, and Eddie followed suit, knowing that he was definitely not her type. The mothers threw up their hands as if the notion was absurd. Still they did not verbally deny the allegations.

As the chuckling quieted, Mr. Dodd took the opportunity to congratulate the grads. "I remember what a chore it was to find the right college. How many college books you had floating around the house and all the different applications. The moaning you did every time your mom reminded you to finish your essays. Then the pins and needles and harassing the mailman when you were waiting for your acceptance letters. Look at you now. All your worry, hard work, and perseverance has paid off. I am proud of all my boys, but today belongs to you, Ed. You and Evie should be proud of yourselves. Believe me, your mother and I had our doubts, mainly about your choice in friends, but you did well, Son." With that they all clinked glasses.

Mr. Somers was not making any move to add his own comments, so Sally chimed in. "Yes! Cheers to you both. We hope you had fun on your adventure and keep your focus on the future. We know that you have something special to show the world, Evie. Go forth and be amazing."

Eddie paused and looked around at his brothers and parents, Evie and her parents. Although he initially thought this was a beautiful moment on a very special day, he quickly realized that they were nearing dessert. He let the appetizer come and go. He let the salad come and go. He watched as eight different dinners were placed on the table. The pasta dishes, pork chops, steaks, fish, and veal dinners came and went. In a moment of panic, he excused himself to the men's room.

As he burst through the bathroom door, he loosened his tie and went right for the sink. He let the cool water splash over his face and tried to calm his breathing. He lifted his face as his older brother handed him a towel.

"Too much to drink, lightweight?" his brother Rick razzed him.

"Very funny. I am sure I can drink you under the table, big bro!" A smile played on Eddie's face.

"I just wanted to tell you that I am really proud of you. I know I made fun of you a little for your career choice, but I'm glad you stuck with it."

"Thanks Rick. I'm proposing to Evie tonight." Eddie let the words fly out like a guilty man in confession.

"What?! Good for you, bro! When?" Rick gave him a congratulatory pat on the back.

"Now. I want to do it here." Eddie felt waves of panic flood his senses as he laid out his plan.

"Well I suggest you try to relax. I also suggest you picture your favorite memory with Evie. Do that now, shut your eyes and think about it," Rick guided him.

Eddie took a second to find his favorite moment from over the years. His face curled into a smile and his eyes popped open when he landed on it.

"Now when you get back to the table, think of that moment, and go get your girl, man!"

Eddie wrapped his brother in a hug. He felt relieved, he felt confident and ready.

"You leave first, and I'll wait a second. Might look odd if we walk out at the same time," Rick said in all seriousness. Eddie shook his head at his big brother and walked out of the restroom with a chuckle.

Back at the table the hot topic was dessert. Who would share, who wouldn't, and how many different desserts to try? Rick returned, and the dessert order was placed. Show time.

"Families, I would like to say a few words." Eddie was wishing he had practiced this part as he stared out into a sea of expectant faces. Rick was smirking at him. Eddie took a deep breath and shut his eyes for a second so he could capture that moment.

"I would like to thank everyone for coming and sharing this accomplishment with us. I know that both Evie and I truly appreciate your love and support over the past four years. I also wanted to give a special thank you to, Evie." Eddie turned toward Evie and pushed his chair back a bit, making space on the floor between them. He looked deep into her eyes as he spoke.

"In only two years of being with you, Evie, you have made me a more compassionate, loyal, and confident man. You have tested me, and demanded the best of me as a boyfriend, and I have done my best to make you happy. On a rainy afternoon in the beginning of our junior year we had a study date in the library. You were already inside, shaking out your umbrella as I came darting into the library and slipped on the floor. My feet were in the air and my ass hit the ground, hard. While the rest of the once silent library erupted in laughter, you calmly walked over to me and extended your hand. You looked down at me and said, 'Oh Eddie, no man has ever literally fallen for me before', and I just looked up at you. Your hair draped perfectly around your face as if it were 75 degrees and sunny out. The moment my hand touched yours, I knew it was true. I knew that I had fallen for you." Eddie got down on one knee. "Evie, I have been the best boyfriend to you that I know how to be. But you make me want more. You make me want to be the best husband to you that I can possibly be. And so I have to ask you, Evangeline, will you let me work every day for the rest of my life to be the husband that you deserve? Will you be my wife?"

That summer they both earned an RN license, moved from Maine to New York, plus fit in a wedding. It was thrilling to Eddie. He was reaching goals and proud of the life he was living. Not to mention, he was in love. The two were great under pressure and took the stress of the summer in stride. However, that was not the case once school began, and bills began, but jobs did not.

They were running on wedding gift money through the summer and had to ask his parents for rent money when they moved into their apartment. Eddie followed a tight grocery budget, and long-distance calls were limited to six minutes. He knew that his wife would be carrying the financial burden soon enough.

"This is not a game, Eddie. Bills are real adult business that we signed up for. You wanted to be my husband; well this is part of it." Evie was doing everything in her power to avoid asking her parents for money. Eddie knew that was the last conversation she wanted to have. "I don't care if you deliver newspapers. Maybe it is time to get creative. Money is money, and as long as it isn't coming from my parents, then I am good with it. But so help me, Eddie, if it comes to down to it, I promise I will dial all the digits of my parents phone number and let you explain this mess to my father."

Tangled Vines of Good Intentions

"Honey, I hear you. I am looking. We are ok. Local jobs are slim, as you know. It is amazing that you got that position at the emergency clinic."

"Not amazing Eddie! Good timing and hard work. I know that you are every bit as capable as I am." Evie was still shouting.

"I have a few yards lined up this weekend. Two houses need mowing and hedge trimming. And if worse comes to worst then I can offer snow shoveling." Eddie knew this wasn't much to bring to the table.

"You are a grown man, Ed." Evie slammed her hand down on the table.

"Please calm down," Eddie pleaded, knowing that she was too far gone to get back at the moment.

"Do not tell me to calm down! We just moved in here. I actually like this apartment. I want to unpack and get settled. I have zero interest in being evicted or living out of boxes until you have a job to cover your half of the expenses, my friend."

"Ok. You are right. I hear you, loud and clear. I am going out now. It was a pleasure talking to you." Eddie had enough for one evening. And per usual, when she was too hot, he made his way down the street to the local watering hole, landscaping money in hand.

The Bar on East was in the center of town and was a sanctuary for most of the businessmen in town. The thought of networking crossed Eddie's mind a time or two. But he thought better of it, wanting to keep the bar a stress-free zone. Eddie was looking for a place to start his career. He wanted to put down roots and find a job to support his family comfortably. He knew that any job would not satisfy him.

September rolled into October and then November with little relief in the house. The fights were always the same. Eddie had no defense. He wasn't ready to settle, and in that small New York town settling meant bagging groceries. He needed more. Evie wouldn't even let him get a word in to

Eddie

explain his feelings; surely she would understand? Where did his understanding girlfriend go? These were deep thoughts he often contemplated while he was seeking refuge at the bar.

It was a cold November day when Evie came home from work to find the cable out. They lived in the second-floor apartment of a Victorian style house. Eddie knew Evie had the decorating sense and watched as she brought the muted beige living room to life with wicker baskets and thick handmade blankets. The walls were adorned with paintings the two had picked up at tag sales, plus a few they took from old college buddies. The kitchen was jam packed with bowls, plates, and gadgets Eddie intended to use; gifts from their wedding. The table and four chairs managed to stay clear of clutter and offered a perfect complement to the placemats Gert made them. The bedroom was sparsely decorated, in comparison. Their full-size bed, a quilt handmade by Eddie's mother, and a small television on top of the bureau. Evie thought it was peacefully simple, and refused to let Eddie change it, not even a wedding photo on the nightstand. The apartment had one bathroom and a small office that served as a storage room for a myriad of random objects that neither had the heart to part with.

Eddie walked in defenseless to the irate wife who was waiting for him. He didn't expect her to be home early, and he didn't expect the cable to be shut off.

"Why I am I home, sitting on this couch, and not watching our television, Ed?" she started.

Eddie was aware of her frosty demeanor. "Hello, honey. How was your day?" He walked toward the bedroom without offering her a hello kiss. As expected, she was up and at his heals in no time.

"Why am I not watching Sally, or Donahue, or All My Children right now, damn it!"

"Why aren't you?"

"I am asking you for fuck sake! The cable is out!" Evie was yelling.

Tangled Vines of Good Intentions

"Did you see if the neighbors have service, maybe there is an outage?" he said calmly.

"Is that how you want to play this, Ed? Are you sure? Cause I am a college educated woman. I had better grades than you. I can save lives. You think I wouldn't call the cable company?"

"Let me get dinner started. Would you like chicken breast with red potatoes or rice?" He tried to comfort, or distract, Evie as he unloaded each food item from his shopping bags and showed it off much like the models on Price Is Right. His attempt to subdue her failed. Screaming ensued. Not in the mood for her dramatics, Eddie left, letting his wife know exactly where he would be if she happened to calm down and wanted to join him.

The Bar on East was a spacious room, bare wood from floor to ceiling, dimly lit with 60-watt light bulbs hanging from outdated light fixtures. There were several wooden tables and chairs arranged on one side of the room and a solid oak bar taking up the other side. Mirrors on the wall behind the bar made for an optical illusion of more space. The stools were well worn, and local pictures hung with pride as decorations throughout. There was nothing flashy about the place, and most times it smelled of beer and dirty rags. But this bar had character.

The bar was surprisingly packed for a Wednesday evening. Eddie snagged the last seat at the end of the shellacked bar, grabbed a handful of nuts, and waited patiently for the bartender to make her way over. "What's all the excitement about?" Eddie shouted over the bar.

"Stag," she yelled back.

"Where's the lucky groom, I have some advice for him!" Eddie said with a smirk. Before he could put in his order, the bartender slid a cold frothy beer his way. Perhaps he went there too often? He took a good long drink and turned toward the crowd to watch the celebration. The room was filled with clean cut men laughing, reminiscing, and drinking.

Eddie

After his third beer, Eddie blended right in. He found the groom at some point before his fifth drink and decided to give him some friendly advice. Extending a hand, he opened with the reminder to put the toilet seat down and finished strong with always have a job. The conversation was easy and as natural as two old buddies. The men laughed and Eddie patted the groom on the back in celebratory fashion. To Eddie's surprise the groom gave him a business card and told Eddie to call him about a job. Confused, but thankful, Eddie slipped the card into his pocket and bought the man a beer. He was not sure what would come of it, but he was having a blast, and made a mental note of how much he enjoyed a good stag.

By the time he stumbled into the apartment, he found a sheet and a pillow tossed on the couch. Grateful to not have to walk all the way to the bedroom, Eddie hit the couch, clothes on, and passed out.

Clearly, Evie was still pissed at him the next morning, because she snuck out without a peep. She didn't bother making him a cup of coffee either, despite the fact that the pot was still hot and there was a dirty cup in the sink. Eddie didn't know the coffee maker could brew only one cup. He needed a cup. His head was throbbing. It took his eyes a minute to adjust to the time on the microwave, and another minute to realize what day it was. He let out some expletives when it finally hit him that he had slept through his first class. No time to lament over the morning coffee, or shower for that matter, he changed his clothes, grabbed his bag, and was out the door. It was going to be that kind of day.

When he returned from class, his head was clear, and he could really take in the events of the previous night. He started to clean up the covers on the couch and return them to the closet. He washed his wife's coffee cup and decided to make himself a pot. He pulled out some leftovers, recalling that he never had a chance to eat dinner the night before, and heated up a plate. As he moved to the table, he found a scathing note from Evie.

> *Sick of this. We are well educated people. We do not need our parents to rub our mistakes in our faces, we simply need to fix our mistakes. Be a man and fix this shit, Eddie.*

This new cutthroat side was something that Eddie had not seen before they were married. She was far less understanding of his flaws and was always urging him to fix them. He tried to recall when this shift occurred, but it felt like he woke up one morning and his sweet bride had turned bitter. Eddie finished his meal and headed to the bathroom for a much-needed shower. On the way he gathered up his clothes from the night before that he left strewn all over in his morning rush. As soon as he grabbed his jeans the business card flew out of the pocket and landed on the floor. Eddie swiped it up and chuckled. He thought about it and decided it couldn't hurt. He would call after his shower.

The voicemail seemed very professional. Eddie stuttered a bit, trying to match the voice of Dr. Ron with the image of the bachelor in his head.

"Um, hello, yes, my name is Eddie Dodd. We met at the bar the night of your bachelor party. I was calling to follow up with the possible job opening in your office. Not sure how much you remember from that night, but you did pass along your business card. So, if you remember me, and still have an opening, I would like the chance to speak with you further. Thanks."

After leaving the message, he decided that he would not mention a word of it to Evie. It seemed silly, and unlikely to him that this would pan out, and he could only imagine what her reaction would be. In fact, lately he couldn't imagine what her reaction would be at all. He was never sure what type of mood she would be in when she came home, or what would set her off during a casual conversation. He felt like he was losing the girl he knew. All over temporary financial problems? Something didn't make sense. Eddie ran out to the store for some fresh flowers and the ingredients to Evie's favorite meal. Tonight she would be home early, and he needed to increase his odds of having a good evening, the only way he knew how.

She was visibly tired when she walked through the door, but the smell of dinner ignited her senses. Eddie greeted her with a glass of red wine. He unloaded the briefcase, books, and purse from her arms, then pulled the winter coat off her shoulders. He guided her to the couch where he draped a hand knit blanket over her. He disappeared into the kitchen and returned with a veggie platter. He sat across from her and looked into her tired eyes. He could still see his love deep in there somewhere.

"I'll share my blanket with you. Wanna come over?" Evie broke the silence with a peace offering.

"Not yet. I have to pull dinner out of the oven in about five minutes. If I crawl under that blanket with you now, we will most likely burn the place down cause I'm not coming out until morning."

Evie laughed out loud. The sound was refreshing. He needed that reassurance. He smiled back and disappeared into the kitchen. He pulled the French onion soup out of the oven just as the cheese started to turn golden at the edges and bubble. The roast beef was already resting, and ready to be sliced for the open-faced sandwiches that would complete Evie's favorite meal.

They talked about classes and current events. They talked about safety alerts and immunizations, AIDS, cocaine, and the future of medicine. It was heavy conversation, but they were engrossed in each other's thoughts and viewpoints. Dinner was delicious; they left the small hand-me-down table to head back to the living room to relax before they could even think about dessert.

Tangled Vines of Good Intentions

Eddie curled up close to Evie under the blanket. He refilled her wine glass, again. Then he gently pressed his lips to her neck, heading up toward her ear.

"No, Eddie. I am gross. I am tired, and I need a shower," Evie said in protest.

"I can help you," he said.

Evie was too tired to fight him off. She giggled and let him continue with his plan to help her. Eddie peeled back the blanket, grabbed Evie by the waist and shifted her so she was able to lie on the couch. She did not resist. He leaned over her body and slipped his hands under her sweater. In seconds, her sweater was over her head and folded neatly on the floor. Then his mouth found her earlobes and made her squeal with delight. But he was determined to help her, so he used his mouth to remove her hoop earrings, a trick that he was sure made her fall in love with him. Her turtleneck was next, then her belt. All the while she was holding back giggles and he was rock hard from the playful exploration of her body. He ripped her pants off in a triumphant move and kneeled over her like she was his conquest. Then gave her a smoldering look that let her know the games were over, as he took off his own shirt and pants. In one fluid motion he lifted Evie from the couch and carried her to the bathroom. She stood, gazing into his eyes. He reached for her bra strap and unhooked it. As the bra fell to the floor he bent slowly to kiss and caress each breast. His lips and tongue moved sensually downward. He could hear her breathing pick up. As he reached her belly button, he turned away from her yearning body to turn on the shower. When he turned back to her, he dropped to his knees, lowered her petal pink silky panties with his teeth, and caressed her full ass cheeks with his hands. She steadied herself with his shoulders and slipped each leg out of her panties. Eddie kissed the patch of hair below her belly button, and with a quick glance up at her, he spread her legs a bit and went in hard with two fingers. Evie gasped and her legs trembled. Eddie had a wicked smirk on his face that he hid while nibbling on her thighs. Once he could feel the heat and warmth of her womanly juices, he removed his hand, stood, and kissed her deeply. Eddie guided her by the hips and they both climbed into the shower. He was unsure if she would be clean by then end, or dirtier than when she entered, but his goal was for sure the latter.

That night as she slept soundly, curled up by his side, he lay awake hoping to hear from Dr. Ron.

Thanksgiving was days away and the two made plans to spend their first Thanksgiving as a married couple in New York. They planned to drive down to New York City, have a nice dinner, see the tree, and spend the night. Not long after they set these plans, they changed, out of financial necessity. Holiday pay was an offer Evie would be foolish to refuse, and they agreed she should pick up some extra shifts at the clinic the morning of Thanksgiving, as well as the day after. They settled on an early dinner at home and then to the town tree lighting ceremony.

Eddie had the morning to prepare a nice meal, making him the target for all the family phone calls. He spoke to two of his aunts, his brothers, both sets of grandparents, and, of course, his mother.

"I am really going to miss you this year, Eddie. The whole family will. Tell me, how are you two getting along?" Gert started.

"Getting along just fine, Mom. Kinda like most married couples would."

"Don't get smart, I'm making sure that you both are happy."

"Yes mother, very happy. Thank you for asking." Eddie tried to disguise his snippy tone.

"Ok. Well then, when are you planning to make me some grandbabies?"

Eddie wasn't sure if he should laugh or be furious. Since it was a holiday, he knew there would be a better opportunity

Tangled Vines of Good Intentions

to tell her his real feelings in the future. "No talk of that yet. I am pretty focused on getting a job so I can get some experience and hands-on learning. But school is going well. Keeping my marks up."

"Smart boy. Please let us know if you need anything financially. I know you have been looking for a position for quite some time now. Don't get discouraged, hun."

"I appreciate that, Mom. I will repay you for the money you sent last month. That has held us over plus I have a few good prospects after the holiday to look into."

"Good. Please keep us posted. Stay warm up there. See you for Christmas. Love you very much."

"Love you Mom. And tell Dad the same. See you soon." Eddie went to the fridge to grab a beer to calm him down.

He adored his mother. They had a give and take relationship. Eddie tried not to give her too much headache, because she refused to take his crap. Eddie recognized that she was a no-nonsense woman, and he respected her for that. Lately their relationship was strained. He loved her so much he hated to disappoint her. It was hard to ask them for money, but it was even harder to take the cold shoulder from his wife. Eddie knew the situation was temporary, but his patience was wearing thin. As he thought about making his mother a grandmother a smile crossed his face.

The sound of the oven timer pulled him from his daydream. They had a wonderful Thanksgiving Day. Evie was happy, the meal was delicious, and the day was a wonderful memory to add to their journey together.

It was early on a Saturday when Eddie received the call. "Ed. You there? It's Rick."

Eddie tried to rub the sleep from his eyes and focus on the clock. 5 a.m. "Rick? I'm here. Go!"

Eddie

"Ed, Dad suffered a massive heart attack in the middle of the night. He didn't survive. Dad died, Ed."

His head spun and his heart began to pound. How could this be? This couldn't be. What the hell happens now? While Eddie was in the middle of a raging internal battle over the news, his brother was frantically trying to get his attention over the phone.

"Ed, Ed! You still there?"

"Uh…I'm…I'm here."

"Can you come down? Mom needs us."

"I'm on my way."

And with that Eddie hung up the phone and set to packing a bag and getting on the road. School was still on holiday break, so he wouldn't miss any classwork, luckily. He jumped in the car and headed to Evie's work. When he arrived at the clinic, they asked him to sit in the waiting room. Eddie felt like he might need a doctor, like the emergency room was exactly where he needed to be. He waited anxiously for what felt like an eternity. His head was empty, he couldn't think, or maybe he was trying not to. And when Evie appeared with a look of concern on her face, he didn't know what to say. He felt her warmth as she sat next to him and gently took his hand.

"What's going on? I am surprised to see you here."

He had no words. He leaned on her shoulder and started to cry. His big manly sobs distracted the others in the waiting room. One woman nearby leaned over with a box of tissues. With that kind gesture, Evie took to the task of getting her husband on his feet and escorting him outside.

"Take a deep breath, Eddie. Talk to me." Evie was doing her best to console him but had never seen him like this before. With all her sensitivity training, she still felt unsure of how to navigate the situation.

"He died."

"Who?"

"Dad."

Tangled Vines of Good Intentions

Eddie was grateful that she didn't press him for the specifics. It was clear that this news was fresh.

"Your father had a gentle soul." She was at a loss. "Go. I will take the bus down when I can. Maybe in a day or two so I can get someone to cover my shifts. Okay? Go be with your family and send them my love."

Eddie held her a bit longer, then dried his puddle-like tears, and turned toward the car. He wanted to put her in the car and bring her. He wanted her to handle the situation so he wouldn't have to think about anything. But he sensed her discomfort and knew this was uncharted territory for them both. As he strapped in for the ride, he could feel a looming dread settle in; this was sure to be an unpleasant experience.

A little over six hours later Eddie was turning onto his street. He recognized the white picket fence around the Moore's house; the first house on the right. He had driven past that fence for years and walked or ran past it for as long as he could remember. But today the fence that once stood sturdy in front of the rich blue two-story house on the hill seemed different. Today he could see every strip of peeling paint, several missing slats, and the general run-down look of the aged fence. In fact, the farther he drove down the street the less and less it felt like the one from his happy childhood. Was this the street his father taught him to ride a bike on? The street where his father pitched him the ball for hours, until he was good enough to play with his brothers? The street where they had family parties, and his father would dazzle guests with a firework show in the heat of the summer? What was so familiar, now felt cold and foreign. There was no life in the winter. There was no life at his own old house. As he pulled into the driveway, he realized that he was at a complete loss for what to do. This would certainly have been a good time to reach out to his dad for guidance.

The front door opened to a small entry way that spilled into the formal living room. The air was thick with sadness and dread, and the couches were full of people whispering and holding hands. Clearly no one was prepared. Eddie was on auto pilot as aunts and cousins gave him tearful hellos. They took his coat and asked him if he was hungry. He was sure that he must be but couldn't focus on that.

"We've been waiting for you. How was the drive down, hun?" Aunt Bernice took his hand and pulled him toward the kitchen. "Everyone is in the back with Father Michael. Rick, his girls, oh, you'll see. But first, you should eat."

"Just a water please, Auntie." His head was spinning. All he could handle was water before having to face the undeniable truth that his father was gone. Father Michael was there as proof of that.

"Now I'm sure you must be starving. We have pie and pot roast." His aunt paused to face Eddie. He felt some relief as she reached up and placed her cold hands on each side of his face. With a gentle authority she squeezed, "You be strong now. We all will be. That's what your father would have wanted." Aunt Bernice pulled Eddie's face down and in for a quick kiss on the check before moving behind him and shoving him into the crowded kitchen. He saw her slip away, headed toward the cupboard of plates and glasses.

Eddie clumsily made his way through a new wave of chatty family members, close friends, and neighbors in the kitchen. He was asked if he wanted some food by at least three people. When he opened the fridge he could see why. There were trays of lunch meat and cheese, mashed potatoes, pasta, and side dishes, each in different cookware. This was an impressive show of love from the group.

Just as his aunt handed him a glass of water, his brother Pat walked into the room. Pat was the oldest, but in that moment his face looked much older than Eddie remembered, the tracks of his tears still noticeable. He opened his arms wide, but Eddie was apprehensive given the room full of people and gave him a quick halfhearted hug in return. As he stepped back,

Tangled Vines of Good Intentions

he saw a quizzical look on his brother's face, but was grateful when he didn't press the issue, and seemed to give him a pass.

"Mom will be happy to see you. She is in the den with everyone else. I'm getting her a cup of coffee."

Eddie nodded to his big brother and turned to face reality. As he made his way through the sea of guests again, a few people asked where Evie was. He replied that she would take a bus down in a few days. He was not able to decipher their curious looks or figure out what the proper protocol was for things like this. He could only focus on one thing at a time, and now it was time to hug his mother and do everything in his power not to break down and cry again like a little baby, or like the scared little boy that he felt like inside.

He made it through the living room and turned the corner to head down the steps and into the den. Rick and his wife were there, Pat's wife and their daughter, his father's eighty-something year old parents, his mother's eighty-something year old parents, Father Michael, and Gert.

He went right for his mother. He held her longer than he should have but didn't shed a tear. She held him tight and grabbed his cheeks to get a good look at her baby boy. She gave him a half-lit smile and they sat together on the couch. Father Michael took his mother's hand and exchanged some hushed words with her. As he stood and turned to leave, he gave Eddie a firm squeeze on his shoulder. Once he was out of earshot, Eddie's mother was quick to fill him in on the situation and ask about the missing wife in the room.

The following days were a blur of tearful greetings and tearful goodbyes. People came out of the woodwork to show support for the family and love for Arthur Dodd. Evie's parents stopped by but didn't bother to ask when she would arrive. Clearly, she had reached out to them. Eddie hadn't heard from her though, or tried to call her, but it hadn't occurred to him to do so. He was feeling like life was moving in slow motion. Almost as if he was watching his life happen without being an active participant. He hadn't cried since his time with Evie, and he knew she would have that effect on him again whenever they caught up with each other.

The morning of the funeral, Eddie stood in front of the mirror assessing his pieced together outfit. By some miracle he had a pair of black pants that fit in his closet along with a snug, pinstriped gray jacket. He had white tube socks to match a white collared shirt, of which he left the top button undone, hidden by a tie that he gave his father years earlier. This was the best he could do. He even had to borrow a pair of shoes from Rick; luckily, they were black.

Gert peered into his room. "Good thing I never got around to cleaning out your closet."

"I wish I had something a little more suitable, or that at least matched. I feel like a high schooler."

"You look fine. And I think you are much taller and hairier than you were in high school Ed." They smiled at each other.

"This must be hard for you, Mom." Eddie was trying not to get sappy.

"It must be hard for you, too. We all lost someone we loved, and who loved us." Eddie pulled his mom into a tight embrace before they headed out the door to make their way to church.

The family was in a small room with Father Michael. He would guide them through the chapel to be seated in the front row once the whole family arrived. Eddie kept peeking into the massive chapel and was a little stunned by the growing crowd. He felt the familiar dread that had shadowed him this whole trip. When it was time to head out, his mother nudged him forward till they made it to their seats. It was still so hard to comprehend, and Eddie knew he was doing his best to go through the motions. As they were all about to sit, Evie walked up. She was quiet and gave hugs all around before taking her place next to Eddie. She reached for his hand and Eddie took comfort when she gave it a squeeze. He glanced at her just long enough for a single tear to betray him and slide down his cheek.

After the service, Gert rode with Father Michael, and Evie rode with Eddie in the procession to the cemetery. She gave him a big kiss but didn't press him with questions or force him to talk.

"Thank you for being here," Eddie said.

"A wife stands by her husband," Evie replied.

She stuck by him for the rest of the day and then asked when he was planning to head back to New York. This was a question that he should have been able to easily answer, but his brain was not looking at the bigger picture. He tried to really think about it before responding. Seems he had been in Connecticut for just over a week, and although there was nothing pressing at home, he knew that being here was like being in limbo. At some point he would have to function in this new reality. Life would have to go on without his father. Even so, he was not sure he was ready to leave.

"When do you go back to work?" Eddie answered her question with a question.

"I have the next two days off. I am due back Monday."

"Ok. I'll speak with my mother, but I would like to drive home with you on Sunday." Eddie had made a decision. Reality would reign once again.

He spent the weekend catching up with family from out of town and enjoying his mother's company. They decided that Eddie would come back for a week around Christmas to help her pack some things.

"Eddie, I know this has all been very sudden. If you need to talk when it sinks in a bit, please call, day or night."

"All right Mom. Maybe it will help to get back into a routine." With mixed feelings he pulled himself from the safety of his mother's arms, to face life once again.

The car ride home was long, and quiet. Neither of them had the right words. In his heart, Eddie knew that the joy of

Eddie

is childhood home was changed forever, and as that resonated, he wasn't sure how he would be able to return.

"I wish this was a dream," Eddie murmured.

"Your father would want you to live your life and be successful," Evie chimed in.

Those were words that he had to ponder. What did his father want for him? What were his hopes and desires and expectations for Eddie's future? These questions and their lack of answers occupied Eddie's mind for the remainder of the trip. How could he not know?

When they got home it was late, dark, and all Eddie wanted was to shower and go to bed. There were three new messages on the answering machine. One from a classmate giving condolences to Eddie. The second was a sales call reminding them to renew their subscription for the newspaper. The last message was a strangely familiar voice. Eddie walked out of the bedroom just in time to hear the man leave his number and say goodbye. He looked at Evie, puzzled. "Who was that?"

"It was for you. Dr. Ron? He left a message, said sorry it has been so long, and that he has a few things that might interest you. He wants you to go by the hospital and see him." Eddie's face lit up, as Evie's contorted with confusion.

"What's that all about?" She asked.

"I will tell you later. It's too late to get into it, but it could be good." And with that, Eddie disappeared into the bathroom.

Going to meet Dr. Ron was nerve racking. It had only been a few weeks, but the Bar on East was dark, and they were drinking; would they even recognize each other? But it was nice to have something positive to focus on. Dr. Ron worked in one of the two local hospitals. He was a primary care physician, and very well known. Eddie wasn't sure, but he thought he caught the receptionist blush when he mentioned the doctor's name.

As Eddie got off the elevator, he immediately heard that voice. He recognized Dr. Ron in an instant. They hugged and acted as if they were old friends. Dr. Ron invited Eddie into his office to talk. His office was a comfortable size. It had several large bookcases, with a rich cherry finish, that matched the round table. His own desk was a darker wood with ornate legs and drawers. There were no family pictures visible, no plants and no personal effects, besides his various degrees that were perfectly hung around the room. Despite the fact that there were no windows, the office felt spacious and uncluttered.

"So, I know that you recently finished school, you made great grades, and you worked steadily in your field of study. What can you tell me that isn't on this piece of paper?" Dr. Ron asked causally as the two sat across from each other at the round table.

"I enjoy cooking, and long walks on the beach." Comic relief was all Eddie could think to do in that moment, and it worked, as Dr. Ron burst into laughter.

"That sounds amazing, but I am married, and I am afraid the position has just been filled. Thank you for your time." Dr. Ron made a gesture of getting up to leave, which was ineffective as he was still laughing hysterically.

"Seriously though, I am a hard worker, and very passionate about the field. I work well with teams and follow instructions well. I am really excited to get back to work, and honestly I think my wife is even more excited than I am." Eddie quickly realized that he could control the pace of this conversation and that Dr. Ron was one of the most laid back and easy going people he had ever met.

"Good, good. Married? Are you following your own advice? Are you happy in your marriage?" Dr. Ron was straight faced as he posed the question to Eddie.

Not sure how to respond, Eddie took a brief pause. "Evie is my everything."

"Nice. I am a hopeless romantic myself. There are lots of women in this field, be careful." Again, Dr. Ron's remarks came without a shred of laughter.

"Of course, Sir." Eddie was at a loss.

"Sir? Oh, jeez! I'm sorry Ed, look at me getting all personal and serious with you. I think you are a terrific guy. I had a blast talking with you at the bar from what I remember, and heck, I am having a good time talking to you right now. Please don't think of me as an overbearing boss type. I want you to be able to come to me and be honest if you need to or come to me if you want to talk sports, or if you simply want to tell me a joke. You, on the other hand, might want to consider making people call you "sir". I want to make you the floor supervisor. You will be head of my nursing team and have about 15 nurses below you. How does that sound?" Dr. Ron paused trying to gauge his reaction.

"Sounds like I am way underqualified!" Eddie sputtered, amazed at the offer.

"Only if you are not willing to learn, my friend," Dr. Ron said casually.

"I am."

"And I am very glad to hear that. Welcome aboard! Now, are you a Yankees fan?"

"Is it a deal breaker if I am a Mets fan?" Eddie could only hold his smile for a second. "Yes, I am a Yankees fan."

They continued to laugh and joke, and an hour and a half later Eddie strolled out with a grin, and a job. He was ready to start living, start providing, and to start making his father proud.

Eddie got take-out that night, lit candles, and waited eagerly for Evie to come home. She was thrilled with the news. She surprised Eddie when she jumped into his arms and gave him deep kisses, then beckoned him into the bedroom.

Tangled Vines of Good Intentions

They had a celebratory quickie before reheating their Chinese take-out and cuddling on the couch. Eddie couldn't really believe the news himself. Dr. Ron offered him the position of head nurse on his staff. Eddie was thrilled for the challenge and knew that he and Dr. Ron would get along really well.

On their first anniversary, Eddie had flowers delivered to his wife's work and made reservations at a new restaurant nearby. He was excited to have the time to talk face to face and reflect on the year that had come and gone in the blink of an eye.

"Ready when you are," Eddie called to Evie who was still in the bedroom getting ready.

"Give me ten more minutes. I am almost ready," Evie replied.

"We have reservations," Eddie reminded as tenderly as possible.

"Fine! If you want me to get all dressed up and leave my hair looking like I worked an eight-hour shift in the ER, then I guess I'm ready," Evie countered.

"Take your time, Dear. But I am sure you will look lovely no matter what." Eddie found marriage to be a bit of a game. It reminded him of Minesweeper. Everything was going your way one day, and the next it was a matter of one wrong move.

Eddie's lips curled into a devious smile when Evie came out in a low-cut black dress with her hair perfectly puffed. Her purple eyeliner and coordinating shadow brought out the emerald in her eyes. She went with a subtle tangerine lip that flattered her complexion. She looked young and beautiful.

"Ok, husband. Your wife is ready." A smile spread across Evie's face and she gifted Eddie with an affectionate kiss on the cheek before heading for the car.

They arrived to see a line forming at the door of the restaurant. Eddie gave the maître d their name, and within minutes they were being escorted through the small dimly lit restaurant. The restaurant featured an open style kitchen. The couple landed a table toward the back, prime location to watch the flames flare and hear the sound of knives in action. They drank white wine and had delicious oysters, which were an accompaniment to the good conversation.

"I feel like we haven't had a chance to talk like this in a long time, Buttercup," Eddie remarked as he gazed contently across the table.

"Well, it really has been a busy year. We have had some hurdles to get through. I am really happy that you love your job. I am also really happy that you found Dr. Ron. He seems like a genuinely sweet guy." Eddie interrupted her with the noise of stifled laughter.

"Don't be fooled. He is a low-down dirty dog of a man!" Eddie interrupted.

"What are you talking about? He is nothing but polite when I see him. And watch what you say, I may not let you go to the bar with him if he is a bad influence." Evie's tone was laced with curiosity.

"I am sure I have told you that the Good Doctor has a reputation around work. He gets what he wants by using his assets, if you catch my drift." Eddie grinned, recollecting some bar stories from his friend's younger days.

"No, I most certainly do not know what you mean? He is married." Evie leaned closer, intent on getting the details from her husband.

"I am not going to make any comments on his marriage. I honestly don't know much about the woman. But I know that the man can flirt. He has a history—before his wife, and I would imagine it is hard to tame that type of wild side." He watched as Evie sipped her wine. She looked perplexed, as if she wasn't sure what to do with the information. "When we go out after work, we tell stories from our past. We laugh about life and go over some of the crazy stuff happening at work. You have no reason to worry. I am not influenced by him. I am a leader, not a follower." And with that they broke into easy laughter and finished their second glass of wine.

"How is your mother?"

"You could call her sometime, you know." Eddie thought he sounded very much like his mother when he uttered those words.

"I like her more than my own mother, that's all I can offer you at the moment. I am just not good at family."

"Evie, you have always done great with my family," Eddie encouraged.

"But really, I have only seen them a handful of times. Plus, the funeral was not exactly a good time to chat it up with them," she said honestly.

"Are you saying you want to spend more time with my family?" He knew her response before she gave it.

"No."

"Right, well then, let's not worry about them. Mom is fine, and she will call if she needs anything."

Eddie noticed her look cautiously at him before continuing the conversation. "What are your thoughts for the holidays this year?"

"I am sure we will have to work. It is still summer, let's not wish away the year." Eddie was short. He continued to quietly eat. As much as he missed his mother, the Christmas after his father passed was harder than he could have expected. His brothers were in and out, helping here and there, but it was Eddie who had to go through his things with Gert. The two of them rifled through a myriad of clothes, photos, trinkets, and memories that represented his father's life. Eddie's heart broke all over again. He lashed out at his mother. They spent more than one evening eating dinner in separate rooms. When Eddie left her, deep down he knew that he needed a break. That being home was just too painful. He thought that leaning on Evie would help, but he found that she truly didn't understand the depth of his loss. She didn't have the patience for his grieving. He rarely spoke to her about it anymore, and he was honestly shocked that she brought it up.

"So, you wanna have sex tonight?" Evie broke the silence.

The two finished dessert, headed home, and Eddie proceeded to make love to his wife. He was slow and deliberate as he removed her black dress. While they stood in the living room. He pressed his lips to her neck and caught the bouquet of the perfume he bought her as an anniversary present. The smell of wildflowers mixed with the natural aroma of his wife's soft skin was enough to get him fully aroused. They moved from room to room biting, kissing, and stripping along the way. He lifted her naked body onto the bed, and they were quickly lost in a passionate dance under the sheets.

As time marched on, Eddie found himself at the bar more and with Evie less. She had a new schedule and they only saw each other for minutes a day, and sometimes the other person was sleeping during those minutes. He didn't think much of it, though. He knew that she was happy working, and he was not about to start a fight over it. Besides, he had Dr. Ron to occupy his time. Eddie left work to head home and change, figure out dinner, possibly shower, and then head to the bar. He would usually beat Dr. Ron there, and was a beer in when his friend arrived. They would talk work or life, and sometimes they wouldn't talk much at all. Eddie tried not to talk about Evie too much, because he noticed that his friend rarely spoke about his wife. Once he lost count of how many drinks he had, he would settle up his tab and stumble home, occasionally leaving Dr. Ron at the bar. On a good night he would make it home and slip into bed as Evie arrived. But the alcohol would always win, and he was usually asleep by the time she made it to the bedroom.

Tangled Vines of Good Intentions

At work the two were completely professional. Dr. Ron trusted him, and he worked hard day in and day out to keep it that way. There was a learning curve to his new job, though, and Eddie took a team approach with the other nurses. The women on his staff were very receptive to this and viewed him as an equal rather than a boss. Eddie loved being one of the girls and listened closely to every juicy bit of gossip that was floating around. He had ears that extended to most departments in the hospital. He rarely ever betrayed his coworkers by gossiping to Dr. Ron.

It was Valentine's Day of '86 when the gossip was just too good to keep to himself. Eddie needed the full story. As per his routine, he stopped home to prepare dinner before making his way to the bar. On this particular day Dr. Ron was already there. The place was close to deserted.

"Hey! You are early. Where are my flowers and chocolates?" Eddie gave his friend a firm handshake.

"You know, I used to love Valentine's Day. Why aren't you with Evie? She is a special woman. I would think she would want to celebrate today?" Dr. Ron asked inquisitively.

"She is working. I think that makes her happy. I sent her flowers…and chocolates!" Eddie felt silly saying it out loud.

"Really man? That was as original as you could get?" Dr. Ron shook his head in disapproval. "Evie is unique. Special. I hope you didn't send her roses. I would have sent her a single flower, her favorite flower, a lily. Then I would have written her a card, and I would have absolutely made her dinner. I mean, you are a better cook than a nurse man!"

Eddie was at a loss. He wasn't used to this level of judgment from his friend. "Well, I know my wife, and she is happier being at work, than at home complaining about what a mess I've made in the kitchen. You are right though; she is a sucker for my cooking." Eddie took a long swig of his cold beer.

"And why aren't you with your woman, Dr. Romance?" He could barely say that with a straight face.

"We don't celebrate that in our culture." Dr. Ron was short.

"I didn't know it was a cultural thing. Wasn't Valentine an Italian guy?" Eddie mused.

"Not sure."

"Well can you tell me, Dr. Romance, about that one year…?" Eddie nudged his friend in an effort to jog his memory.

"Why do you keep calling me that? Who have you been talking to, and what do you think you know?" Dr. Ron pointed his finger in Eddie's chest. He was serious.

"Easy, buddy! I heard a funny story about how you decided you would ask all the single ladies on the floor to be your Valentine. And they were very grateful when you brought them all red roses…" Eddie paused to take a drink and observe the reaction.

"Oh boy! Guilty as charged. That was one of my first years in the position. I wanted to keep everyone happy, especially on Valentine's Day. What is so wrong about that?" Dr. Ron tried to put on an innocent act.

"And…and I heard that some of the women got a special gift."

"Jeez Ed! Keep it down! Are you kidding you heard that at work?" With his head in his hands Dr. Ron told his side of the tale. "You have seen our department. We have some attractive girls, and they are sweet, and funny, and flirty."

Eddie interrupted, "I heard that you were the flirty one."

"Look. I am not going to apologize for what happened. Let's just say that I got a little personal with some of them, but I didn't hear anyone complaining." Dr. Ron said with finality in his voice.

"Oh, I'm guessing you won't hear anyone complaining now, either. You have a bunch of happy customers." They both broke into hardy laughter and clinked glasses to celebrate Dr. Ron's expression of manhood.

"Ed, I believe in love. True love. The kind that is transcendent. The kind that people can see and feel. I have learned a lot over the years, and lately, about the timing and the reality of this delicate jewel. It doesn't come to everyone, most people think they have it, but they don't. When it's the real thing it will hit you like a freight train that you never heard coming. And worst of all, once you have been run over, I have no clue how to pick up my limbs and keep going without it."

Noticing that this omission made his friend a little sad, Eddie instantly deduced that it wasn't his wife that he was transcending with. He truly felt bad for his friend for finding himself in that position. He offered him a shot to ease the mood, and put away his Dr. Romance jokes, at least until the next year.

Eddie always invited Evie to the bar, but she never went, it was mostly a timing thing. A few times he tried a couple's get together, but quickly found out that Evie and Dr. Ron's wife did not have much in common. Evie went on and on about how stuffy she was, and how boring spending time with her was. Eddie took the complaining as a clear message to only get them together when absolutely necessary. Dr. Ron seemed more than happy to hang out without his wife, leaving Eddie to believe that maybe he and Evie shared the same opinion of the woman. Dr. Ron became a friend to both him and Evie, and that felt like a win to Eddie.

"Hey babe, let's go!" It was a beautiful day in October of '86 and Eddie had tickets to a Yankees game. Naturally, Evie wasn't ready yet, whether her hair wasn't puffy enough, or she couldn't find the right outfit to wear, he never bothered to ask anymore. "You look good! Will you be comfortable in those shoes?" Eddie was practically gawking at his wife in tightfitting jeans with high heeled black boots. Her sweater skimmed the top of her jeans and Eddie could see her tantalizing skin peeking out as she swayed in her boots.

Eddie

Eddie watched as she completed her game day look with popping cherry lipstick, then turned to face him, tapping her boot expectantly. "Ok then, let's go."

"Does my hair look okay?" Evie's voice filled the silence in the car.

"Of course. You look like you dressed up for the game."

"Is there something wrong with a girl wanting to look nice Ed? I mean I wear scrubs all day, for crying out loud! Please do not forget that I am a young woman. Despite being leaps and bounds more mature than you are, I am only 24 years old," Evie said with an air of sass and seriousness.

"Well, I hope you aren't leaping and bounding in those boots. People can break bones at any age, I see it every day." Eddie played the comedian. He used it to keep his occasionally tense wife calm.

"You are so funny," she said dryly. "Do you want me to ride in the back seat?"

"No, no. I mean, you may be the young one in the group, but Dr. Ron seems to be in good health, and I think he will be comfortable riding in the back," Eddie said with a smile.

Eddie kept his confusion to himself watching Evie fidget with her makeup in the passenger fold down mirror as he pulled into Dr. Ron's driveway. His wife was becoming far more complex as time moved on.

"Hey, buddy!" Eddie greeted him as he opened the door.

"Hi! Who's excited for the game today? Evie, you look stunning," Dr. Ron said as he settled into the back.

And just like that Eddie watched his moody wife blossom into the chatty young woman that he once knew. He could feel her aura change to something far more positive, and happy. And although he couldn't put his finger on why the change, he was grateful.

They were all fans, and genuinely thrilled to see the game. They made their way to their seats with snacks and beers in hand. Eddie started a system where each person would take

Tangled Vines of Good Intentions

turns making drink runs. The system was working smoothly, until it wasn't. During the last few innings of the game, Evie went up for her run. At a break in the action, Eddie recognized his wife's absence and decided to head up, use the bathroom, and see what was keeping her.

To his surprise, she was sitting in the middle of the concessions area in a folding chair, surrounded by medics and security, with an ice pack covering her ankle. Surprise was probably what he should have felt. He could very quickly deduce what happened, and he was sure it had everything to do with her heels.

"Can you walk? Is it a break or a sprain?" He quickly knelt in front of her to assess the situation

"Oh hey! Thank goodness you are here. I tripped." Evie played it up.

"Yes. I see. Can you please give me some details on the injury? Is it a break?" Eddie pushed back the crowd of young muscular security and pulled the ice from her ankle. He noticed the broken boot heel lying beside her. The number of men fawning over her gave him pause. He knew that Evie was most definitely a woman who could handle pain and expected everybody else to do the same. He further assessed the injury and then her and was sure that she was enjoying the unnecessary pampering. "You look good, hun. Would you like to come and enjoy the last few innings with us?"

"Yeah. I think the ice helped. I can elevate at my seat," Evie agreed.

Eddie thanked the medics and security as the couple turned to head back to watch the game. As they started back to their seats, Dr. Ron was heading up the stairs in search of them both.

"Oh no! Those poor boots!" He seemed shocked. In the blink of an eye Eddie watched him swoop Evie off her feet. He was speechless as Dr. Ron gingerly carried her down the stairs and planted her in her seat. Dr. Ron then positioned her so that her ankle was resting on his lap.

Eddie

"Well you made that look easy. You might as well carry her home!" Eddie laughed at his own joke, while the other two gave him a half-hearted smile.

School was over, both Eddie and Evie were gainfully employed, 1987 was over, and life was stable. And then everything changed. Eddie came in from work one January afternoon to change and head out to meet Dr. Ron at the bar. To his surprise, Evie was home. She was crying, balling her eyes out on the bathroom floor. She was already in her pajamas when Eddie found her, curled up in a fetal position on the brown tile floor. She seemed shocked to see him rush in. He got down and opened his arms wide, but she pushed away. She made her way to her feet and sprinted into the bedroom, slamming the door behind her. Confused, Eddie tried to talk to her through the door. He could hear her sobbing into the pillows. He had no idea what was going on, what he should say, or what he might have done wrong, and the only solution to this unknown problem that he could think of was to cook.

He ran out to the store and stopped by the bar to let Dr. Ron know that he couldn't join him. He found his friend already three deep, much earlier than usual. Eddie didn't have time to worry about Dr. Ron. He only had time to give him the rundown of what was going on at home.

"Hey, Evie is going through something, and she's locked herself in the bedroom," Eddie blurted out.

"That's not going to fix anything," Dr. Ron said with a hint of frustration that Eddie picked up on.

"Right. But I have no clue what she is upset about. I'm going to try to talk to her if she will let me."

"Are you sure you want to hear it? Maybe wait a little bit? She might be easier to talk to after you've had a few drinks?" Dr. Ron slurred a bit.

Tangled Vines of Good Intentions

"Sorry buddy, she needs me," Eddie replied as he left the bar.

When he got home from the store the bedroom was quiet and he assumed she was asleep. So, he set to work cooking up some stew and homemade rolls for when she woke up. All the while Eddie was racking his brain trying to figure out what could have upset her like that. Was someone dead? Did she get fired? Did she cheat? Did he? Eddie quickly ruled out those options, thinking that her dramatics were not a suitable reaction in any of those cases. As the clock ticked on later and later, Eddie patiently sat waiting. The bedroom door finally creaked open as Evie ran to the bathroom and was behind closed doors yet again.

Before Eddie could make up his mind to knock on the bathroom door or not, the door opened, and she walked quietly into the kitchen, with blotchy skin and swollen eyes.

"Let's eat," Eddie said softly. Evie nodded her head in agreement and went right for the pot of soup. Eddie could see she was starving. Two bowls and three rolls later, they sat silently at the table. The silence was maddening. When Eddie reached for her hand she pulled away, her eyes glistened with threatening tears. Eddie sat frozen as big wet tears sprang from her eyes. He tried to speak, but she held up her hand and shook her head. Before retreating to the bedroom and locking the door, again, she looked at Eddie and told him that she was pregnant.

Eddie didn't know how to react, but it seemed like Evie was having enough of a reaction for both of them. Hadn't they talked about kids eventually, possibly, maybe? Eddie was unsettled by the thought that his wife did not want to have children with him. Perhaps this was a timing issue, or it was too much of a surprise for her to take in at the moment. He had no clue what was going on in Evie's head, but it was not the reaction he expected. How could she not want to tell him? They had been home together for hours and she only looked at him twice. This was happening to both of them, but Eddie had never felt more detached from her. He was deeply hurt and confused by her actions, by her reaction. Not knowing what else to do, Eddie settled in for a sleepless night on the couch.

The next morning he woke to Evie standing above him, fully dressed, with her purse in one hand and a suitcase in the other.

"I am going to Carol's for a few days. I need to talk to someone and clear my head."

"What about talking to me? We need to have a conversation about this. I am here for you, to help you with…" Eddie was interrupted.

"I'm just not ready yet, Ed. You can help me by giving me a little space right this second." And with that she turned and left. Another closed door.

This whole episode felt very surreal. What was the big deal? People have children every day. They were both healthy, young adults, with solid educations and good careers. This was totally doable. That Evie was always full of surprises. Once the door closed, he sat in the emptiness for a minute, then let out a beast like, cathartic, yell.

"AAAARRRRRGGGGGHHHHHHHH! What the fuck, Evie!"

There was nothing Eddie could do but go to work and wait it out. He never expected that he would have to wait so long. Evie stayed at Carol's for a full week, only calling once. Eddie was left to guess and assume what she was feeling and thinking. His own emotions, running wild and wreaking havoc on him all week. This did not seem fair. Eddie went straight from work to the apartment to check for signs of Evie, and with no luck, he ended up at the bar. This was the routine for five straight days, and each night he went home to an empty apartment. He cooked dinner for one a few times, and sat at the kitchen table and ate alone, then when he was tired of the silence, he made his way back to the bar to get good and drunk to numb the pain. This was a new type of pain for Eddie, different than losing his father; this was sharper, more like betrayal.

"I know this has to be hard for you. She won't talk to you at all?" Dr. Ron asked.

"She won't take my calls. I just don't get it. Why would she want to be apart at a time like this?"

"I don't know. She is hurting. Her emotions are very complex. I am sure she never meant to hurt you." Dr. Ron seemed at a loss for words, but genuinely distraught at the situation Eddie found himself in.

"She doesn't have to hurt me. We just need to talk about it. I have no clue what is going on in her mind right now. I can't believe she is doing this. It has been days man. Days!" Eddie slumped his head on the bar in a sign of resignation to his feelings.

"Barkeep, two shots please." Dr. Ron did the only thing he knew how to do. "To the woman who left. May she return soon, and may she bring happiness with her."

"Thanks buddy." Eddie warmed to his kind gesture, as his throat burned with the harsh shot of brown liquid.

Of course, Dr. Ron was not thrilled with the baby news. Dr. Ron was a bachelor at heart. He did not want kids, as far as Eddie knew. Eddie could never imagine that he would be ready to give up his freedom.

"I am sure that she is clearing her head. She is going to be a great mother," Dr. Ron trailed off.

"Yes. We...we...she...I can be a parent, too. Together. We have to do it together." Eddie stumbled to get his thought out.

"You will. I am sure. You just need to give her time and space," Dr. Ron offered.

When Eddie could no longer sit up straight, his friend asked the bartender to call them both a cab. That was the third time that week. Eddie was late for work the next day, for the fourth time that week. Part of him believed that if he hadn't been with the boss the previous evening that he would for sure lose his job. He did the best he could to go through the motions and get through each day one hour at a time. Dr. Ron made that very long week bearable for him.

On Saturday evening, as Eddie was sitting down to dinner, she came home. Eddie noticed from the moment she walked in that she was different, maybe even a little sad. She looked the same but radiated a much different vibe.

"I am ready to talk now, Eddie." They sat across from each other at the kitchen table. He offered to make her a plate, but she shook her head.

"Honestly, I never thought about having kids. Not seriously. I am not ready. I don't know if I will ever be ready. I might have never chosen to get pregnant at all. But here we are, in a very sticky situation. I don't think it would be very responsible of us to have this baby and then give it up for adoption. So it is feeling like we have no choice at all. We have to make the best of it." She exhaled.

Eddie was speechless. A woman, about to be a mother, talking about making the best of it? She didn't want kids, ever? Who was this person, and how could this ever work? Without a word he got up, grabbed his keys and headed for the door.

"Hey! I thought you wanted to talk about this!" Evie sounded shocked, and furious.

"Sounds like neither of us have much of a choice." And with that he hit the bar. Hard. He was drinking to stop the feeling of dread that had settled in. He was alone, until he wasn't. It was about closing time when Dr. Ron slid in next to him.

"She still isn't home?" He asked his friend.

"She is. We're having a baby," Eddie slurred.

Dr. Ron helped his friend out of the Bar on East that night and brought him back to his apartment where Evie had piled pillows and a blanket on the couch for him. Eddie passed out with worry still heavily weighing on him. Evie was home, but he was still feeling so very alone.

They never talked about it again. They were having a baby. He was thrilled, and she was less than thrilled. Eddie felt disconnected from his wife. They both went through the motions while she was pregnant, smiling when sharing the news with friends and family. They went to several baby showers, and they even started looking for a house that spring. To Eddie, it felt like they were never really sharing their true feelings, or never really being honest about anything. He couldn't make her laugh anymore, and a part of him wanted to stop trying. This was not the woman he fell in love with, and there was nothing he could do to get back in. She locked him out of her head, her soul, and her heart, but at a time that was supposed to bring a couple so much joy. Eddie simply didn't understand. They could do this together, easily. Why didn't she see that?

"There are two open houses today, would you like to go?" Eddie started casual conversation one rare Sunday morning when they were both home together. He had just rolled out of bed and Evie was sitting with a bowl of cereal at the kitchen table. Eddie had circled the house listings in the newspaper the night before and left them on the table.

"Sure, but I have some errands to run before work. We need to be back here by 1 p.m." Evie never turned to look in his direction.

"Okay. I can be ready in ten minutes."

"That's great for you, but I am going to need at least twice that. Not only do I have to find something suitable to wear out in public, but I have to finish eating and clean up. So sorry that I slept in on my morning off. I didn't realize you had plans for us." Evie's volume rose as she annunciated each word.

Eddie

"Take your time. I am in no rush. Did you get a chance to look at the listings?" Eddie knew he had to tread carefully.

"Really? I woke up, put on my robe, and poured my cereal. I was eating it peacefully." Evie looked him square in the eye this time.

"Right. I am going to get in the shower then. The listings are circled, if you are interested." He slipped out of the room, shaking his head, confused at what just happened.

"Give me a damn minute, please!" Evie shouted behind him.

Eddie found sanctuary in the bathroom, or any room where he didn't have to face the many moods of his wife.

"Let's go Ed." An hour later, Evie stood at the door, purse in hand, ready for the open houses.

"Great. Which one would you like to see first?"

"I don't care," she responded flatly.

"Did either description seem more appealing to you?"

"What does it matter? Let's look at both."

"Okay." Eddie ushered her to the car and said a silent prayer.

"I don't like this neighborhood," Evie offered as they pulled up to the first house. "Don't care for the house color, either."

Eddie knew better than to add a response. They looked around silently at the three-bedroom, two-bathroom, '40s build. It was one level, with an outdated kitchen, but a nice size backyard. He could see the potential but was having a hard time getting a read on his wife.

"This one has great charm, and lots of storage space. It won't be on the market for long," The realtor pointed out as they made their way back to the front of the house.

"What do you think, Honey?" Eddie turned to Evie.

"There is a smell in here. I can't stay here much longer."

And five minutes later they left, ready for the second house.

"Are you feeling okay? Would you like to go home?" Eddie asked gingerly.

"If the next place doesn't smell like burnt meatloaf, then I should be fine. I know we have to do this, Ed. I am painfully aware that I am pregnant, and I have zero intentions of raising my child in an apartment if I don't have to." And with that, she swung open her door and started toward the next house.

They did a more thorough walk through of this one. Eddie noticed that Evie seemed more interested, which worried him, because this house was over budget. Back in the car she was willing to start the conversation.

"That had potential. We need to re-carpet, paint, landscape, and possibly update the bathroom," Evie started.

"But it only had one bathroom. And that kitchen needed more space," Eddie said, offering his opinion.

"Is this how things are going to go? Every time I have something positive to say, you are going to shoot me down?"

Eddie could practically feel her heating up. "No. Just wanted to highlight all of the pros and cons. I liked the yard, and the basement has potential."

"Fine. Seems that's not the one." Evie ended the conversation there. Eddie was not looking to continue the aggressive banter, and he left it alone. He wanted so badly to wrap her in a bear hug and tell her that things didn't have to be so stressful, that they would find a suitable house, and be a happy family. But he didn't, he couldn't. He was not completely sure that things would happen that way.

He was truly surprised when Evie threw him a 26th birthday party that May. It was a nice evening. There were a handful of coworkers who had blended into friends, and the other couples who lived in their building. Evie ordered giant sub sandwiches and had a variety of chips and dips spread around the kitchen. It was simple, but sweet. Eddie felt hopeful for the first time since the day she told him she was pregnant.

He noticed Dr. Ron having easy conversation with Evie; she even let him feel her belly. Eddie would have thought it odd since he only touched her belly when she was asleep, but it looked very natural, like she might for one second not completely hate being pregnant. Dr. Ron made her smile. Eddie was so grateful to see his wife like that again. He fought back the ping of jealousy and remembered that Evie didn't walk out on Dr. Ron for a week in the beginning of this pregnancy. They just picked up where they left off.

There was little room to laugh or try to make Evie smile in their recent conversations. Her back hurt, her feet hurt, her breasts hurt. She had very specific meals that she would and would not allow him to cook. She hated the way she looked, she hated the clothes she had to buy, and she had acne now, which she more than hated. It was one honest thing after another. There was little that Eddie could do, especially since it felt very much like she blamed him. He marked off the days on the calendar hoping things would change when the baby came.

And on August 11, 1988, the baby came.

Cassandra

On January 26, 1992, they welcomed home a beautiful daughter. She was 7 lbs., 9 ounces, with chubby cheeks, dark hair, and rich brown eyes. She was quiet during the day, and loud at night. Her brother was the only one who could sleep through her wails. She was here, and everyone was trying to make it feel normal.

Cassie was an unplanned child in every sense of the word. She was using all her brother Brian's hand me downs, including his bassinet, blankets, and even clothes. She didn't have a room of her own when she got home, she barely had diapers. She was an unhappy baby, and there wasn't much anyone could do about it. She challenged the routine already in place and forced her parents to divert their attention from her big brother. Cassie turned the whole family upside down.

The first year flew by. She took her first steps in daycare, and she said her first word in daycare. When she wasn't at daycare she was attached to her brother. Sometimes they were home with one parent or the other and sometimes they were at Carol's house. Her little life was a hustle and bustle of being shuffled around. Since she was an infant, the chaos was her normal and she thrived. She was independent and determined, which were key to success in this family. She hit all the right milestones, no matter who was there to see them. With each passing day Cassie's skin became richer and richer with pigment, and her brown curls fuller and thicker on her tiny head. She was the baby sister, at least, that was her title.

By the time Cassie was two, the joy of a new baby had long since disappeared and turned into the stress of another child to look after and schedule around. She was walking, talking, running, crying, and making giant messes that seemed impossible for such a tiny human to manage. She started the day with her mother, getting Brian ready for the bus, and getting herself dressed for work, before the babysitter arrived. Her father relieved the sitter and spent the evenings helping Brian with schoolwork or playing with toys that were not suitable for toddlers. Cassie's father would make a big dinner on the days he was off, and when the stars aligned and they were all at the table together, it was quick, and quiet. Brian was the star of the show. He went on about the things he was learning, the kids he didn't like at school, and the newest episode of Power Rangers.

As Cassie started to find her way into the family, she really latched on to her brother Brian. He was patient with her and would share his Lego blocks, or let her watch TV with him when he got home from school. He would talk to her when they were together, and she noticed that.

Her earliest memories were of hayrides in the orchard with Brian, Aunt Carol, and her girls. Cassie would chase her brother through the corn maze, determined to keep up and not get lost. She could never keep up, and could never find him, but she was laughing and smiling the whole way through, while gazing up in awe of the corn stalks. The fall also reminded her of trips to the grocery store with her father to pick up warm apple cider donuts. This was the only time she remembered doing something special with only him. The fall air was cool and crisp, and her father always bundled her in hat and matching scarf. The two would make a quick trip to the special store, then bring the donuts to the park. Cassie watched over them in the back seat, as the smell of cinnamon and warm brown sugar tickled her senses. The plan never changed, they would start at a bench and split one before playing on the swings and heading back home to put away the other groceries. Although her childhood was not full of memories, the ones she did have were priceless to her.

When she was four, the sitter quit, and it was back to daycare. She enjoyed the small class setting and playing with other kids. The time at daycare was far more relaxing than life outside of it. Her days were often a blur of daycare, her brother's soccer practices and games, and back home again. She had frequent play dates at Auntie Carol's house, which felt very much like her second home. Aunt Carol, who was her mother's best friend, but not her actual sister, was a stay-at-home mother to three girls. Her house had dolls, and coloring books, movies and games. Aunt Carol had more toys than Cassie had at her daycare. Cassie always ran to her oldest daughter's doll house. Jillian wouldn't let her sisters play with it, ever; only Cassie. It came with a family of four and a little yellow dog. Cassie gingerly played with each piece, creating scenes and dialogue between the characters. She was lost in a tiny world of perfection that she had total control over. She didn't mind so much not having a dollhouse at home, or any dolls, that weren't Brian's, because it felt like she was always at Carol's, and there it was special. She never noticed how long she was actually at Carol's, because she loved every minute of it. Most of the time her mother was there too, but busy having adult time with Carol and Brian was glued to the TV.

When she turned five, they had a cake for her at Carol's house. She arrived with her mother and brother, to the whole house smelling like chocolate. She ran to find Aunt Carol, jumped in her arms and gave her a big squeeze. There was one chair in the kitchen that had a pink balloon tied to it, and Cassie felt like a princess all through dinner, sitting up a little straighter than usual. Each of Carol's daughters had taken the time to make her a birthday card, and Jillian drew a picture of the dollhouse on her card. Cassie could remember feeling overwhelmed with happiness and love that day. They all sat together and laughed as the girls told school stories and Brian chimed in with his jokes. They sang to Cassie as she blew out the candles on her chocolate cake with pink frosting. And they all hugged goodbye as the Dodd's layered up with coats and hats and headed home on that snowy evening in January.

Home was not a place full of laughter and joy. Home was quiet. Brian was Cassie's best friend, and if it was okay with Brian, then it was all right with her. Brian was the best part of her home. In the spring they played on the swing set in the backyard. They caught caterpillars in a jar and dug through the mud to pull up worms. Her life was fun, it was all she knew. Cassie never questioned why her mom and dad didn't talk much, or why they didn't do fun things all together, or even why they didn't hug her as much as they did Brian. She didn't ask them why she couldn't have her own dollhouse, or why she couldn't paint her room another color besides beige. She recognized that she had grandparents, but she never saw them, and never felt comfortable asking.

When a new boy started at her daycare, who was African-American, Cassie was curious when his mother had curls close to her own. At times when his mom came into the room Cassie would just stare. Her curls were a little tighter than Cassie's, and less frizzy. She looked so beautifully put together and always had bright lipstick on.

"Well, aren't you a pretty little girl. What's your name?" Cassie was caught staring as she picked him up one afternoon.

"Cass…Cassandra." Talking to strangers was not her favorite thing.

"Hello, Cassandra. And how old are you?"

"I am five years old. I had a chocolate cake with pink frosting for my birthday," she said proudly.

"Well that sounds delicious! And look at your hair! Those curls are such a mess! Did you play hard today?"

Cassie was not the type of little girl who cared about her hair. Most mornings she held back tears as her mother tried to pull a brush through her head. She tried not to think about her hair at all.

"Can I fix your barrette?" The new boy's mother seemed nice enough. Cassie stood frozen in front of her as she deftly twisted her curly mass into a braid. This was the first braid Cassie had ever had. She let a tear fall, but not out of pain, but out of overwhelming joy as she looked in the mirror and grabbed and twisted her braid.

"It is so awesome! Will you teach my mom how to do that?" Cassie didn't want this to be her last great hair style.

"I would love to! But I have to go home with Charlie right now. It's time to get dinner ready for his dad and big sisters. It was very nice to meet you Cassandra."

Cassie couldn't stop talking about her braid, and how nice the new boy's mother was, and her excitement was only amplified when her father told her that they were having spaghetti and sauce for dinner.

"She said she would teach mommy how to do it!"

"That sounds very nice, but I am not sure that your mom has time in the morning for all that."

Cassie felt a bit deflated. "Why do I have curly hair and not mommy?"

"Well, genetics is a very tricky thing. Sometimes there are dominant and recessive genes for certain traits. When you get a little older, we will explain it more. Don't worry. You are beautiful exactly the way you are. Now eat, please."

Cassandra

Spaghetti was her kryptonite. She ate, and enjoyed her braid, and tucked away the conversation with her father. When you are five you notice more and forget less. Things around you start to feel different, and you are powerless to change them. When you are five, people treat you like a child and never ask for your opinion. You have an opinion you have feelings anyway.

Eddie

In the fall of 1988, Eddie was in charge of the move. He got boxes, packed boxes, labeled boxes, and moved boxes. Plus, he painted the new house, although he did not pick out the colors. Evie cleaned what she could, and window shopped the latest home trends with the baby on her days off. It was a one level, three-bedroom home with a nice backyard. All that was missing was the dog and picket fence.

"Eddie, I really need you to get the painting done in one day. I am not going to expose Brian to paint fumes, and it is much easier for me to be home with him." Evie was hell bent on painting the house before unpacking and settling in. Although she agreed to keep the sage green in their bedroom and cream color in the other two bedrooms, the wallpaper in the bathroom had to go, and the living room mauve color was not going to work with Evie's color pallet. Eddie suggested several beige tones and was quickly rejected each time. It took the biggest paint sample pallet that he could bring home to find a soothing enough color for her. Eddie wasn't brave enough to mention that the new color looked very similar to the current one. The two continued their conversation as they moved into their bedroom, one of the only rooms with furniture.

"I understand. Believe me, I do not want to be away from you guys. Dr. Ron will be here for a few hours tomorrow and we should have it all done." Eddie felt horrible that the timing of the move was so close to the birth of their son. Brian was only a few months old, and Evie was stressed out with late night feedings, sleeping for only three hours at a time, and now putting her out for the weekend. Eddie knew he had one shot to get this place painted.

"Oh, well that is great news. I will fix some sandwiches for you guys and leave them in the fridge." Her tone became noticeably more lighthearted.

"You don't have to do that, honey." Eddie was grateful for the offer but didn't want to put more on his wife.

"No. I want to. End of discussion. I will zip to the store early in the morning, if you will watch Brian, then I will fix you guys some lunch and head over to Carol's so you can get to work." Evie seemed pleased with the plan.

"Sounds perfect" Eddie said calmly.

Dr. Ron was quick to offer his help. And when he wasn't chatting it up with Evie, he was very helpful. He and Eddie had already moved furniture into the bedrooms, under Evie's direction, spent hours trimming bushes and cutting down the overgrown lawn, and now were about to throw on a new coat of paint. Eddie was impressed at the Doctor's hands on approach, as he wasn't sure he did any of these things at his own house. Not only did Dr. Ron know his way around hedge trimmers, but he also had an amazing ability to navigate Evie's moods.

The next morning Evie put her plan into action. Eddie spent his alone time with Brian just watching him sleep in his crib. The two had bonded already, and Eddie knew that his son was now his whole world.

"Ed, help me with these bags?" Evie was shouting as she burst through the front door. Not only did she wake the baby, but Eddie jumped right out of the rocking chair. He uttered some unsavory words before comforting the baby and heading out to see what version of Evie had come home from the store.

"You startled the baby. How much did you buy?" Eddie asked, noting the bags already being unpacked in the kitchen.

"You're welcome. It was really no trouble to do some shopping for you and our child. God forbid Ed! There is only one more load out there." Sassy was Evie's best side these days.

Eddie leaned in to give his wife an appreciative kiss, and was quickly rejected, which was not a surprise; however, it was a bit of a surprise when she wouldn't take the baby.

"I am going to jump in the shower. What time is Dr. Ron coming?" Evie said as she gave Brian a kiss on his fuzzy round head.

"Maybe 10 minutes?" Eddie was confused, she had showered the night before, but he was not about to stop her.

Twenty minutes later, Eddie and Dr. Ron were watching Brian inch around on a blanket in the fresh air outside in their back yard. The men were chatting about the football season so far, when Evie joined them.

"Nice to see you Dr. Ron. I really appreciate all your help. You are a great friend to Eddie, and to me." Evie was being genuine, and her honesty struck Eddie. He couldn't recall the last time she had said something heartfelt to him.

"I am very lucky. And you are looking beautiful today, Momma." Dr. Ron was the only person that Evie would let call her that. Eddie wasn't even sure she would allow Brain to say it.

"Oh, you know that's not true. What I wouldn't give for a manicure and a haircut!" Evie batted her thick eyelashes over her striking green eyes. Eddie was mesmerized at how beautiful she was, even now. Her curves were more luscious, and her breasts had tripled in size. Eddie knew his friend was

Eddie

being polite, but the words were so true. It was not lost on Eddie that he could not flatter her like that anymore, but it did make him feel good to see her youthful smile, even if it wasn't directly aimed at him. Evie was thrilled to have Dr. Ron over, and Eddie was thrilled that Evie seemed herself.

After some time, Eddie had to leave the backyard and start prepping for the task at hand. Once the drop clothes were down, he had to steal Dr. Ron away.

"I hate to interrupt, but is one of you going to help me paint today?" Eddie yelled out the back door. He watched as Dr. Ron got to his feet and hugged Evie gently.

Evie turned toward Eddie and offered him a wave. "I already packed the car. Call me at Carol's when you're done."

Eddie walked out and met her as she made her way to the front. He gave her a quick kiss on the cheek and had a quick conversation with Brian about being on his best behavior at Auntie Carol's house.

"Goodbye. I love you," Eddie said as she walked away.

"You too. Have fun!" Evie replied without looking back.

Eddie had so much hope in his new family, new home, and new life. He had hope that Evie would soften into her old self, and that she would soften to being a mother. Hope that this little baby would make his parents a stronger unit. And hope that they would all be happy.

Eddie rolled over and instantly caught a whiff of rose petals from Evie's locks. It was a heavenly smell that ignited his manhood. With his eyes still closed her snuggled in closer and began to nibble on her ear.

"What the hell? I am still trying to sleep." She may have been groggy, but the tone was very clear.

"You can snuggle with me and fall back asleep. I want to hold you," Eddie said innocently.

"I am not a baby. He is in the other room if you want to hold something," Evie said, adding distance between them once again.

"Evie, you are a stunningly beautiful woman. I want to show you that I love you and appreciate you."

"Waking me on a morning that I can sleep in is not the best way to do that. Please let me sleep, Ed."

Not wanting to press the issue, he left her alone. And he was left alone, with the memory of how warm an inviting her body once was.

It was around Brian's second birthday when Eddie's hope stared to run out. Evie was at Carol's almost every night. Brian was with the sitter all day until Eddie came home. Eddie was with Brian four nights a week, feeding him, bathing him, and putting him to sleep. He was only two. So full of life and love. He had teeth and was running all over the house. He had beautiful blonde hair and his mother's green eyes. He was talking up a storm, and he loved books. Eddie loved the time they spent together. They went to the park together and spent hours going back and forth between the slide and the swings. They hung out at home in the yard chasing balls and flying kites. And when naptime rolled around, all it took was a warm bottle and a place on Eddie's chest as they rocked in his oak chair. Eddie wished that they would do things as a family. They did have dinner together at least one night a week, but that was the extent of the together time. On those nights Evie would crawl in bed after Brian was down, and watch TV until she fell asleep. He was once again feeling a disconnect. She was back for a minute, but he just couldn't hold on. They were strangers.

One afternoon, Eddie came home to relieve the babysitter, knowing Brian had a cold. Evie had not been home, so Eddie called her job, but she was not at work. Assuming she was at Carol's, Eddie took Brian out to the pharmacy to get him some medicine. On the way, he drove past the bar, slowly, to see if Dr. Ron made it there yet. Eddie squinted, then his eyes opened wide and he slowed the car to a crawl. He blinked in disbelief and paused a second too long. As the car behind him laid on his horn, Eddie hit the gas. Brian was screaming in the back, frightened by the car horn, and Eddie was lost in thought as he arrived at the store. As he pulled Brian out of the car to soothe him.

"Bri, I am pretty sure I just saw your mother in that bar." The moment the baby heard the word Mommy his head jerked to look around and he repeated the word over and over. Realizing that he was no longer dealing with an infant, Eddie decided to keep most of his conversation to himself. Eddie struggled with the notion of Evie and Dr. Ron. Dr. Ron was his best friend, so he shouldn't be worried, but everyone knew about his smooth-talking ways. Eddie couldn't prove it was her, or Dr. Ron for that matter; he was in a moving car. But he knew the bottom line of the scenario; if she was cheating, he could lose everything, including his son. He paused and squeezed Brian tight in his arms as that revelation really hit home.

"Right. Daddy loves Mommy, and Daddy loves you Bri. I am not going to go looking for trouble. I know nothing, until I actually know something. I am not going to risk losing you. Ever."

Feeling better after their man-to-man conversation, Eddie got the medicine and started home. When he passed the bar, he did not see Evie, nor did he see Dr. Ron through the glass. He would put this day in the past. But he waited up until Evie got home that night. She came through the door with a bounce in her step and seemingly in a great mood.

"Oh! You startled me. What are you doing up?" She was genuinely shocked to see Eddie sitting at the kitchen table waiting for her.

"I wanted to talk to you."

"Now? I'm tired Ed. And I need a shower," she whined.

"Your son has a fever. I had to go out for some medicine. I wanted you to know."

"Well, good thing his daddy is a nurse. I will check on him in a minute," Evie replied.

"I would like us to spend more time as a family, Evie."

"Eddie, this conversation needs to be saved for another time. Let's have dinner together tomorrow and we can talk about what's on your mind." Evie tried to brush him off.

"Were you with Carol all afternoon?" Eddie didn't want to sound accusatory, but he did.

"Are you concerned about my whereabouts? I am a grown woman; you don't have to worry about me. I went to run some errands after work, and then dinner with Carol and the kids." Evie disappeared into the bedroom, unwilling to continue with the conversation.

Eddie wasn't going to let this go that easily. He would be sure to make this the topic of their next dinner conversation. He wanted to at least try to be a family, for Brian's sake. Evie was a mother, and a wife, and that should mean something to her. He would have to work on his approach. If he was too honest with her, she was likely to throw her dinner plate at him. He would never expect that from the Evie he used to know, but this version was full of emotions and outbursts, and surprises.

The next morning, they coordinated schedules and set a date to have a family dinner. Eddie planned a full menu, something that he enjoyed doing, and made sure to have some of Evie's favorites, including scalloped potatoes and a roast. Dinner went better than Eddie expected. He was careful with his words. He told her that he loved her and missed her. Neither could deny how quickly Bri was growing, and Eddie used that as the platform for wanting more family time. They would never get these moments back; he would never be a baby again. It seemed to work. Despite the fact that Evie came into motherhood with her share of issues, she truly enjoyed spending time with her son. They agreed that they would have family time three nights a week and at least one weekend evening. Eddie avoided landmine topics, and didn't bring up Dr. Ron, nor did he say anything about her responsibilities as a wife or a mother. He didn't mention Carol either. The agreement to spend more time together was a win. A big win for Eddie and for Brian.

They played the part of a happy family very well. Evie was home for dinner most nights. She had light conversation with Eddie and started giving Brian his baths. She would put him down for bed, and then head out to meet Carol for a night cap, or so she said. Eddie wanted badly to believe her. He wanted to believe that she was with Carol, and not anyone else. He wanted to believe that she just smelled like the bar when she crawled in bed, and not like Dr. Ron's expensive cologne.

Eddie locked the door on the roller coaster that was the 1980s and hoped the '90s were a smoother ride. It was sometime in February of 1991 when Eddie lied to Evie by asking her to go to a dinner conference with him, which was not actually dinner, and not actually a conference.

"I really appreciate you coming with me tonight, honey. It means a lot to me." Eddie could feel his pulse quicken as they approached their destination.

"Why are you being so weird about it? I happened to have the night off, and the topic will be useful to us both." Eddie thought he heard a hint of suspicion in her tone.

"Right then. Here we are." He pulled into a tall charming brick building that he must have passed a hundred times before without giving it any thought. He studied the details of the brick, it looked historic. For a brief second the image of his wife knocking it over with the force of her anger flashed in his head.

"Where are we? Is this the Wright building?" Evie turned to him in total confusion.

"Yes. I believe it is. They have cleared out the basement for the speech." Eddie tried to avoid eye contact.

"I thought this was a dinner conference. I am starving, Ed!" Evie's voice began to escalate.

"Did I say that? I apologize. I am sure they will have something. And I promise I will take you out afterwards." Eddie turned to get out of the car, in hopes that she would follow suit.

"We need to pick up our son afterwards, but you better believe you are going to the McDonald's drive thru on our way home." She seemed satisfied with her solution.

They walked through the double doors and entered a lobby. There was a greeter with name tags.

"Hello, and welcome. Please fill out a name tag and make your way down two flights and to the left. We are happy to have you with us tonight. The Doctor will be joining us soon." The woman at the door inspected their name tags before pointing them further down the stairs.

"Evie, this is not a work conference. I lied." Eddie didn't stop walking and ignored Evie's slowed pace. "We are about to walk into a couples counseling session." Eddie stood outside of the room they were directed to, while Evie was frozen 15 feet away. He walked toward her, partly to avoid yelling, partly to stop her from running away, and partly to beg for forgiveness.

In a soft voice Evie said, "Why would you do this to me? Why would you lie to me about this? It's humiliating." As Eddie opened his mouth to speak Evie raised one finger to silence him.

"And look at the position you have put me in. What do I do? Turn and leave so you can tell a room full of strangers that I am a terrible wife, or I can go tell a room full of strangers that my husband thinks I am such a terrible wife that he had to lie to me?" She paused to exhale. Eddie could feel her rage emanating.

"I am going to find a bathroom, and compose myself, while I weigh my options." Evie turned and started for the

Eddie

stairs. Eddie was grateful that she kept her voice down, but it didn't make him feel any better.

When she returned, he was waiting for her at the bottom of the stairs. He looked at her and said, "I want to do this together. Lying was wrong. But I love you, and that feels right." Evie shook her head in acknowledgment and they both proceeded to the room.

It was spacious, but sparse. The brick walls were painted white and it had a sterile feel to it. There were about a dozen folding chairs set up in a large circle. At the front end of the room was a sign in sheet, and some pamphlets. A table of crackers, cookies and other refreshments was available on the opposite side of the room. All the while the bitter smell of burnt coffee permeated the air.

This was not a surprise his wife took lightly. Evie was quick to share with the group that her husband brought her there under false pretenses, that he lied to her face, and that he might have a problem. Leave it to Evie to spin things. Still, she didn't leave. She sat and pretended that she was perfect, but she didn't leave. They listened to other couples talk about their triggers and stressors and how they managed their busy lives. The therapist talked about putting too much stress on our partners, and ourselves and how happiness is a balance. Despite the circumstances, Eddie was pleased with himself for getting them both there.

Seething mad, Evie refused to speak to him for several days after the meeting. When she finally come around, she made her feelings very clear. It was evening and Evie was home watching television in the bedroom. Eddie had put Brian down and was finishing up the dinner dishes. He made Evie's favorite pie for dessert and noticed that she hadn't cut into it yet. It had been about a week of silence, and Eddie knew it couldn't hurt to try. He warmed up a healthy slice of sticky pecan pie and added a heavy-handed scoop of vanilla bean ice cream to the plate of sweet delight. He tiptoed passed the baby's room and slowly pushed the bedroom door open. She looked at him, and he immediately noticed her lip twinge when she saw dessert. This was his opening.

"I made you some forgive me pie." He proceeded with caution. Evie took the plate without hesitation and shoveled in a mouthful of gooey pie filling and creamy ice cream. "I want us to be happy together. But it just seems that I can never do right by you, and I would like to fix that," Eddie started.

With her mouth half full Evie quieted her husband. "Shh. Please. Don't talk for a minute. Let me just finish one more bite in silence. Hang on." She ate, and he watched, quietly.

"Listen. I do not want to talk about the past. I do not want to go to group therapy. But I also want to be happy. If you find a therapist that is agreeable to us both, preferably a woman, then I would be open to considering going once a month to a private session, twice a month at the most. Now that's that. Those are my terms. Let's move on."

There was no mention of his deceitful actions. Apparently, that was something she could overlook. Eddie was over the moon. "Thank you. I accept." He moved next to Evie on the bed and gave her a kiss on the cheek.

"Do you want to watch Doogie Howser, M.D. with me?" Evie extended an olive branch.

"I thought you'd never ask!" Eddie stayed close and they snuggled in to watch the show.

"You really out did yourself with this pie. Might have to stop talking to you more often." Evie smiled.

Eddie knew that Brian was old enough to start understanding the relationship between his parents. He wanted to set a good example, and what's more he wanted his son to be able to communicate in his own relationships, something that Eddie and Evie could never get right. Plus, deep down, Eddie still wanted to get his girl back, and truly thought therapy could help. He wanted to be a happy family; he believed that they could still be a happy family.

Eddie

They went to therapy faithfully for months. The sessions were built on listening and respecting your partners' feelings, while working as a team to find healthy resolutions to conflicts and challenges. Some sessions ended up in arguments and agreeing to disagree. A few sessions attempted to help them with communication and listening to each other's concerns using a series of hypothetical situations. Each person had to express their honest feelings about the situation and then listen to the other's feelings. Then the therapist had them use real life examples. Eddie wasn't sure which example to choose, so he started with a softball, house chores. Evie listened, while he delicately expressed how he felt overloaded with all the inside and outside chores. He felt good getting it off his chest, but Evie wasn't exactly jumping at the chance to do housework. She simply said she would consider his feelings and try to be tidier at home.

Eddie wasn't noticing much of an impact. They were still on different schedules and weren't making the effort to spend more time together. Eddie had to ask all the questions when they did have a minute to talk. Evie never volunteered how her day was, or how Carol was, or anything. And when their son turned three, they divided the list of things to do and put on a happy face for their guests. Still, they kept going to therapy and that was all Eddie needed. He wanted to believe that she was trying.

The year came to an end, much like it had started, cold and quiet. Eddie had therapy, and he had Brian. He needed Brian, and he still loved Evie. He resigned to this being his life. And resolved to make the best of it.

A few weeks into January, on a cold afternoon, Evie dropped a bomb on Eddie.

"Let's adopt a baby!" She said, exploding with excitement. Eddie was too stunned for words. Was this a joke, a trick?

What would possess them to do such a thing? They were still trying to keep the family of three happy and functioning. And why is she so excited? This was not her reaction the first time around.

"Evie, this sounds like something we really need to think about for a while."

"But why? There is a baby at the hospital, and I want her. I don't want some stranger to have her. This is my chance. She is waiting for me. We can do this, now!" Evie was so confident and determined. There was clearly something that he was missing. This made no sense to him at all.

"Evie, I don't understand? When were you at the hospital? And why is this your chance? This reaction is so different than the first time around."

"That was over three years ago. I now know what it's like to be a mom. I don't want this baby to go to a stranger Ed. I have seen her. It's like she was meant to be mine," Evie pleaded.

"Seriously, this is all a bit much for me. I am going to go out for a while and think on it." Eddie didn't know what else to do.

"Ed, you need to get on board. I want to tell Brian tomorrow. This is happening."

Feeling like he had no say in his life was a feeling that Eddie was all too familiar with. He went to the bar, the same place he ended up when he found out they were pregnant. Eddie was confused and angry. Why does she get to make all the decisions? Evie couldn't pressure him into adopting a child, could she? But Eddie was a sucker for her smile. Happy Evie was the woman that he was married to, the woman that he stayed for. He would gladly live 50 miserable years if he could see that happy girl, that magic smile, every now and then.

Dr. Ron was there, already blitzed. "Glad you're here, my friend! It's been a rough week." Eddie sensed that he was more stressed than usual over the past few weeks but didn't press the issue.

"It has been a strange day, for sure." Eddie agreed, and they both lifted a glass to that.

"Wanna talk about it?" Eddie was happy to avoid his own problems for a minute.

"Oh, the usual…girl trouble." Dr. Ron said as he threw back a shot of something brown.

"Yikes! That bad?" Eddie pressed.

"Well, let's just say that I am not as good at it as I used to be. I am losing focus. Getting sloppy, and that can only lead to trouble."

Eddie did not want him to fill in any more details. He was assuming a million different things as it was. Although Eddie wanted to believe that his friend was loyal to him, he had a nagging suspicion that he wasn't.

"What brings you down here, pal? Haven't seen you in a while. Fight with Green Eyes?" Dr. Ron asked.

Eddie did not like the fact that Dr. Ron had a nickname for his wife, or that he knew the color of her eyes. He ordered a shot of the brown stuff.

"She wants to bring home a baby," Eddie said bluntly. When he didn't hear a reaction from Dr. Ron, he turned to look at his face. He looked pale.

"No, fucking way." Dr. Ron was finally able to express himself.

"Yep. I was shocked too." Eddie said.

"No, I mean, don't. Do not take that fucking baby!" Dr. Ron was loud. Again, Eddie was totally confused by the reaction.

"Why do you give a shit?" He shot back.

Dr. Ron took a second to compose himself. "I just want you to be happy. Is now the best time for another kid? Haven't you and Evie been a little off lately?"

Eddie did not want to admit that he had a point. He was stilled surprised at his passionate response. Why did Dr. Ron care so much?! And why shouldn't they have a baby? Eddie loved Brian more than he ever imagined he could love anything. He was well taken care of. He was a happy kid. Plus, he and Evie were in counseling, and that meant she was trying. Maybe a baby was another way for her to show that she was still in this marriage. Eddie was glad he bumped into Dr. Ron that night. He was glad his friend doubted him, because Eddie was going to prove him wrong.

As Eddie stumbled into his house that night, he peeked in on his son sleeping soundly, and smiled. He made his way to the bedroom, stripped off his clothes and climbed in bed with his wife. He kissed her neck until her eyes opened and she turned towards him. He whispered to her that he was on board and kissed her more. He hadn't kissed her in a long time, and he forgot how much he loved the shape of her body. He began caressing her. Suddenly, Evie flipped the script, and hopped out of bed. Before he knew it, she pulled him to his feet. Eddie was positioned behind her, as she leaned forward. He stood facing her ass cheeks. He rubbed them, and gave her a little smack, before diving in. Intimacy with Evie felt more like checking off an item on the to-do list. He knew that things changed after pushing out a baby, and he was just happy to be there, trying. He couldn't stop himself from exploding inside her with excitement, after a few short minutes. The show was over, without even breaking a sweat.

Evie looked into his eyes and said, "She will be coming home in three days, January 26th."

They both moved to their respective sides of the bed and fell asleep.

Cassandra

The summer of 1997, Cassie's parents told her they were getting a divorce. It seemed to come out of nowhere. One night they were out on a date, and the next night they were going to live in separate states. The news spoiled Cassie's favorite spaghetti dinner.

"Now kids, don't be upset. We both love you very much, and we will both see you as much as we possibly can," Evie added.

"Mom, I don't get it? You two won't be married anymore?" Brian asked cautiously.

"That's right kiddo."

"And who is moving to where?" Cassie heard the panic in Brian's voice, and it brought tears to her eyes.

"We have thought very hard about this Bri. We want you and your sister to have a happy normal life, we want what is best for you both," Her father started. "You can tell us what you want to do, but we were thinking that you would stay and live with me, and your mother and sister would move to Connecticut," Eddie finished, waiting for a reaction.

"Mom is leaving?"

"I won't be far, and you can come visit anytime you want." Cassie's tears were only encouraged by the tears spilling from her mother's eyes.

"This really bites," Brain remarked.

"Do you have any questions Cass?" Her mother turned to her.

"No." Cassie had no comprehension of what was happening. She felt a helplessness come over her that she wasn't sure what to make of. She couldn't grasp what was happening.

But no one took the time to discuss what it all actually meant. They continued on with their dinner, as if that was the end of it. No one explained the magnitude of leaving everything she had ever known and starting new without her brother, without Auntie Carol, and without her father. But then that might have been the crux of the problem between her parents.

That evening Brian seemed to take the news better than Cassie. It felt like a win to keep your friends and your home, plus get rid of your little sister. But to Cassie, Brian was more than a sibling. He was the one that she looked up to. She was allowed to play with all of his toys, even his G.I Joe dolls. He pushed her around in her red and yellow Little Tykes car when it was nice outside. They were backseat buddies, sharing snacks and laughing as the other stuck their hand out of the car window. They took turns sneaking the raw cookie dough off the pan before Evie could get them into the oven. Brian challenged Cassie to keep up with him on bike rides, or when running through the woods. And at only five years old, she knew that there was much more that she would need her partner in crime for. Brian was always there. A constant that Cassie didn't want to be without.

They went to the TV room to watch a show before bed that night, and all at once Cassie felt unsure of her future, more than that, she was scared. She grabbed Brian's leg protected only by his Spiderman footed pajamas, and cried, screaming and sobbing through the entire show. She wanted to hear that they would still be best buddies and great friends, just a little farther apart. That they could talk on the phone and send letters and pictures back and forth. She wanted him to tell her that she would always be his sister, but in that moment all he could do was let her hang on and cry.

It was late when Evie and Eddie carried their sleeping children from the couch and tucked them into their beds. Eddie returned to the couch and Evie settled in their bedroom for the last time.

Cassie left her home, her father, and her brother. She left her daycare, Auntie Carol and her girls. She left her favorite ice cream shop, and the bench near the pond where she and her dad would feed ducks in the summer. She left without a fuss. She didn't refuse or throw a tantrum, in fact that never occurred to her. Her parents made the rules, and Cassie followed them, it was that simple. But as she drove away from all she'd ever known; she couldn't help but feel like there was a little piece of her heart that was broken. She had never been this sad before. And being five years old, she probably wouldn't ever forget the feeling.

Evie and Cassie had a two-bedroom townhouse style apartment in the same town as Gert. Cassie had no more yard, no more Brian's room, no more Brian. When they arrived in Connecticut, they went to dinner at Evie's parents' house. The big white house was stuffy, and Cassie was afraid to touch anything. Cassie was left to watch television most of the evening, while the adults had a heated conversation in the next room. Minutes before her show was over, Evie snatched her up and told her to say goodbye. Sally and Bud did not hug her, they merely waved. Cassie followed suit and waved back.

Tangled Vines of Good Intentions

A few days later Gert came over to visit. She brought Evie a bouquet of wildflowers, and a new Barbie for Cassie. This was her first ever Barbie doll. Cassie was stunned. The doll had dark curly hair, kind of like her own, and a mocha complexion, kind of like her own. It was wearing a short green shimmery halter party dress, which complemented the medium purple eye makeup outlining her oval eyes. Cassie hadn't spent much time with Gert that she could remember, but was immediately comforted by her warmth, and thrilled with the gift. And when Gert offered to help Evie with Cassie, until they were more settled, Cassie felt like it was the first good thing to happen in a while.

Gert started picking her up from daycare during the week and watching her until Evie got home from work. Cassie enjoyed seeing Gert. She liked the way she smelled like a bouquet of flowers everywhere she went. She loved the soft grey color in Gert's eyes. She loved her round face and wildly bright red framed glasses. Most of all, Cassie loved how she felt when Gert hugged her. The softness of her body and the comfort of her embrace created a moment for Cassie where the only thing that mattered were her and Gert. A truly wonderful moment. It soon became apparent the affection was mutual.

It was Cassie's first day of school in her new town. They had only been there for a few weeks, some of her clothes were hanging in the closet, while others, were hanging out of boxes. Luckily her mother bought her a new outfit for her first day. As she slipped her feet into her black patent leather shoes, a single tear trickled down her face as she thought about how Brian was supposed to wait at the bus stop with her. She was pulled from her thoughts as Evie called her into the kitchen. In her new yellow stretch pants and lace trimmed oversized t-shirt top, she grabbed her bag and went downstairs. Evie added a few hair clips to the mass of dark chocolate brown curls that was Cassie's head, and commented that they should find a hair stylist soon. Cassie grabbed her lunch and kissed her mother goodbye. She would not see her again until the next day. The now familiar routine of their lives had Evie working a twelve-hour day from 10 to 10. Gert pulled into the driveway as Evie and Cassie were headed out the front door to wait for the bus. Cassie smiled for the first time that morning, feeling the love from her grandmother, as Gert wrapped her in a big tight embrace.

"Looking good Cassafras!"

Cassie couldn't help but catch Gert's enthusiasm.

As she shuffled through the halls trying to stay single file with her classmates, Cassie felt alone. Everything was so unfamiliar. She was one of twenty kids in her class, several of whom already knew each other from daycare centers, or through their older siblings. The kids congregated in their own groups during class time, leaving Cassie feeling like the odd man out. The teacher was nice enough and encouraged Cassie to reach out to new people and give it time. So, she tried to sit with a boy who looked exactly like her brother at lunch, but he already had enough friends to fill every seat. With few other options, she sat at the far end of a table half full, never making eye contact with the kids at the other end. As she looked around at the room full of kindergarteners, loud and laughing, sharing snacks and making friends, she couldn't help but feel very different than this group, mostly because they were all the same. Every girl was wearing a dress, tights, white shiny shoes, and a ribbon in her pure blonde hair, while every boy wore navy or khaki pants and a shirt with a collar. Naturally, the shirt complimented their fair skin and light-colored eyes. Cassie didn't know that so many people from different families could look so similar.

The school was an older, one story brick building. The walls were light blue and displayed large bulletin boards outside of every classroom. Some with art projects from the older kids, others with upcoming school events and some were specific to a classroom. The library looked more fun than Cassie remembered. She remembered going to the library once back home with Brian and her dad, but it was not like the one at this school. The school library was very colorful and had lots of things to look at. Glass cases displayed history projects and art projects from students. There was a section of the room with blocks and toys, books everywhere, and even a handful of computers. Plus, it had big windows and she enjoyed looking at the garden at the base of the flagpole near the bus drop off.

Her new elementary school was a great place to learn and play for those who were excited to be there. Although she was intrigued by the daily activities, painting, writing, and reading, she had a hard time making friends and she was quiet. Everyone asked her why her hair was so curly, and if she had to wear sunscreen in the summer. Cassie was not sure what their questions meant. Back home no one cared about her hair, and neither did she. And honestly, she didn't ever feel any different than everyone else, until now. This was the first time Cassie noticed that she didn't look like them, and it mattered.

"Mom, why is my hair curly? No one else at school has my kind of hair." It was eating at Cassie.

"What do they say about your hair? Never mind them. You are beautiful! Look in the mirror, that's proof." Evie was brief.

"But why do all the other girls have blonde hair?" Cassie pressed.

"That is what God gave them. Your looks are a gift from God. They are part of the goop inside that makes you special and different." Cassie couldn't quite grasp the finer details of the conversation. "You don't need to worry about why you don't look a certain way, you need to be happy with the way your goop made you," Evie said.

"Am I different than, Daddy, and you…and Brian?" Cassie was not fully aware of the question she was asking.

"You have your own goop, so do I, so does Daddy, and Brian, and every person on the earth. I wish my goop gave me big brown eyes like you. Now please do not worry about the kids at school. They have their goop and you have yours. Time to shower and get ready for bed, now." Evie was adamant.

Cassie was confused but pacified with her mother's goop theory. And she didn't want to think about being different than Brian. Or the possibility that she had to leave Brian because she was different. With a shutter, she shut out those thoughts and went up to get ready for bed.

Cassie was slow to adjust. Taking on a new state, a new apartment, a new school, and new people. By the time Christmas break rolled around she had one new friend. They exchanged Christmas cards on the last day before break. Cassie was delighted with the massive amounts of glitter her friend added to the handmade card. The girls embraced in a long hug before the end of school that day. It was a nice feeling, an accomplishment, and she hoped her friend would still be there when they returned from break.

She didn't have high hopes for Christmas that year. She knew this life was not as joyful as her old life. She missed being a family very much. She even missed her mother, who seemed to always be working now. But to her surprise and delight, her mother was home as Cassie stepped off the bus that afternoon. She ran through the parking lot and flung open the apartment door. Cassie stopped dead in her tracks and had to blink twice to believe what she was really seeing. Had Santa come early? She launched herself in the air and latched on tightly to Brian. He smirked and let her hold linger a bit longer than he'd like.

"Hey, Sis," he said in his slightly squeaky voice.

"Brian, Brian, Brian! I can't believe you are here! We have so much to do, so many games to play, and I have to show you my Barbie. I missed you," she squealed in delight.

"First things first," Evie cut in, "Why don't you guys get your hat and gloves and we'll go out and get a tree."

Both kids gave an approving nod and went to gather their gear. Cassie pulled her hat and gloves from her backpack and was ready to go, while Brian pulled his coat from the nearby coat closet. Cassie sat in the back of the Corolla, letting her emotions show in a smile, so big her cheeks started to hurt. Brian sat in the front and played with the radio, as Cassie sat thinking in the back. She was trying to remember her favorite Christmas at home, although that was harder than she thought, so she focused on her last Christmas. There was a tree that she and her mother decorated with lights and balls of every color. It was taller than her mother and smelled like fresh cut Christmas. She remembered shopping for gifts for Brian and Mommy one afternoon at the mall with her father. The stores were beautifully decorated with garland, snowflakes hanging from the ceilings, wooden reindeer in snow covered forests, and gingerbread houses. The mall was full of people and full of spirit. They picked out a new RC car for Brian and went to a special store to find something for Evie. Cassie loved visiting the jewelry store because all the sparkly stuff was at eye level. She pressed her nose to every case, each one more impressive than the last. Her dad suggested Cassie pick out a charm. She went to work picking out something that she thought her mother would like. After much deliberation, she picked out a three-dimensional silver heart charm, with a purple stone in the center.

"Perfect." The word was out of her mouth before she realized that she was speaking aloud.

"Do you have imaginary friends now?" A big brother jab was launched her way and pulled her from her warm memory.

"No! I was thinking something in my head." Cassie gave a weak rebuttal.

"Knock it off you two. It's time to get a tree!" Evie said.

Cassie couldn't remember ever seeing that charm around her mother's neck, but she was still hopeful.

Cassie couldn't help but notice that her mother seemed almost joyful with Brian here. She liked this version of her, and hoped it was here for a permanent visit. She secretly hoped Brian was on a permanent visit too. The week was amazing. It was as if they had never been apart at all. The three of them had meals out at restaurants and went to the movies. Cassie was lost in all the excitement. So, lost that when her bubble burst on Christmas Eve, she was completely blindsided.

They family was gathered at Gert's house. Kids were running around and playing with new gifts. Adults were gathered in the living room telling stories and drinking eggnog. The fireplace was blazing as flames reflected in the silver balls and tinsel adorning the Christmas tree, and carols were playing softly in the background. The doorbell rang.

Evie glided to the door in an ethereal manner that caught Cassie's eye. A man appeared. He was tall and had hair, lots of hair. Evie's face was bright and cheery as she took his hand and brought him in to meet the family. Cassie was frozen. She wasn't sure if she should run and tell Brian, or if she should run and hide. Who was this stranger? Why was he there now, on Christmas Eve? She didn't move, until Evie was standing right in front of her, with him at her heels.

"Cassandra, please grab your brother and come into the kitchen for a minute," Evie said excitedly.

Slowly, Cassie wrapped her head around the instructions and tried to give her feet the message to move.

"Now, please Cassandra," Evie urged. Her feet heard the message this time.

Cassie ran in search of Brian but wasn't able to explain what was happening. She had no clue. The two stumbled into the kitchen, shoving the other to go in first.

"Guys, this is Joe," Evie started. "He is my new boyfriend. He will be spending the day with us tomorrow." She paused. "Say hello, please."

The kids were speechless. They spit out a greeting and were gone as quickly as they came. Brian went back to the toys and seemed as if nothing had happened. Cassie was confused. She was not sure that this was ok. She wondered how her mother had time to meet a new friend. How will she have time to see her new friend and see Cassie? She escaped to her grandmother's room. Cassie looked in Gert's floor mirror and saw tears streaming down her face. She strolled around the room, trying to distract herself. She peeked out the windows and watched the snowflakes cover the ground. She climbed up on the queen-sized bed, and made her way under the heavy coverlet, then Vellux blanket, to slip between the crisp sheets and curl up. That was the end of her evening.

Christmas came and went. The gifts were great, and Cassie drank in each second she had with her brother, not knowing when she would see him again. She didn't have much of an opinion of Joe. All she really wanted to do was have some time alone with her mother to talk it over. She wanted to get a hug and hear that there would be enough time for both of them, but that conversation never happened.

As vacation came to an end, so did Brian's visit. He gave her a big hug and was picked up in a car that looked oddly familiar. And just like that, her normal routine was back in full swing, and she was relieved to have her alone time with Gert back. She needed someone to talk to.

"Who took Brian home, Gram?"

"I'm not sure, honey. Did someone pick him up?" Gert seemed caught off guard by the question.

"I couldn't see who was driving. It was a silvery car."

"You know, that could have been your Dad." Cassie searched Gert's face for a reaction; for an emotion. How was she supposed to feel about this?

"But he didn't come in, he didn't wave or anything. He didn't want to see me?" The tears welled up, threatening to spill. Gert pulled Cassie close, and held her for a minute,

CASSANDRA

buying time to figure out how to make the situation any easier.

"I think he is still very sad that he doesn't get to see you every day. I am sure that he thought it would make you sad if he said hi, and then turned around and left. He didn't have time for a visit. When he is ready, I am sure he will spend some time with you, little one."

"But I really don't understand?" Cassie couldn't hold back her tears. This new life was no fun.

"I don't either. I don't know why your mom and dad can't get along. But I promise I will always be here when you need me." Gert held her a little tighter until the tears subsided.

The end of kindergarten brought new challenges and feelings for Cassie. She wasn't focused and often times was reprimanded during class. She never made more than her one friend, and she still had this nagging sense that she didn't belong there. Joe was still around, and Evie not so much. She missed her brother, and her dad, and hoped for a summer visit. Luckily, she had Gert.

No one came during the summer. She spoke to Brian over the phone briefly about his summer plans. He was off to basketball camp and then vacation at a lake with his friends' family. He would turn 10 that summer, and Cassie would miss his celebration. She ended the conversation begging Brian to write her, or send her a post card, or call her when he was back from his trip.

Cassie had summer plans of her own. She was at her own version of summer camp, Grandma Gert's. Evie and Joe took off on a three-week trip to who knew where. For all Cassie knew, her mother was at home enjoying her time alone. But it didn't matter. Cassie was in her happy place. This was the person who she loved the most, and who loved her right back.

They played in the yard with the sprinkler and worked in the garden. Gert had all kinds of flowers, from poppies to orchids to bright pink peonies and various shades of purple Iris. The two baked cookies and made peach pie. They often had dinner outside on the patio and sipped cool iced tea with fresh mint leaves. Cassie was having so much fun she didn't notice that her three-week stay was extended.

One evening after dinner, Gert made Cassie an extra-large sundae, and they sat at the kitchen table eating together. It had all of Cassie's favorite toppings: nuts, chocolate shots, Oreo cookies, and hot fudge. This was the evening that Gert had to tell a six-year-old that her mother had moved away and left her and was not coming back anytime soon.

Gert

"Bernice, I simply don't understand kids these days! I mean, I tried to tell Ed not to marry that girl in the first place, but never in a million years would I have thought he would have agreed to a divorce, especially with children involved." Gert needed to vent to her sister, although the '97 Fourth of July picnic might not have been the best setting for the conversation. As she grabbed another cold beer from the cooler, she continued her rant, "And don't even get me started on the adoption. Who does that? Out of the blue, no conversation with your spouse or family? I still have never met the girl. It's like my son morphed into a completely different person and forgot how he was raised. I am furious with him. Just because his father died, why does that give him the right to stop visiting his home, and keep the grandbabies away from their grandmother?" Gert let out a long sigh and sipped her beer.

"You do have a car, Gert. Nothing is stopping you from visiting your son and his family," Bernice chimed in.

"One would think, but every time I tell Eddie I'm coming he has an excuse. The kids are sick, Evie is working all weekend, or he is doing some home repairs. What does he want me to do, let him live his life and never reach out to him again? I mean, fine, but then you call me and tell me you are getting a divorce, and expect me to do what? Be happy for you? I will be if that means I get my son back."

"Gert, you will always be there for your son, and your grandkids, whether you see them once a year, or once every ten years, right?"

"Of course, Bern."

"Well, then focus on the things you can control, and do a serenity prayer for the rest." Bernice wrapped her sister in a loving embrace as they both chuckled.

Gert used Bernice as a sounding board as often as she could. She and her sister were only two years apart. They relied on each other for honesty and gave each other much needed breaks from reality when they were together, laughing and reminiscing. They liked the same genre of music—top '50s pop, something with a beat, but nothing vulgar; the same books, murder mysteries the kind with a romantic twist; and the same men, strong, rugged, and delicious smelling. The pair also frequented the movie theater on senior day to catch the latest Oscar hopeful or historical remake. They had similar parenting methods, based very much on their own upbringing. Now in their older age the women both had glistening strands of silver and snow-white hair, cut in a fashion forward and ever-elegant bob. Bernice, however, visited the salon monthly to make sure her grays were covered with a golden brown that she was more accustomed to. She didn't mind getting older, but she sure did mind looking older. Gert, on the other hand, wore her natural hair color with pride, as she did every wrinkle, sag, and flap. Her body was beautiful to her. She didn't worry about the bulge that was created in the back when she fastened her bra. She wasn't concerned about the extra pounds that had settled in her waist over the years; in fact, she more often than not attributed those pounds to many years of successful pie baking or birthday cake celebrations with her boys, family, and friends. And when she played with her grandkids, they all burst into laughter as her grandson ran his fingers over the lines in her forehead and said they looked exactly like his favorite snack—raisins. Her body was a map of a life well-lived and a woman well-loved.

It had been more than ten years since her husband left the earth and she had to create a new life. With all the boys out of the house there were fewer people to look after. Her oldest son, Pat, lived about an hour away with his wife and three children. They came down for dinner with her once a month. Gert still loved to set the table and prepare a formal meal for her family. Although she usually had to make boxed macaroni and cheese for her grandkids, she was committed to finding a home-cooked meal they would eat. Picky eating was one thing that Gert didn't understand about that younger generation.

Her middle child, Rick, moved out to California with his wife after being offered a job. Gert was thrilled for him, but her heart broke to let him go. Logically she knew that all her children were successful, competent adults that hadn't needed their mother in a very long time, but she felt better knowing that they were all close by if they did. With Rick gone, Gert needed to stop lamenting over the family time that she didn't have and start enjoying the alone time that she did.

She kept her house spotless and her gardens weedless. What used to be Pat's room was now a library with soft purple walls and frilly drapery over the large window. Eddie and Rick shared a room until Pat left for college. Gert painted it a soft spring yellow and purchased a new bed with ornate wrought iron headboard for the space. After the much needed decorating the room was transformed into a calm and inviting guest room. Her room was also on that floor, but she didn't make too many changes. The little details, like his coin jar on top of his chest and the antique chair that they picked out together, still reminded her of happy times with her husband. The den was de-cluttered of years of her boys' sporting equipment, toys, and games. Gert moved the bunk beds downstairs and created a hangout space for the grandkids. She cleared out a separate part of her basement and turned it into a small art studio for her to dabble in watercolors or acrylics, depending on the day. With all the changes she made after her husband passed, she had no intention of touching the kitchen.

Fall brought fairs, and competition. Gert submitted pies, jams, and relishes to several town fairs each year. And was never without a blue ribbon to show for it. She was well known with the locals and had a good community of friends, despite her competitive side. She busied herself with bi-weekly garden club meetings, which also kept her on top of all the local gossip. However, when she showed off a picture of her newly adopted grandbaby, she inadvertently made Eddie their target. They all smiled and commented on her lovely dark features, only to turn around to their husbands and girlfriends and speculate about where the baby came from. Lately, she found herself dodging the conversation of her youngest child's impending divorce. Despite the fact that he was hundreds of miles away, Eddie's dirty laundry spread quickly. But when the conversation turned to business there was not a more skilled green thumb in town than Gert. Her passion and willingness to roll up her sleeves and get her hands dirty made her the envy of the club. The ladies respected her, despite their many opinions of her son's life.

Her conversations, and her overall relationship with Eddie had become tense. He visited once a year, if she was lucky, and never brought the kids. Gert made her way up when Brian was born and stayed for a full week to help around the house. Evie didn't seem very grateful for her visit, but she did keep her busy running to the store and here and there to pick up things for the baby. When Cassie came it was only a weekend visit. Gert had every intention of asking questions, like why and where did this baby come from; but she was distracted by the enthusiasm of her grandson. Brian loved the attention, and he took every bit of it that she would give him. Gert never asked the tough questions. She watched Eddie and Evie interact as a couple; she felt the tension. After that visit she was convinced that they were hiding something, and that something was not quite right with the whole situation. As the months turned to years, Gert never made her way back for a visit.

She was in uncharted territory with the news of Eddie's divorce. She couldn't help but feel disappointed. She and her husband had high hopes for their children. They wanted them to create loving and nurturing homes and fill them with babies. It never occurred to either of them that one of the boys would not be successful at it. It troubled her that she was on the outside of Eddie's world and couldn't get in to help him, or even hear him. He never talked to her anymore, not about the important things. He could have come to her when he was feeling the strain and pressure of marriage. They could have talked about it together. She was well aware that he didn't need a mother 24/7, but she never imagined that she couldn't be a friend or confidant.

She remembered so clearly the evening that he told her he wanted to marry Evie. Gert had to hold her tongue; she knew it was not the right time, but he just wouldn't hear her. Once Eddie left the kitchen that night, Gert felt a sinking feeling in her stomach. All she could do was shake her head, until she was rejuvenated by the arms of her love. Arthur slid into the seat next to her on the bench and wrapped his arms around her. She was a sucker for his charms as he kissed her forehead and told her that he was proud of her. Her husband knew that she was not a big fan of Evie, and even more, he knew that she was fiercely protective of her boys. Gert let Arthur calm her nerves and fill her heart with hope as he did every time she was fretting over something that he truly believed would be okay. She trusted him. Their love was built on faith and trust and had never failed her a day in over 25 years.

And so Eddie would be divorced. She didn't know what that meant for his children, or where he and his wife would end up. With more questions than answers, all Gert could do was wait until he gave her more information. But when he finally did give her more information, it was equally devastating and hard to hear. He told her that he would be staying in New York with Brian, and that Evie would be back in town with the little girl. She thought Eddie's solution was ludicrous. How could that be the only option? What was Gert to do, hold her tongue? But knowing what she had with Eddie was already delicate, that is exactly what she did.

With Evie moving home and not Eddie, the future seemed so unsure. Evie had always rubbed Gert the wrong way. Gert was appalled when she learned of the issues that Evie had growing up with her parents, and how she had essentially cut them out of her adult life. The information came out over time after they were married. When Arthur died, Gert had a flood of friends calling and stopping by in the following months. Dotty, a member of her church, brought over a poppy loaf and the two had tea and talked about a variety of things, most surprisingly, Evie.

"How is the happy couple doing? I didn't see much of them when Arthur passed," Dotty started.

"Honestly Dot, Eddie is taking the loss very hard, and I just didn't have the heart to press him about it." Gert paused to sip her tea. "She didn't come down with him, but they did leave together. There is something that rubs me the wrong way about that girl. I know she has a strained relationship with her parents. That's never a good sign," she continued.

"Funny you should mention that. My nephew went to grade school with the Somers girl, and I have heard some stories." Dotty set the bait.

"Like what?" Gert wasn't sure what she was expecting to hear.

"Well, she is the only daughter to a well-off family and she practically hates them. Her parents gave her anything she wanted, and she still defied them every chance she got. When she was younger, it was a bad attitude, but as she got older, from what I heard she was a real piece of work. She never followed their rules. Snuck out of the house a few times. Didn't do chores. I heard they practically kicked her out when it came time for college," Dotty said with a serious face.

"I can see that snotty attitude in her now. She is always out for herself." Gert shook her head in despair.

"I mean, you never really know what is happening under someone's roof, but it is a shame that such a beautiful girl can be so difficult," Dotty finished.

"Yes. I don't know if she has grown, or changed, but I sure hope so. She has some big issues that I wish my Eddie had been smart enough to stay away from." They continued their tea over less concerning matters.

She could forgive unruly teen behavior, but for an adult to turn their back on their parents? Gert tried to ignore the stories and judge Evie fairly, but after several different people had similar comments, Gert decided to have a chat with the Somers.

After Brian was born, and with newly developed pictures from her visit with him, Gert decided to meet with Sally. She called Sally, who was thrilled at the idea of having her stop by. Gert did feel a little bad for using her grandbaby as bait, but she wanted to get to the truth. And so, on a crisp fall afternoon, the two women visited and laughed over pie.

"I appreciate you letting me come over. You have a lovely home." Gert noticed the plastic covered furniture in the living room but decided not to ask.

"Nice to have you. And I have heard so much about your award-winning pie! I'll grab some plates and forks," Sally said politely.

"Are you and your husband planning to go up for a visit?" Gert couldn't help but notice the beautiful kitchen that Sally had, and the top of the line Kitchen-Aid mixer that she herself was still saving up for.

"Honestly Gert, we have lost touch with Evie since the wedding. I mean, she stayed here for the weekend after your husband died; may he rest in peace." Sally didn't make eye contact as she continued to move back and forth between the kitchen and the dining room table.

"Eddie has been distant since his father's passing. But I will tell you that they both seem thrilled with that beautiful baby boy." Gert tried to lift the mood.

"I was a little surprised to hear they were expecting." Gert could sense that Sally wanted to elaborate on this.

"Oh? Why is that?" She offered.

"My Evie is a free spirit. She never once mentioned becoming a mother or being a wife for that matter. I mean half of our blow-ups were about just that." Sally hesitated. "Oh, don't let me bore you with our family troubles." She started to cut into the pie.

"It isn't a family without some trouble. I have three boys, remember?" Both women smirked. "I am happy to listen," Gert said kindly.

"Well, it's just that she was…is my only child, and it hurts so deeply that we never connected. Everything I told her to do she would do the opposite. Everything that was proper for young ladies made her run in the other direction, no dresses, no heels, to get her to do her hair was a challenge some days. She simply wanted to disobey—all the time. That was the only thing that made her happy. She tells us that we put too much pressure on her, and always made her do what we wanted her to do, but we just wanted her to be a lady, and be happy. But be a lady first," Sally exhaled.

"We can only do so much. There is no instruction booklet. I am sure she knows that you love her." Gert was not sure what to make of it.

"We send her a birthday card every year, and I tell her in there." Sally went quiet for what felt like an eternity. "Let's see this baby boy!" She perked up.

Over the years Gert formed her own truth that Evie was a difficult child who still held a grudge against her parents when they were only trying to love her the best way they knew how. She felt justified for not warming to her. Of course her most difficult child would be drawn to another difficult child. And now Evie would be back in town. As hard as she tried to make sense of this nasty situation, she came up empty handed. Gert decided that she would do her best to be cordial in an effort to spend time with her granddaughter. She would be the one to tell Cassie that her daddy loved her, knowing full well that Evie would not. The curious little baby was now a part of a broken family. Still unsure of where she came from, or if she was a planned decision, Gert felt compelled to make sure Cassie understood that she did have a loving family in Connecticut.

When Gert went out to meet her after she was born, she was instructed not to talk about the adoption. Gert almost laughed out loud at the request.

"Eddie, you do see the complexion of this little girl, her big chocolate eyes, don't you? You do see the blonde hair and green eyes on your biological child? How would you like to avoid the topic of adoption?" Gert had a right to know the logic behind lying to a child.

"Gert, we are not telling her yet. When she and Brian are older, and if and when the question comes up..." Evie started.

"Oh, it will come up!" Gert was quick to interrupt.

"And we will deal with it when she is able to understand the situation." Evie made it clear that this was the end of the conversation by getting up and storming out of the room, baby in her arms.

Eddie explained that they were trying to offer Cassie a normal life. They didn't think a child should have to wrap their head around the specifics of being adopted. She had a family that was her own, no matter what everyone looked like. Eddie also explained that Evie wrote a letter to Cassie about the adoption, which they planned to give to her on her 18th birthday, if not before. He truly believed that if no one mentioned it, no one would notice. But Gert couldn't help feeling like it was an extremely unfair position for this little girl to be in. Her only hope was that she was a resilient.

Once the two had arrived and settled in their new apartment; Gert felt obligated to reach out and begin the process of building a relationship. Trying to be friendly, and to see her granddaughter, Gert invited Evie and Cassie to family dinner with Pat and his family one Sunday before school started. Gert was growing very fond of Cassie. She was unlike any child Gert had ever interacted with before. She was smart and thoughtful. She was caring, not snotty or rude. Most importantly, she was a very go-with-the-flow type of kid. She didn't ask too many questions. Gert was happy to pick her up from daycare and watch her in the evenings. Cassie was way easier than her boys had been, that Gert could remember anyway. She was looking forward to introducing her to her cousins and Aunt and Uncle. Pat's kids were a few years older than Cassie, but the youngest of the three was a girl, and Gert expected them to hit it off.

Gert

The menu for the evening was on the simple side. Gert was not interested in making a separate meal for the older grandkids, so she went with lasagna. She started the sauce early that morning, so the herbs and spices had time to marry before she added the meat. She was going with no bake noodles to keep things easy, salad, and summer squash. Knowing full well that Cassie would happily eat whatever was put in front of her, Gert crossed her fingers that the other three wouldn't make a fuss. She and Bernice picked up salad ingredients and both French bread and fresh Italian bread from the store that morning. Gert planned to make her own croutons and Cesar dressing. More important than the dinner, naturally, was the dessert. It didn't take long for Gert to settle on making apple cranberry pie with pecan caramel ice cream, from scratch. And she enjoyed every minute in the kitchen.

Her guests were all very prompt, and Gert had just enough time to whip up some dip and slice some fresh veggies while the adults chatted; the kids disappeared outside. She envied how easy it was for kids to get along. The adult conversation was awkward to say the least. Despite warnings from Bernice, Gert thought it would be ok to have Evie in the mix with the family. Evie had always gotten along with everyone, or so she thought. Luckily, Evie brought wine. After Pat's first glass, he excused himself to head outside and catch up with the kids. Gert was left with the two women, feeling very much like she missed her boys; they were so much easier to talk to. But she did her best to keep the conversation light.

"Anybody catch Ally last week?" Gert asked excitedly.

"If I am home by then, I am asleep by then for sure!" Evie shook her head.

"I think I have only seen one episode or so- what do you like about it so much, Mom?" Deb thought she was asking a simple question, but Gert knew she had to keep her cool and not spend the next hour going on and on about her new favorite show.

"Well, let me tell you! It is smart, and funny, so funny, with great characters. I mean Richard Fish! There is also a dancing baby." Laughter escaped her, despite the disinterest from Evie. "I mean, it is a good story, and I think you should try it again. Can you believe we are rolling into September once again? It amazes me how quickly the time rolls on."

"I could handle a few more weeks of warmth, but my three need to get their butts back in school. I miss the structure, and I lose track of who is where sometimes!" They all giggled with Deb and agreed on her point. "Is your little one excited for school Evie?"

"I think so. She hasn't been too talkative lately. Once she gets into a new routine, I am sure she will be glad for it."

"Has she done a school visit, or taken a trip on the bus?"

"No. We were a late enroll. There should be an orientation coming up soon, so she will get to tour the place."

"Poor thing. I bet it is a hard transition." Deb shook her head.

"She watched Brian get on the bus, and has been to his school a bunch, so I think she knows what to expect. She is strong, much stronger than anyone gives her credit for. I never worry about her." Gert could sense the defensiveness creep into Evie's voice and posture.

"You girls will have the pleasure of tasting one of my ribbon winning pies tonight, with a twist. I am adjusting my spices to see if I can get a new flavor into an already delicious bite. A very important task, because fair season is right around the corner as you might recall." Gert did a quick subject change.

"You know your grandkids are already talking about the fairs. The girls want to see the animals, and Nate wants to go down the giant slide on a burlap sack. I love that they love the fairs. I mean, you really have to growing up here in New England." Deb took the last sip of her wine.

As the conversation continued Gert filled up their glasses and excused herself to the kitchen to check on the pie and uncover the lasagna. When she returned the topic shifted to Evie, and how she was adjusting to being back in Connecticut. Leave it to her daughter-in-law to make things awkward all over again.

"You know, I didn't exactly plan this Deb. I thought I would have more support in Connecticut," Evie snapped.

"How are your parents then, supportive?" Deb was not shy.

"I saw them a few weeks ago, they are doing well, thank you for asking."

"And how is Brian?" Gert knew Deb was walking on thin ice. Brian was the golden child, Evie adored him.

"He needed to stay with Eddie, to keep his friends, and his sports. I was trying to disrupt his life as little as possible," Evie started.

"But doesn't matter about the little girl. She is resilient right, won't notice moving into a white neighborhood with a bunch of strangers in a town she isn't familiar with." Deb was going in for the kill.

"Saved by the bell!" Gert exclaimed awkwardly as the buzzer in the kitchen ended the round of jabbing between the two. "You two play nice and call in the kids, would you please?"

"We aren't all perfect like this damn family." Gert heard Evie mumble clear as day as she headed for the door.

At least the kids were getting along well. They all played together and laughed together, and never thought anything of it. Dinner conversation was directed at the little ones. Gert loved catching up on the latest movies, or Hollywood hunk from her oldest granddaughter. Apparently, the group Hanson was a hit with both girls, and her grandson saw the summer blockbuster Men in Black twice at the movies and was requesting the VHS tape for his birthday. They also talked all about school and if they were ready for the first day in a few weeks. This was a topic that Cassie could chime in on. Gert listened intently as she told everyone that her and her mother already went to the nearby mall to pick out an outfit for her. Gert was relieved to see a smile reaching from ear to ear the whole time she was talking.

And as quickly as they all arrived, they all packed up to leave. One slice of pie was the lone survivor. Gert loved Sunday dinner because everyone left early, giving her enough time to clean up and catch her show. She was proud of herself for getting everyone through the first family dinner with their additional family members. Who knew how many more dinners this new group would be having now that Evie was back in town?

As Gert was preparing to head to her garden club meeting the next day, she got an unexpected call from Pat. He started by thanking her for dinner, and then rolled right into the reason for his call.

"Ma, honestly, didn't you think it was a little strange having Evie there?"

"Well, I didn't stop to think about it, I guess. She lives here now, and Cassie needs to spend time with family. I highly doubt Evie will spend time with her own parents now that she's here!" Gert tried to defend her decision.

"I get that, Ma. And I feel for her, but I don't feel like she is part of our family anymore." There was a long silence on the line. "I just think that it would be more comfortable if in the future she wasn't invited to our Sunday dinners. You can certainly have her over. I mean, I never thought you two were best buds, but that's up to you."

Gert was mentally cussing out her youngest child for even giving her a reason to have this talk with Pat, and for making her defend a decision that she wasn't sure she could defend. "Look sweetie, Evie and I are not best friends. But she was part of this family for a long time. She is also the mother of my grandson. I will not close my door if she needs help. I know this is not a new town, but this is a new situation for her. If you prefer not to have Evie for dinner, I will do my best to accommodate your wishes. However, I will not turn my back on that little girl, ever. There might be occasions when you have to see them both. Please don't make me choose between my family members." Gert could feel herself getting a little heated.

"Fine Ma. Don't get all bent out of shape. I was just saying that intimate family dinners are awkward. Cassie seems like a sweet kid. I think my daughters are jealous of her hair. They wouldn't shut up about it the while ride home," Pat said.

"You didn't tell them, did you?" Gert was instantly panicked.

"No. You only told us a hundred times not to. But if it comes up, we will tell our kids the truth. Deb and I can't support lying to our children."

"Understood. Well look hun, I am on my way out the door to a club meeting," Gert said.

"Ok. Good talk. Love you Ma."

"Love you too. Kiss the babies for me." Gert needed to clear her head after that call.

Gert was true to her word and limited the family time with Evie. It was Christmas when they all were together again. It was then that Gert finally understood what Pat meant. It was that moment when you look around and see kids playing happily, adults laughing over childhood stories, and thinking that nothing can slice through your Christmas spirit. And then Evie did. Gert started to get a sense of what Eddie had to deal with. The girl was downright selfish. Which Gert knew all along, but to be in a relationship with someone like that must have been torture.

Tangled Vines of Good Intentions

Gert felt closer to understanding Eddie's situation after having Evie in town for only a few months. Still, she had never been more distant from her son. He drove down to drop off Brian but didn't stay the night. They sat for coffee and that was it. He had an aversion to the house, and somehow Gert was thrown in the mix. She could sense that he had so much pain from losing his father that he couldn't separate her from the equation. It made her sad, and angry. She told Eddie rather sternly that he needed to get professional help, and that he was not setting a good example for Brian. And while she was being honest, she point-blank asked Eddie how he intended to be a good father to Cassie if he lived in another state and never bothered to visit her?

"Are you serious right now? Evie took her. As far as I am concerned, she has always been Evie's child. I am doing my best, but I want nothing to do with Evie. Just give me some time to heal Mom, please. You couldn't possibly understand." Eddie was exasperated.

"That's just it Ed—if I don't understand then a five-year-old certainly won't. You are the person that she calls Dad. And now you barely call her. What is she supposed to think? What am I supposed to think? Who taught you to turn your back on your family like that?"

"Well one thing is for sure, you and Dad never taught me anything about heartbreak and divorce!" Eddie snapped.

"We did our best to prepare you for life. There are twists and turns that no one can imagine or prepare for Ed, but I thought we gave you the tools to make good decisions and take responsibility for your actions." Gert was furious at the 'poor me attitude' that her son had.

"I hear you. I am taking care of Brian. He will have everything he wants. He will be happy. I am being the father that he deserves."

"And there is the point I am trying to make…who is being the father that Cassie deserves?" Gert let out a heavy sigh in the silence that followed. Clearly Eddie was not having this conversation anymore. He finished his coffee and left.

Gert resigned not to let her father's absence be a factor in Cassie's life. Gert saw the girl almost every day and was happy to build a special relationship with her that might fill the void of not having Eddie in her life.

And when Evie decided to invite her new boyfriend to Gert's house, uninvited, on Christmas Eve, Gert knew that she was done putting in the effort with Evie. She was done trying to play nice and holding her tongue. She was done being in the middle of the relationship and she was done supporting either of Cassie's parents.

In the months after Christmas, Gert worked on her relationship with Cassie, as her Grandmother, her parent, and her friend. It was clear that she was being left behind. Eddie spoke to her once a month, if that, and Evie was showing her stellar parenting skills by spending her days off with her new beau and leaving Cassie with Gert. Aside from all of her anger and disappointment, Gert had so much love for Cassie, and it thrilled her that they got along so well, so easily.

"Good morning Gram!"

"Good morning Cass. Don't you seem chipper today? Wave to your mother." As Evie pulled out of the drive, Gert already had a few ideas for how to occupy Cassie on her snow day off from school.

"I am excited that I don't have to go to school today cause it is snowing, and I like the snow, but most of all, I like being here with you." Gert was touched by the sincerity of the six-year-old.

"Well, I am very happy you are here, Love. First things first, did you eat breakfast yet?"

"Nope." Gert saw concern cross the little girls' face.

"No worries! How about some eggs and toast, or French toast? I think I have some cinnamon toast crunch if you feel like cereal?"

The two went straight for the kitchen to get their snow day started off on the right foot. After standing in front of the open fridge for at least two minutes, Gert realized that decision making was not this child's strong suit.

"Okay, time to close the door, or you are going to have to put your hat, coat and gloves back on to stand in the kitchen. Have a seat at the table please, Missy, and I will fix you something to eat." Gert watched Cassie take her seat on the bench at the table and proceeded to play with her pen and notepad. "Don't lose my grocery list now."

"I won't. I was just going to draw you a picture," Cassie replied, without breaking from her doodle.

Minutes later Gert set breakfast in front of her and carried a plate over for herself. Cassie had already started on her cinnamon toast and seemed to be enjoying it.

"Did you finish your reading assignment that is due at the end of the week yet?" She decided to do her usual school check-up. Without making eye contact with Gert, Cassie slowly shook her head left to right. "Well it is a good thing that we have a copy of that book here. How about you get a few pages of reading done, and then we can have some fun."

Cassie's eyes lit with curiosity and excitement. "What fun things are we going to do today, Gram?"

"I have a whole list of things in mind! We can wash the kitchen floor, scrub the toilets, and we better shovel the driveway and rake the roof."

With a mouthful of eggs, her granddaughter let out an infectious laugh that Gert couldn't help but mirror.

"What's so funny? Do you think I should throw you up there on the roof and you can shovel all the snow off?" Gert continued with a smile.

"No! I don't want to go on the roof," Cassie giggled.

"What do you want to do then?" She waited and watched her little gears turning. They had spent enough time together that she could almost guess what Cassie's favorite things to do were, but this was their first winter together, and Gert had some things up her sleeve.

After a brief delay, and a few more bites of toast, Cassie responded, "Um…can we color, and play cards, and maybe watch a movie?"

"Great choices! All very fun things that we usually do together, but I had a few other things in mind, some wintery things." She had her full attention. "What do you think about building a snowman?"

"Yes! Cool! I wanna build a snowman! Do you have carrots? I remember the last time I played in the snow, my brother Brain and me rolled up two big balls. Daddy had to come outside and lift them on top of each other. And then he rolled a little ball and plopped it right on top for the head. Daddy let me push a carrot in his head to give him a nose, and then Brian used rocks to make two black eyes. But I can't remember… can't remember…his mouth?"

"We can use anything we find, anything you want. Did you guys name your snowman?" She loved when Cassie carried on. The world seemed far more optimistic from a child's point of view.

"I don't remember. But after we were done building him, my brother starting throwing snowballs at me. He chased me all over the yard!" Cassie said through her grin.

"There will be none of that today! Gram will play in it, but throwing it is a whole different story. Do you like hot chocolate?"

"Yeah! Daddy used to put smellows in mine."

"He put what in there?" Gert was looking forward to hearing this explanation.

"Have you ever had a smellow? They come in a bag, and you buy them at the store. I think they are kinda chewy, and sticky, but I don't know what's inside them. When you put them in hot cocoa, they get a little melty, and it's so yummy. Do you have those here Gram?" It was clear that Cassie believed the word smellow was in the dictionary.

"I think I might have something close, but it is called a marshmallow."

"Mash-marshmallow." Cassie played with the word in her mouth. "What do they look like?"

Gert went to the cabinet and pulled out a bag of mini marshmallows.

"That's a smellow! You do have them! They make the cocoa so yummy." Cassie was so excited, and confident, that Gert decided that the grammar lesson was not needed.

"Great! And what else can we add to the list today? Would you like to do some baking?"

"Yes! Yes! Yes!"

Gert was not surprised by the response. Cassie was a great helper in the kitchen and seemed to enjoy watching Gert in her element during pie season. "I was thinking Tollhouse cookies?"

"My favorite!" Cassie exclaimed.

"Sounds like we have a pretty full list of things to do. Can you remember what number one is?" She looked at her with a serious, but not stern face. Cassie shook her head up and down and got up from the table. When she returned Gert watched her place her reading book next to her on the bench and proceed to finish her breakfast.

As summer rolled around Gert was hit with a new reality. Evie stopped in unexpectedly with Cassie. She sent Cassie to play outside while she had a talk with Gert. Not knowing what to expect, Gert tried to stay calm and open minded. As they stepped into the kitchen, out of earshot of Cassie, Evie burst into tears.

"I miss Brian," she said. Tears ran down her face in an honest display of a mother's pain. Gert poured them both a glass of iced tea and they sat at the kitchen table. "I need to go back to Brian."

Not sure what to say, Gert tried to comfort Evie. "Well you can still go back."

"Gert, I'm just not sure what I am doing as a parent. I feel like I have to hurt one child to meet the needs of the other. But I still fall short. I miss Brian. He is my baby."

"Being a parent is tough. I still don't have everything figured out. But things will be ok if you put your children first." That was about all the sage parenting advice Gert could muster. Her next suggestion would be to grow up and stop being so selfish. It was on the tip of her tongue.

"Joe and I would like to take a vacation, alone, for a few weeks. Would you be willing to watch Cassandra while we are gone?"

Not really feeling like she had any choice, Gert hesitantly said yes. "Just make sure to leave me your travel plans and number where I can reach you."

And this would be a lesson Gert would not soon forget; never trust Evie, because she would always pick selfishness.

It was two weeks into their three-week vacation when Evie called to tell Gert they were not returning to Connecticut. Gert was now responsible for a six-year-old whose mother skipped town, and whose father didn't want to be involved in her life. She was beside herself. Her natural instinct was to call Bernice, but Gert knew Bernice would have seen right through Evie's trap.

As she dialed Eddie, she tried to imagine how the conversation would go. She wanted to hear that he would be down as soon as he could to pick her up; she tried to will the words out of his mouth. And again, what she got was a smack in the face. As if Gert had not taken enough garbage from the Eddie-Evie situation, Eddie did not jump at the chance to come and reunite his daughter with her brother. Instead, Eddie told his mother that he was engaged. He said that he would be starting a new life and moving on from the pain that Evie caused.

"Mom, not only did she break my heart when she left, but she made me question our entire marriage. I wonder if she ever loved me at all. She cheated on me, Mom." Eddie took a pause, perhaps hoping for some reaction from Gert, but she was not on the same page. "And when I think about the adoption, I still don't understand what her motivation was. Was a baby one last real attempt, and it failed too? I know that Cassandra would be a walking reminder of such a hurtful situation. A walking, talking, eating breathing reminder of a painful time."

"You are creating a painful time for me right now, Ed! I don't even know what to say. Put your children first. That's the one thing you should have learned from your father and me. And we sure as hell taught you about forgiveness. Honestly, she is innocent. You two plucked her from the hospital; she could have had a different life Ed, but *you* wanted her!" Gert was practically screaming into the phone. Luckily it was late, and Cassie was upstairs sleeping. "Are you honestly telling me that you are building a new happy life and you do not want your daughter in it?"

"Yes. I have thought about it, and I need to do what is best…for Brian. I'm sorry."

"For Brian, or for you?"

"How would I explain to Brian why he doesn't look anything like the child we are calling his sister? And how do I explain to Cassandra that she has another set of parents out there in the world. Ma, I truly don't know how to handle the adoption thing, especially on my own."

"What about this new wife? I'm sure she could help you out, assuming you even told her?" Gert could feel the conversation spiraling.

"We have talked about it. She supports my decision."

"Well she sounds like a peach! You have a knack for picking up woman who like to run from their responsibilities."

"Hey. Calm down. I know this is a crappy situation, but it isn't Susan's problem."

"You need to listen to yourself! It isn't Susan's problem, it isn't your problem, apparently, or Evie's; but it sure is my problem. Ok, well then you can start that new life without me, too. It's been a pleasure being your parent Ed, but I will not support this decision. You walk out on Cassandra and you walk out on me." Gert hadn't realized the tears blurring her vision, or the sweat beading subtly around her forehead.

"Don't do this, Mom."

"Don't do this, Ed."

"I have to. For me, for Brian."

"But not for Cassie. I see. Well you know how to reach us if you change your mind." And with that, Gert hung up, and sat quietly sobbing in the den. She had failed as a mother, her son had failed to be a father, and the one that suffers is Cassie. Gert decided right then that she would not throw a pity party for her granddaughter. This was the shit hand she was dealt, and they would make the best of it together. It was the next phase of both of their lives. They were together, and Gert had the chance to teach her that she could find family anywhere, that we only get one life, and you have to make the best of it, and that she was strong enough to overcome anything. Not entirely sure how to do this, Gert focused on step one, telling her that her mother was gone.

Gert found herself in uncharted territory. Girls were very different than boys. Cassie was strong, talkative, and smart, but so sensitive. She took a while to settle in, as one would expect. When Cassie was in elementary school, Gert spent as much time in the principal's office as she did. The general theme seemed to be her listening skills, or lack thereof, and her inability to share.

First grade show and tell was rapidly approaching and Cassie seemed excited. Together they thought of a long list of things

Tangled Vines of Good Intentions

Cassie could bring with her that were special to her. Never thinking that there could be a downside to show and tell, Gert was shocked to receive a call from the principal on that day.

"Mrs. Dodd, Cassandra was sent to my office today for shoving another student outside at recess," the principal began.

"I see. And what exactly happened." Gert knew from raising her boys that there was always more to the story.

"Apparently another student asked to see her doll and Cassandra refused and pushed her to the ground."

"That's it?"

"Well, we cannot allow children to push, or hurt other children Mrs. Dodd." The principal started to scold Gert.

"Right, no, I agree. I meant, was that the end of the altercation. I want to be clear about what I am walking into. I appreciate the call, and I will be down within the hour to discuss this further." Gert was not pleased with the interruption in her day.

Cassie was sitting in the office with her head hanging, clinging to the Barbie doll that Gert gave her when she moved back to Connecticut, dried tears chalked her cheeks. Gert checked in with the secretary and took the seat next to Cassie.

"Why am I here Cass?" she asked as she hugged her granddaughter close and gave her a kiss on the top of her head.

"Because Jenny tried to take my Barbie when I told her she couldn't hold it. I pushed her away when she reached for it, and she fell and scraped her hand."

"Did you ask her nicely, not to touch your doll?"

"No." Cassie was still staring at her feet.

"And why didn't you want Jenny to hold your doll?"

"I didn't want her to ruin it or get it dirty."

"I see. Can I please see your doll, Cass?" Gert knew that Cassie was super attached to this particular doll, which is why they both thought it was the best item to bring.

"Now Cass, isn't this the doll that you have had for over a year now?"

"Yes. You gave it to me as a gift, don't you remember?" She lifted her head to be sure Gert knew the significance of this Barbie.

"I remember. And do you remember over the summer when your cousins were here and you all played with your Barbies? Even this one?"

With a sigh, Cassie replied, "yes."

"And I am almost positive that this doll has been outside in the garden a few times with you, and through the sprinkler once or twice, right?"

"Yes."

"Are you sure that you didn't want to share because you thought she would ruin your doll?" Gert knew her point was clear and was hoping for the rest of the story now.

"No."

Gert waited in the silence. She gave Cassie a chance to collect her thoughts, as little tears dripped down to her lap.

"She was making fun of my Barbie because she isn't the same color as the real Barbie. I didn't want her to touch my doll, because Jenny is mean."

"That was mean. It sounds like her words were very hurtful."

"Yes, they hurt me first."

"Right, but that doesn't mean that you have the right to hurt someone back, Love. She made you feel sad, and then you made her feel sad, but did that make you feel better? Cause it looks to me like those are sad tears."

"No. I do not feel better."

"Okay. Well then, I think we need to brainstorm and come up with some things we can do to make you feel better when someone hurts your feelings and pushing or hitting will not be on that list. Understood?"

"Yes, Gram."

"Now I have to go talk to your principal. You wait here, and we can continue our conversation on the way home."

"Okay."

Gert was angry as she entered the office and shut the door. She was not sure why only one side of the story was told, but she had a few thoughts on that.

"We meet again, Mrs. Dodd. This is becoming a regular thing. We should have tea," the principal quipped.

"I am not happy to be here, nor am I staying long enough to sit down. I know what you are going to suggest, and you know the answer is no. I would like to inform you that Jenny had some unkind remarks about the ethnicity of the Barbie doll, and that is what fueled Cassie's response. I plan to have a conversation about her behavior. What I wish I didn't have to talk to her about over, and over, and over again is why people think she is different, and not equal. I will talk to my six-year-old again about how all people are different, and how to handle bullies. So, I will ask you, how does this school deal with bullies?"

"Um…well…I was not informed that Jenny made any remarks. I will look into it further, but the pushing is the matter at hand." The principal stumbled over her words, clearly caught off guard.

"Yes. Understood, I will handle that, without therapy thank you very much. The response to the teasing was not okay, but Cass won't push people if they are kind to her. These kids are so young, and they are simply reflections of the adults in their lives, and what those adults are teaching them. I promise to handle the reaction, if there is someone to stop the action in the first place. Thank you for your time, I have to go, need to put a pie in the oven. Have a nice afternoon." And with that Gert left before the principal could say goodbye. She didn't need to hear it.

The school didn't have much to say that Gert found valuable. Every meeting the principal presented the same solution. They wanted to send Cassie to special classes with fewer kids and more one on one attention. Gert was quick to shoot down this plan. It was not her intelligence that was the issue. The school suggested therapy a few times, and Gert almost went for that, but decided this was something they would have to work out together. If Cassie was angry, she could tell Gert, if she was sad, she could tell Gert, and together they would find a solution. Plus, the thought of telling a psychiatrist the story of Cassie's life, and then asking that person not to tell Cassie, sounded like a recipe for disaster.

Although Gert was not a fan of keeping Cassie's adoption quiet, it seemed to not come up all that often. Cassie recognized that she looked different from the other kids at school but hadn't yet thought about why she looked different than her family. There were times when she was picked on at school for her dark features, or her tan complexion. And in those moments, Gert would give her a big hug and simply explain that people need to be more kind, and that she shouldn't want to be anyone else, because all the greatest, most special people on the planet were unique. Gert wasn't hiding the fact that she looked different, but she wasn't offering her an explanation for it either. She knew deep down that Cassie was naïve enough to not even think that her mother wasn't her birth mother, or her father, or her brother, or even that Gert wasn't her biological grandmother.

Cassie never questioned if Gert loved her, but she never stopped asking about her mother. Gert knew Cassie honestly believed that this was her only family, and never thought twice about it. They carried on with their lives, because different was their normal. Gert assumed the day would come when Cassie was a teenager and she would ask the question, or maybe a few questions, but until that day arrived Gert wouldn't worry about it.

Eddie did mail the handwritten letter to Gert, the one that Evie penned when Cassie was born. She didn't read it, simply placed the sealed envelope in a well-hidden spot and vowed not to lose sleep over it. It was not her secret to tell. This was a decision her parents made, and Gert could only pray that she didn't take the blame for their choices. She prayed a lot.

As the weeks rolled into months and the months flipped to years, Gert found herself invigorated by the lightheartedness of her preteen. Cassie took time to enjoy the little things, and many of those were things they could do together. When she wasn't over at a friend's house, Cassie was eager to help weed the garden, or pick the vegetables. Gert was thrilled when Cassie requested her own section of garden when she was about ten. They transformed a small section of lawn into rich tilled soil that she was able to transform however she wanted. She pitched in with dinner clean up, and even cleaned up her room after the first time Gert asked. Gert was amazed at what a quick study she was when it came to cooking and baking. Her boys never much cared about the process, just the results. She appreciated having someone around that was genuinely interested. Gert loved Cassie's brains. With each passing year she was more and more thoughtful, insightful, genuine, and sweet. Gert noticed her doing better in school and enjoying it more. She was excited to attend science fairs, and chorus concerts. Cassie was a wonderful child, and Gert felt like she was doing a decent job at being a parent to her. When Cassie needed to be reprimanded, Gert didn't often let her off the hook. Although she did enjoy letting her play hooky occasionally; they always went to the movies and then out for lunch. Gert was grateful for her life with Cassie and couldn't imagine a life without her.

And when either of her other parents did come around, Gert was quick to protect her baby girl. It was the end of Cassie's eighth grade year when Gert received an unexpected call from Evie. She wanted to know how Cassie was and wanted to see her.

"I am not sure, Evie. She is having the time of her life right now with graduation, and I don't want you around killing the mood." Gert didn't ever want her around but knew she probably couldn't stop Evie.

"Graduation! Yes! That must be soon, a week or so away?" Evie pried.

"Yes, next Friday. They are having a full ceremony at the school for the kids. We have plans to get her a new dress, and she is excited. Let the girl be happy, Evie."

"Ok. I won't rain on her parade. This is a special occasion, although I would like to get her a gift or something?"

"Why don't you call or send a card. She used to ask about you often. I imagine it weighs on her that you have been absent for so many years. She is moving into teen hood, Evie, she is a sensitive person, and I don't need you getting her all wound up."

"Gert, I never intended to hurt her, or anyone for that matter. I know that it looks that way, and I'm sure it feels that way to her, but I have grown up too. I was a bad parent for leaving, but maybe better than if I had stayed. I knew I was leaving her in the best hands."

"Evie, all I am saying is that now is a bad time. Think of her for a change," Gert interrupted.

"But that's just it Gert, I was trying to think of her when I left. I was a mess. Made some poor decisions and couldn't face her. I am changing, and I want her to see that."

"It's been nice chatting with you. Call your daughter once in a while. That will be a big change for her." And with that Gert ended the call. Not sure if she should believe Evie, but leaned towards no.

Cassandra

It was June 3, 2006, and eighth grade graduation was only six days away. Cassie and Gert spent hours strolling through department stores picking out the perfect dress. They bounced from store to store as Cassie tried on short dresses, long dresses, printed dresses, and solid dresses. Even when she rejected five different dresses, she was still grinning from ear to ear. Finally, she found a long spaghetti strapped, green floral dress that she paired with a white cardigan. They both liked it very much, but quickly turned their attention to the rest of the plans for Cassie's big day. A family picnic was set for the afternoon after her ceremony. Cassie had even called to invite Brian and her father, but both had plans. Cassie was learning to live a happy life without those members of her family, but one question always remained; why did she have to?

Life with Gert was special. They had a bond that seemed unbreakable. Cassie never wanted for anything, and always felt at home. She knew she was lucky but couldn't shake the hint of sadness she still felt when she thought about her mother.

When she heard the news that her mother would not be back all those years ago, she felt betrayed. Her heart felt that terrible breaking feeling that she remembered once before. She so desperately wanted to know why her mother left her. Young kids are resilient; they bounce back from everything, their tears dry quickly, and there is always something new to capture their attention. Cassie had heard that a million times. But she knew young kids have memories too; they hold on to the things that hurt them and carry it with them on their journey through life.

And on her special day, she was glad she had Gert by her side. She knew that her Grandmother was proud of her, and that warmed her from head to toe. With her curls tamed by a hairdresser and her fingernails coated with sparkly polish, she proudly stood with her class, among her friends, and thought back on how much fun middle school was. There were class trips to the zoo, fancy art museums, and her favorite, Broadway shows. She loved her chorus concerts and dressing up for Halloween at school. This fun life was made possible by Grandma Gert, and Cassie couldn't wait to explode off the stage and give her a big hug. And as the school band started to play the final number, Cassie looked around for Gram. Through the sea of balloon bouquets in school colors that decorated the gym, and the risers full of photo flashing parents and restless little siblings, Cassie instantly thought of a "Where's Waldo" book. She was on cloud nine, the thrill and excitement of the day filled her up and spilled carelessly from her grin and giggles. But then a face caught her eye. Cassie stood paralyzed, trying to absorb what she was seeing, trying to figure out if it was real. She blinked hard, and the person was gone.

"Cass, stand next to me for a minute!" Her friend Brittney caught her in a daze and turned her around for a picture. "Say cheese, Cassie!" Brittney demanded.

Cassie contorted her face into something that satisfied Brittney, then turned back around. When she did, Gert was standing right in front of her with open arms. As they embraced, she could feel her confusion melting away and the thrill return.

"Congratulations, baby girl!" Gert exclaimed! "Now it's time to party!" Gert watched Cassie get flooded in the chaos of her friends wanting pictures and let her enjoy this moment in time.

Soon enough they were home putting up decorations and preparing trays of food for the party. Cassie so admired Gert's young spirit. She never saw stress or worry on her face, and to her, Gert made being an adult look fun and easy. It was one of the things Cassie loved most about her grandmother, she made everything more fun!

The rest of the afternoon was perfect. Family, friends and laughter. She invited four of her best friends and they played Frisbee and kickball in the warm evening air. They all had become very close in middle school. Two girls had braces put on and taken off. One girl had a grandfather pass away, and another had parents that went through a divorce. The girls were able to lean on each other during these tough times, when everyone else at school seemed to judge them. They shared happy times too, school dances, crushes, sleepovers, Friday nights at the local movie theater and some good old girl time at the mall. Cassie realized the importance of friends, these friends, people who you could talk to about your problems, and they always made you laugh. Now all five girls would embark on a new journey together in a few short months, high school.

As the party died down and Gert and her sisters were starting the clean up, Cassie sat pensively on the back porch. She looked out at the fireflies floating in the dusk and thought about how much she was looking forward to being a grown-up. She was lost in thoughts of finding the love of her life and wearing a big puffy white dress that she and Gert would pick out together. She wanted three or four children and wanted

Gert to watch them all while she was at work. And she wanted a fancy job in advertising creating commercials for beauty products and snack chips. She would go to work after she put her children on the bus and be home for dinner with her family every night. And every Friday should be pizza night, she decided.

"Did you have a wonderful day?" A voice snuck up behind her and shattered the peacefulness that filled the air.

Cassie was hesitant to turn around, in fear that the voice she thought she was hearing, wasn't actually her mother's.

"Yes." That was all she could muster as she stood and looked at her mother face to face. She was immediately shocked at how short her mother was. Cassie was only an inch shorter. Evie was slimmer than Cassie remembered, but her skin was still a beautiful youthful porcelain.

"Come here and give me a hug! You look so grown up, and beautiful. I've missed you!" Evie said warmly.

Cassie was wondering where Gram was. This felt like a moment when she needed someone by her side; she felt vulnerable and lonely and maybe even sad. But she did as she was asked and fell into a slightly awkward hug with Evie. Questions flooded Cassie's head. There was so much she wanted to say, and ask, but the moment still felt so surreal she could barely speak in full sentences.

"You must be wondering why I'm here, huh?" Evie said, and Cassie nodded slowly in agreement. "Well, I wanted to bring you a graduation present. I know that I have been gone for a few years, but that doesn't mean that I stopped thinking of you for one second. I was hoping we could start fresh and maybe be friends?" Evie waited for a response.

Cassie was stunned. Was she happy that her mother was here, or was she pissed that her mother wanted to be friends? Did this mean that her mother was back? And how did she know about her graduation? It was all a bit too much for Cassie. She burst into tears and ran into the house to find Gert.

"Gram, how did she know about my graduation?" Cassie sobbed.

"She called me last week to ask me when it was and said that she had a present for you. She didn't tell me where she was at the time. I asked her to call you. I never invited her to the house, nor did she tell me that she was coming. Baby girl, I am as surprised as you are. But remember this, no one is perfect, and some people deserve a second chance. Only you can decide who you give that chance to." Cassie held Gram tight, even after the weeping stopped.

Cassie sensed that Gram was being honest, and clearly not happy to see Evie. But Cassie knew this situation was, and had always been, between her Evie. Evie was waiting in the kitchen for some sign of life. She had cut herself a piece of cake and was pouring herself a cup of coffee as the two walked in.

"I didn't mean to upset you, Cassandra!" Evie perked up immediately. "I know you must have questions and be feeling emotions that I just don't understand. But I have a present for you," Evie continued, while handing Cassie a letter-sized envelope.

Cassie looked at the envelope and knew she had to make a choice right then. Would she let this woman back into her heart? Of course the answer was yes, because that is where she always wanted her to be. She desperately wanted to love and forgive her mother, so accepting whatever was in the envelope was her first step. Inside she found a plane ticket to Florida. Her jaw fell open slightly as she gave her mother a quizzical look.

"Isn't it exciting?" Evie squealed. "A girls' trip—you and me and sunny Florida!" she added.

"Oh. Oh, wow. I don't know what to say. Thank you? Thank you." Cassie was not really sure how to feel, or what to say. Conflicting emotions were running rampant through her mind. She decided to latch on to the one that was excited about Florida. She had heard many stories from her friends about traveling to Disney World, or family visits to Tampa Bay, but Cassie didn't have any stories of her own. She and Gert made a point to go to Vermont every fall to see the foliage and shop around at some of the local shops. That was a special trip that Cassie really looked forward to, but this…this was a real deal vacation with a swimming pool and a beach with crystal blue water! Yes, Cassie would choose excitement for the moment.

"Where are we going to stay? When are we leaving? Will there be a pool? Can we swim with dolphins?" She rattled on, as a grin tugged at her checks.

"Well, our flight leaves first thing in the morning, so you should start packing."

Without a second thought, Cassie hugged them both and ran off to start packing.

"Where are we going?" Cassie asked as they sat quietly in the back of a taxi, on their way to the airport.

"I have a few people to see while we are on our trip, and a few stops to make. Then we can check out the beach," Evie said happily.

Cassie immediately noticed how carefully she chose her words, and how vague her response was. "But where are we staying, what hotel in Orlando?" she pressed.

"Don't worry, it will be wonderful! Everything you deserve to celebrate your big accomplishment." Evie was clearly trying to pacify her.

And in that moment her excitement was replaced by dread as her hopes of a beautiful tropical vacation were tainted with the thoughts that she was now leaving the state with a woman she barely knew and had no clue where she was actually going. Cassie shot a glance at the driver and hoped like hell he couldn't see the panic in her eyes.

As promised, they arrived in one piece to the Orlando International Airport. At least Cassie could say that she'd seen palm trees. They promptly rented a car, drove the red Chevy Malibu off the lot, and hit the highway. They were on their way. Cassie thought better of asking more questions, and settled in for the drive, as the GPS alerted them that their destination was one hour away. She tried to picture what a city called Mascotte would look like. She dozed off imagining the soothing rhythm of the ocean waves rolling up on her toes as they danced in the sand.

When she woke, there was not a beach in sight, and not a lot of palm trees either. In fact, there were pine trees. Cassie rubbed her eyes and tried to get her bearings. The first thing she noticed was that she was alone, in the car, in a parking lot. She was hot, even with all the windows down. There was a note on the dashboard, but Cassie decided to take in her surroundings a bit before having to deal with the reality of the situation. She opened the door and got out to stretch. Her thighs left a shine of sweat on the tan leather seat beneath her. She checked her watch and noted that they had probably been in Mascotte for an hour already. They were parked in front of a small brown industrial looking building. Cassie took a short walk to the end of the seemingly quiet street and read the large sign planted firmly in the ground; Mascotte Family Dentistry. Perhaps Evie had chipped a tooth on the way to the hotel?

Cassie strolled back to the car to grab the note. After reading it, she was even more confused. It said that Evie went in and would be back in an hour, and not to come inside. By Cassie's calculations her mother was running late. Cassie sat and scratched her head a bit. It never occurred to her that she needed to "catch up" with her mother, that she no longer knew what she was doing, where she was living, or who she was living with. Until that moment it never occurred to her that she wasn't living happily ever after with Joe somewhere.

The more she thought, the more she realized that it was very possible not to know your own mother, and that was a sad realization. To top it off, the stranger parked her at a dentist's office in Nowheresville, Florida and disappeared inside. She let out a laugh. Seemed like a good alternative to running in the building claiming that she was kidnapped.

Evie finally appeared with a serious look on her face. "Good morning, Sleeping Beauty."

Cassie watched her face relax a bit as she slid into the rental car, firing up the engine.

"Hungry?" Evie asked.

Cassie had so many questions she didn't know where to start. But she sat and took in a face full of air conditioning. "Yes, very." Cassie was brief with her reply, although she desperately wanted to say more.

"What are you thinking about?" Evie's voice broke Cassie's train of thought.

"I would like to know why we were at that office, where we are going, and what happened to Joe." Perhaps that was not an exact response to Evie's question, but Cassie felt good about it.

"Oh. Well these are questions that we can discuss over some food. Let's try out this diner." Cassie was amazed, and annoyed, by her mother's skill to avoid questions.

"Where do you live now? And do you talk to Brian, or Dad? How are they?" Cassie pressed on.

Evie pulled into the first open spot. "Get out of the car Cassandra. We can talk inside." Evie unbuckled and Cassie followed.

She held her tongue as they sat and stared intently at the menu. The restaurant looked like it had been there for a million years. There were rips covered in clear tape in the maroon leather seats of the booth, a noisy air conditioner blowing in the side window, and a stench of grease and coffee that Cassie had never quite experienced before, being swirled around by two shaky ceiling fans. But she was starving and decided to focus on ordering. She decided to stop the questioning for a moment, so not to mess up her chances of getting a meal. All she had to eat that day was a bag of peanuts on the plane.

"Y'all ready to order?" a friendly waitress asked, with an odd twang in her voice.

Evie and Cassie ordered their meals and waited patiently for their food to be ready. There was light conversation between them, with Evie not giving much away.

"Joe and I split up about five years ago. After Joe was Peter, and he and I recently split up. It has been a very hard time for me. I really loved Peter," Evie confessed. "I was thinking that this trip would be a great way to take my mind off of him. Focus on you and I having some fun!" Evie shined a bright smile in Cassie's direction, but it was not reciprocated.

"But why are we in this town? And why were you at the dentist's office?" Cassie started again, ready for some answers.

"Here we are folks!" The twang was back, and interrupting Evie's response.

"Thanks so much," Evie said to the waitress. She dug into her chicken salad sandwich and side salad, without a glance at Cassie.

Feeling like she would have a better result after some nourishment, Cassie turned her attention to the cheeseburger and fries that was plopped in front of her. It looked delicious and surprisingly tasted even better.

As they walked toward the car Cassie could feel her renewed energy, she was even feeling a little defiant.

"Where are we going?" She stood at the passenger door giving Evie an expectant stare.

"Get in the car, Cassandra." Evie's voice was calm, her tone casual. Still, her lack of response was not appeasing her daughter. Cassie did not budge. Evie sat in the driver's seat and rolled down the passenger window to communicate with her daughter.

"Now, please Cassandra. There is no need for you to make a scene."

"Do I need to ask the question again? I am not getting in the car without knowing where I am going." Cassie was in full blown teenager mode, hand on her hips, head cocked, and prepared to do whatever was needed to get an answer.

"It is getting late, let's go to the hotel, and call it a night."

"I need to know the name of the town, and the distance to get there, Evie." Cassie shuddered a bit as she addressed her mother by her real name. It frightened her how naturally it rolled off her tongue, as if they were no longer related.

With that, Evie unbuckled and got out of the car. Cassie was caught off guard at how quickly she sailed over to her side. Before she could blink, they were standing face to face.

"Look, call me what you want, but I am the adult here and you will listen to me. We are going to the hotel. I don't care what town as long as we head north. You can pick the town for all I care! We need to be in Ocala by 9:30 tomorrow morning. I have another job interview. Now get your ass in the car before I help you in." Evie stood still. Cassie could feel the heat radiating from her body.

She was experiencing information overload and crumbled under the pressure of her seriously intimidating mother. This was new. Never had she been yelled at before. For a split second she wished her mother had stayed gone and never dragged her to this bug invested, hot, pine tree full, beach-less state. Tears of anger and defeat pricked her eyes. She turned away from Evie and got in the car, slamming the door.

It was a very quiet ride. They drove the approximately one-hour trip with a static-filled radio station on at a constant hum. After passing a few small hotels with no vacancy signs they turned into Ocala Saddle Suites Motel. Her mother got out while Cassie was left to take in her surroundings. She could see that there was actually a horse farm in the distance. She had seen so many things that she never expected were in

Tangled Vines of Good Intentions

Florida, that she was starting to question what state the pilot really landed in. The red two-story hotel building looked older, and there was no pool in sight. It was near dusk, and Cassie was certainly hoping that everything looked better in the morning light. Evie hopped back in and drove around back to another building.

"This is where we are staying. If you would like to sleep in a bed instead of the car tonight, I suggest you get out now." Evie was all business.

Cassie sulked her way out of the car, grabbed her suitcase from the trunk, and followed her mother to the door. There was a thickness to the cool air inside the room, and a bit of a stale smell. Cassie instantly noticed the two twin size beds and was relieved.

"I am taking a shower," Evie announced.

"I am calling Gram," Cassie said, matching her mother's dispassionate tone.

"Use your own phone, please." Evie was sure to get that in before shutting the bathroom door.

For her thirteenth birthday Gram bought her an LG flip phone. Cassie was elated. All her friends had phones, and she was finally in the club. It was dark purple and covered in stickers and plastic gems. As Cassie pulled out her phone, she noticed two very alarming things: first that the battery life was at 15%, and second there was no service at the Horse Farmhouse in the middle of Nowheresville, Florida. Completely frustrated she grabbed the room key and her phone and went outside.

Holding her phone awkwardly in the air, she made two laps around the parking lot, and was about to head in another direction when her battery blinked a 5% warning. Feeling defeated, she decided to continue her walk anyway. Her mind was racing, but the warm evening air seemed to seep in and cloud all the noise in her head. Before she knew it, she had made it to the horse fence. She climbed up and sat on the highest plank of the rough wood. Lost in a dark shadow, a brown horse brayed, scaring her right off her pedestal. As she laid on the ground, she giggled at her own fright. Cassie stared up at the clear sky and hundreds of bright shining stars. For the first time all day she felt okay, calm even.

And all at once, the peacefulness disappeared as shrieks from her mother pierced the air. She was yelling her name frantically. Startled, Cassie sat up and looked around to see headlights in the distance and again heard her mother yell.

"Now she cares?!" Cassie thought aloud. She trudged off in the direction of the terrible noise, hoping to stop it as soon as possible.

"I'm here! I am right here!" Cassie picked up the pace as she moved toward Evie's car, afraid that something was wrong. "What is going on? Everything ok?" Cassie shouted, and waved her hands, finally catching Evie's attention. Evie slammed on the brakes and jumped out of the car with lightning speed. With the door still open she ran toward Cassie and flung her arms around her.

"What happened? Are you ok?" Cassie gasped as her mother squeezed her harder than she expected.

"Jeez! You had me worried sick! I thought you ran away or got taken by a stranger or something!" Evie held back tears. "I came out of the bathroom and you were gone, no note, no nothing. I looked outside the door, in our parking lot, and not a trace. Why would you run off like that?! Were you trying to scare me to death?" Evie was wound up.

"Mom! Mom. Breathe! I was trying to get cell phone signal, but no such luck. I didn't realize I was gone for so long. I didn't mean to worry you," Cassie said.

They stood quietly, Evie still holding Cassie tight. It was as if the information made it to her ears but hadn't been received by her brain yet. After several minutes, Evie said "Let's sit and talk." They got back in the car and Evie drove toward a picnic table she passed during her search. Cassie followed, as her mother got out and walked over.

Tangled Vines of Good Intentions

"Cass, I am sorry I have been so secretive about this trip. I didn't want to come down here alone, and I thought it would be nice for us to catch up a little bit. I am amazed at what a smart and beautiful teenager you have become, and I need to treat you like one. Last I remember, you were my little girl with those bright brown eyes looking up at me, asking me to do your hair. Part of me thought I could bring that little girl with me." Evie took a deep breath.

"Part of me wishes I was still that little girl too, but only if I could change a few things. I never really understood what was happening, but it was because you would never tell me. You can tell me now. I can take it," Cassie said, half expecting Evie to spill her guts.

"Oh brown eyes, how I wish I could tell you about my life. But that is a ride you are not quite tall enough for. One day, maybe. For now, you deserve the truth about this trip. Peter and I split, like I said, and I've been feeling a little lost. So I thought I would try to make a move, a fresh start, in sunny Florida. I have job interviews set up tomorrow, Saturday, Monday and Tuesday. We will have Wednesday to ourselves and be back to catch our flight in Orlando on Thursday. And I did not tell Gert the full story this time, so no need to be angry with her."

And with that the two decided to start their trip over. It was a business trip, then pleasure. Cassie made Evie promise to take her to a beach before the trip was over, and she agreed. They headed back to the hotel room and gave each other a big hug before bed. With the lights off, Cassie tried to make sense of things. She was replaying the whole day in her head. She felt really good about spending the next few days with her mom, and honestly a little excited about having someone to visit in Florida, if they stayed in touch. But Cassie couldn't stop hearing the same line over and over: her mother said "I did not tell Gert the full story, this time…" What did that mean?

It felt like 3:00 a.m. when Cassie heard Evie in the bathroom the next morning. Before she knew it, her mother was standing over her, dripping wet hair droplets in her face.

"Rise and shine! Let's get this business trip started so we make it to the pleasure part sooner!" Evie said cheerfully.

Wiping water from her face, Cassie slowly sat herself up and tried to adjust to the sunlight that now filled the room. She was ready to try to have a good trip with her mother. She was ready to make an attempt at getting to know her again, and she was ready to move forward with her as part of her life. Cassie had always wanted that and hoped like hell her mother did too.

The day went by uneventfully. After the morning interview, the girls toured the area a bit. Evie wanted to see what the neighborhoods were like, the grocery store, and if there was anything interesting in the city. In Cassie's opinion, there was not. This was a boring place. The horses were the most exciting part, despite the fact that they didn't fit into her idea of Florida. They had lunch at a local hole-in-the-wall spot before continuing to stop number two.

"That town was a pretty dull. I think you might die of boredom there," Cassie offered.

"Thanks, for your input," Evie said with a smile.

Next stop was Gainesville. Cassie was instantly impressed as they rolled through the streets of the college town. Her eyes jumped from building to building and logo to logo. She was entranced. She had never seen a college like this in real life. It was grand and beautiful. It looked rich and enchanting. Cassie felt an electricity in the air. College held the power to bestow great knowledge and hope upon its many students.

"How about we get out and take a look around?" Evie suggested.

"Can we? We shouldn't. We don't go to this school," Cassie said seriously.

"We can. And we will. And I bet you could get into this school when the time comes. Let's grab a brochure and take a tour."

And with that, the girls spent the rest of the afternoon taking a campus tour, strolling around nearby shops, having ice cream, and truly enjoying each other's company.

"Oh! Let's check out this place. Look at that awesome butterfly made out of soda cans!" Cassie stood at the store window for a second, before grabbing her mother and pulling her inside. "All of these handmade creations are so cool!" She was lost in the artsy shop.

"So does this mean you want to be an artist? We can check to see if UF has a fine arts program."

Breaking her focus for a minute she turned and looked quizzically at Evie, "Why would you think an art student? I mean, Gram and I paint together…and I love art class at school, but no. I do not think I want to be an artist. A photographer maybe!" She said, as she picked up an alligator figurine made of silverware.

"Photography! I used to love taking pictures back in the day! Do you have a camera?"

"No. Gram let me use hers a few times. I think I am going to save up to buy one next year."

"Well it is a great hobby."

Finally satisfied with her time in the shop, Cassie turned to the door with her mother trailing behind her.

"So what do you want to be when you grow up Cassandra?" Evie continued the conversation.

"I guess I'm not really sure, but I think advertising is awesome. I like watching commercials and thinking of new ways to make something look good or sound exciting. But I also like writing. So I don't know yet." Cassie had no reason to hold back. It felt good that her mother cared to ask.

"Well keep those grades up and you can do anything you want," Evie added.

"Can we go in here?" Cassie's spotted a souvenir shop and her face lit up. She picked up a magnet and a stuffed gator wearing a Florida Gator's t-shirt for Gert.

After walking and talking until the sun went down, they jumped back in the car to find a hotel and settle in for the night. Cassie would mark this as a very successful vacation type day, with more pleasure than business.

"Well that was a bust!" Evie returned to the Chevy, exasperated.

"Not a good interview?" Cassie asked, curiously. They had not yet discussed exactly what was going on inside the air-conditioned buildings that Evie spent so much time in, while Cassie was left to sweat it out in the Florida sunshine.

"Boring, stuffy, old farts. They wouldn't appreciate my talents. Fuck'em." This sentiment brought a smile to Evie's face. "What next?" She looked to Cassie expectantly.

Luckily Cassie had been busying herself with tourist booklets that she grabbed from the hotel when they checked in. She was prepared for this question.

"They have a cool looking place called the Butterfly Rainforest where the butterflies actually land on you! And there is an art museum called Samuel P. Harn Museum of Art. It has a wide range of arts from Asian to contemporary including a photography section." Cassie paused, and looked up from her pamphlet. She waited anxiously for a response.

"Huh. Hmm. And do these activities have an admission fee?"

"Only one. Butterfly Rainforest." Cassie was quick and accurate.

"Let's start with the Harn and see where the day takes us from there!" Cassie giggled as Evie flashed a wild smile and hit the gas.

Tangled Vines of Good Intentions

Cassie was struck with all the beauty in the art museum. It was an enchanting place. More life-like than some of the museums that she had visited in New York. She stood, stared, shifted her head, and admired. One piece in particular held Cassie's attention. She was captivated by a portrait of a mother holding her baby, and in the picture, they were both crying. At first, it was the soft curve of the newborn's cheeks and its chubby arms that caught her eye, then it was the mother. Her tears left shiny tracks down both cheeks. Her face did not emanate the natural excitement that Cassie thought new mothers had. Her face didn't give any sign that this baby was special to her, or that she cared about its tears. The more Cassie looked, the more she saw that the two were one in the same. The baby who felt alone and scared would one day be an adult, alone and scared.

"And what has you captivated over here, contemporary art?" Evie strolled over to Cassie. "Oh my. What a beautiful photo, on such a horrible day," Evie noted. "It's nice of you to show so much emotion, Cassie. Earth to Cassandra?" Evie gave her a little nudge to break the trance.

"Huh? Oh. I was just looking at this picture. It doesn't look like that mother cares about her child at all." Cassie missed all of Evie's previous comments.

"Did you read the info? That's the only way to really know what is going on in the scene. You have to get the photographer's perspective." Evie paused. "That's not her kid," she added.

The words were slow to translate in Cassie's brain. She attempted to add the new information to her equation. Oddly, it made more sense. That look was the look of a woman who did not want a child. A mother's love could not look like that. Cassie was almost relieved.

"What is going on in this picture?" She asked, glancing toward the info plaque.

"This is a scene outside of a daycare center on the morning of September 11th. The woman could see smoke from the

Pentagon building from the daycare steps. She was facing that horrific scene. It probably isn't her baby. I am guessing that poor woman is overcome with so much emotion that she couldn't help the baby if she wanted to. Did you cover that in history class?"

Cassie tried to break her fixation on the photo, to respond to Evie's question. With a deep sigh, she shook off her confusion, and decided not to let this image haunt her. She was forever curious about the love of a mother. Although her mother was around when she was a baby, she couldn't remember ever feeling deeply connected to her. Like there should be a bond created at birth that wasn't quite right between her and Evie. It had always bothered her more then she let on. "Um. No. High school, I think." Cassie was short, and she moved on to the next exhibit.

The afternoon slipped by while they were in the museum. Cassie was preparing to go around a third time, before Evie ended the adventure.

"How about lunch? I need food, or you will end up dragging me to the car and driving me around for the rest of the day," Evie joked. "I gotta say, it is nice to be with a self-sufficient child."

Cassie was not sure how to take that, she never had anyone to chat with about what she was like as a baby. She had no clue if she was fussy, or easy, or how old she was when she took her first steps.

At lunch they made jokes about blue-haired old ladies and the Red Hat Society that was so prevalent in the area, as they ate at yet another funky diner, this one with chrome chairs, sticky floors, and fly tape.

"Mom, what was I like as a baby?" Cassie causally asked while chewing on her BLT.

"Delightful!" Evie deflected.

"No, really. Do we have a baby book? Did I have hair when I came out? Who held me first?"

"Cassandra. I'm sorry but we did not have a camera at the time. Pretty sure your brother broke it, or the dog ate it or something. There are a few pictures floating around when you were about 9 months old. You were very round. Your head, your cheeks, those big eyes."

Cassie listened intently and watched for signs that this was her loving mother, who adored her newborn baby.

"It was a late morning delivery. Everything went smoothly. Dark hair on your head. Your brother was amazed when we brought you home! He was thrilled and asked to hold you and feed you. He wanted to burp you, but he wasn't quite strong enough to hold you up on his shoulder. I remember like it was yesterday how he would tell me that he had to be the best big brother, and that he was going to cook for you and feed you. We had many nights with mashed vegetable glop all over the kitchen, the floors, not to mention you and your brother were unrecognizable!" Cassie watched Evie beaming and giggling as she recalled the scene.

She tried to remember, tried to tap into those happy family feelings. She saw the love in her mother's eyes, but for a moment she thought it was because of her brother.

"Anyway, time flies! You were an adorable baby and we all were very lucky. Now eat." She noticed her mother seemed pleased to have tied that conversation up so neatly.

"Will you send me some baby pictures?" Cassie added between bites.

"I will," Evie assured her.

And with that, the two were ready to continue exploring. They hit a few more shops and the Butterfly Rainforest. They spent the rest of the day in Gainesville and returned to the same hotel for a second night.

Sunday morning was quiet and peaceful. Cassie slept well. When her eyes slowly opened up to assess the room around her, it was surprisingly dim. She checked the clock and was shocked by the time. Flipping the covers off, she looked around for signs of Evie. After checking the bathroom and her bed, she headed for the door to see if the car was still there. As she reached for the knob, she saw a folded piece of paper sticking out of the door jam. It was from Evie, letting Cassie know that she was out for a run and they would leave shortly after she got back. And with that, Cassie set to showering and packing to hit the road.

Not altogether hating her summer trip, she did wonder how her friends would react to the news that her mother lied about the vacation and they did not spend the week at the beach. But Cassie figured that if she wasn't surprised, they wouldn't be either. Then her thoughts turned to Gram. She hadn't been in touch with her since they landed days ago. She thought about her and what she was up to at home but didn't want to think too long. This was the longest that they had ever been apart.

"Oh, hey there! Ready to start the day? Let's do this!" Evie sprung through the door full of spirit and sweat.

"Shower is free," Cassie said sarcastically, while crinkling her nose at Evie.

"Watch your tone, or I will hit the road just like this, keep the windows closed, and hold my arm up in the air so you can get a whiff!"

"Oh my God! So gross!" Cassie was impressed at her mother's wit. That was a trait she didn't remember.

As they hit the road, she tried to imagine what it would have been like to take a trip to Florida with her whole family.

"Where is Brian? I can't remember the last time I got an update. I think I have a postcard from Washington, D.C. from two or three years ago. Do you ever talk to him? He calls Gram once a month, but I am usually not around," Cassie asked. She tried to hide her feelings about her lack of a relationship with her brother.

"Oh, Cassandra. Teenage boys are really hard to figure out. Brian bounces from here to there and seems plenty happy to do so. He recently graduated vocational high school and is attending a school back home in the fall," Evie said.

"So you talk to him from time to time? Do you see him?"

"I have seen him recently. He is a smart, happy guy. No love interest yet, but I am not sure that I would be the first to know that."

"That's good, I guess. Will you tell him I said hi…and tell him about our trip?"

"I will! Great idea. Oh, I spoke with Gert this morning. She is fine. Sends her love," Evie added casually.

Cassie perked up with the mention of Gram, but it was a reminder that she still had not spoken to her. While she was enjoying the feeling of freedom that came from venturing far away from home without your true parent, she missed sharing the new experiences with her firsthand. Cassie never imagined going through life without Gert. She was the person that knew her the best, was always honest with her, and never left.

"I told her that we were traveling from town to town and exploring different parts of the state. I explained that we were always on the go, and that you would call when you could." Cassie understood that her mother was being very clear about what version of the truth Gram was privy to.

The ride was over an hour with traffic. They rolled into the sleepy town of Palatka before three in the afternoon. They checked into a decent lake front hotel and decided to spend the rest of the day lounging around and soaking up the summer sun.

They settled in for the night, and all of Cassie's thoughts were on her family. Even though she spent most of her life without them, she believed in the love of family. She could see it through friends, and Gram, and cousins and aunts. Cassie never gave up hope. She wanted to love them all again, and part of her had never stopped.

Monday's appointment was set for the afternoon. Cassie and Evie made it a pool morning. They had good light conversation and were getting along well. She was happy to have alone time with her mother, and secretly wished they had more time together. The two ventured to the downtown area to grab some lunch before heading to the local pediatrician's office for Evie's interview.

"Why did you decide on Florida?" Cassie asked.

"Who doesn't like sunshine? I have a whole lot of life left to live and I need a little more excitement. This state has potential," Evie said optimistically.

"What happened to Paul or Perry? You know, the new guy."

Evie choked on her coffee as she let out a surprised laugh. "That would be Peter. Paul was long before you," she said with a wink. Cassie noted her pause and hoped her mother would continue. "I thought we were solid. I loved him, he loved me, period end of story. After a few months things got stale. The flame died out, and I was looking in the mirror in shock that I was stuck again," Evie signed.

"So you just up and left him?"

"No, it wasn't quite like that. Have you ever had a boyfriend, or a crush?"

"Uh…I don't think so. There are a few guys that I think are cute," Cassie replied with a shoulder shrug.

"Okay. Well love is sometimes confusing. People can feel like they are in love but then it turns out not to be right. Or sometimes people have a real love and it slips away, and then they are left chasing that one special feeling that they will never get back. When you let yourself love you need to be clear about what you want and what you don't. I do not want to feel bored or stuck in a relationship. So, I told Peter how I felt, and that I needed something more." Evie was calm during her explanation.

"And he let you go, just like that?"

"He let me go. He had no choice. I let him go first. It was hard, and very sad, but I had no other choice." Evie turned her attention to her meal and made no effort to offer Cassie any more insight into her love life.

Cassie followed her mother's lead and finished her sandwich. Still, she couldn't help but think that there was more to Evie's tale.

After her appointment, the usual house hunting ensued. There was lots of flat land in Palatka. There were some sheep, cows and horses. Things seemed spread out, and Cassie felt like she was lost in the country. There wasn't a house in the whole town that would convince Cassie to move there.

The girls had a quiet evening back in the hotel room. Cassie used the opportunity to call Gram.

"Hi Gram! I miss you so much." Cassie almost didn't realize how much until she said it.

"Love! So good to hear your voice. I was starting to get worried. Are you doing okay? Getting along okay? Having a good time?" Gram fired questions at Cassie.

"Well, I thought we would be at the beach by now, but mom had a few business things to take care of. I think the rest of the trip should be beach time though. I saw some horses."

"I see. And are you two getting along?" Cassie sensed that there was something that Gram was worried about.

"Yes. It has been pretty good so far. We went to an awesome art museum the other day too. I miss you." Cassie could feel homesickness creeping in, or what she thought it would feel like anyway. She stayed on the line with Gram a bit longer, to assure her that she was okay and that her mother wasn't treating her badly, or starving her, or anything crazy like that. And once she was satisfied, Cassie said goodbye to her favorite person in the world.

She lay in bed staring at the stains in the drop ceiling and listening to the air conditioner turn on and off. She thought about her life, the family she had, then lost, and was not sure she would ever get back. Having this time with her mother opened up so many questions. As hard as she tried to leave the past in the past and enjoy the present, Cassie couldn't help but feel like the past might shape her future. She would need to get her mother talking.

The morning came too early and they were back in the car again. Cassie was not terribly interested in cars, but was impressed that this one still smelled new, and grateful that the air conditioner was powerful. She watched the world through her window, watched as each pine tree faded away and a palm tree grew in its place. As the warmth of the sunshine tickled her arm, she rolled her window down and leaned her head out to see if she could smell the ocean. Not sure of what that smell would actually be like in Florida, she giggled at herself amused by her own excitement. She was about to have the vacation that her friends all talked about.

The girls found a Motel 6 within walking distance of the beach. Cassie had her bathing suit unpacked even before Evie got the room key.

"Would you like to go to the beach or the pool?" Evie asked.

"Are you seriously asking me that question?! Beach, beach, beach!" Cassie was practically shouting.

"Ok. You change, and I'll grab some snacks before we hit the beach," Evie said.

Cassie changed and was ready to go, but there was no sign of her mother. She pulled back the heavy drapes and took a good long look at all the passersby, none of which were her mother. After standing for a few minutes she gave up, sat on the edge of the bed, and clicked on the television.

A full 30 minutes passed, and Cassie popped up to do a window search again. This time she did spot her mother. She appeared to be rustling around in the trunk of the car. Cassie watched as her mother pulled a souvenir water bottle with pink fluorescent lettering, and a turquoise beach bag out of one plastic shopping bag. From the looks of it, Evie was loading up the new beach bag. Then Cassie watched as she opened a bottle of juice, and a bottle of something else and poured them in unequal parts into her souvenir cup. Once her mother shut the trunk, Cassie slipped from the window and jumped to the middle of the bed, preparing for her arrival.

"Let's do this! Sunscreen on?"

Cassie was bouncing impatiently on the bed. "Yes. I never use sunscreen. I am ready already," she whined.

"The sun is much stronger here in Florida; besides, skin is skin, no matter how dark you already are. Skin cancer happens in all types of people. Plus, as a woman, you should know that sun exposure increases fine lines and wrinkles. And, as a nurse, I can't let you out in the sun without protection." Evie completed her public service announcement around the same time as she finished lathering Cassie's back and shoulders.

"I'm not as old as you, wrinkles don't concern me," Cassie giggled.

"Very funny. And yes, I may be almost 44 years old, but I still look good, thanks in part to our friend Mr. Sunscreen."

"Did you get me a drink too?" Cassie asked, curious to see what information her mother volunteered.

"Water bottles!" We are set. Let's go!"

Daytona Beach was everything Cassie hoped for. There were people all over the street and pouring out of every beach shop they passed. She took in all the details of this new world. Motorcycles and convertibles lined the streets. The air was a mixture of salt and sweat, food and sand. She felt a thrill deep inside. It was amazing.

They dropped a blanket and spent the next six hours chasing the waves, building sandcastles, people watching, and napping in sunshine.

Evie was sound asleep when Cassie emerged from the ocean for a break. Still curious, Cassie walked around the sleeping body and picked up her souvenir cup. She tried to smell through the straw but ended up jamming it into her nose. She took a suck, but all that was left was bad tasting air. She coughed dramatically and chucked the bottle down. She then proceeded to shake out her wet hair all over her mother.

"What the?! Cassandra?! Are you kidding me?!" Evie sprung up and stumbled to her feet. She stretched her arms and tried to acclimate to her surroundings.

"What time is it, you little monster?" Evie slurred.

"I think it is close to five." Cassie watched as her mother seemed more disoriented than expected.

"Well, how about that," Evie giggled. "How about we clean up and go out to eat at a nice restaurant. Maybe someplace with a band?" She clapped her hands with eagerness.

"Sounds good to me!" Cassie was not going to ask any questions; she wasn't going to mess with Evie's good mood.

It was a night that Cassie would never forget. They had dinner outside at a seafood restaurant overlooking the beach. Cassie took in the breathtaking colors painted vividly in the sky as the sun slipped away. She watched people clear the beach and listened to the sound of the ocean. Evie ordered a strawberry margarita and let Cassie have a sip. She hated it. But she enjoyed the vibe of the restaurant and had no desire to spoil her mother's fun. After their dinner they went downstairs to a large bar type restaurant where the band was jamming and entertaining a lively crowd. Evie had a few more drinks while Cassie tried the Key Lime pie. And then they both proceeded to dance the night away.

It was around one in the morning when the two decided to listen to their screaming feet and started the one block walk up the street to the hotel. Clinging to each other for support, they slowly stumbled back to the room. Evie hit the bed and didn't move. She made no effort to change, or even get under the covers. Cassie decided that this was a side effect of the alcohol and made a mental note for when she was actually old enough to drink. She left her mother snoring gently on top of the bed.

The next morning Evie woke confused that she was still dressed. Cassie was sleepy, a little cranky, and starving. They decided that breakfast was more important than showering and headed out in search of pancakes.

"I had fun. Lots of fun." A guilty smile creeping up on Cassie's face, as she recalled the completely carefree evening she had.

"I have a slight headache. Perhaps we can dial back the fun a bit today?" Evie said honestly.

The rest of the meal was quiet. They both needed the nourishment, and that was the focus. When they got back to the room, they decided on a little pool time. Evie was asleep in minutes, and Cassie was left to take in Daytona on the last day of her Florida vacation. They both agreed on another restaurant by the beach with open air seating for dinner. Their last dinner on this vacation.

"Thank you for bringing me along with you," Cassie started. "What do you think your next move will be?"

"You know, I kinda like it down here. But the beach is really where it's at. I guess I will have to wait and see if I get any job offers," Evie replied.

"So do you still have a job back home? Wherever that is."

"Yes. I do. I don't love it. I work evening shifts, nursing. I think I'm a little bored at home, honestly. But I am between places at the moment since I had to move out of Peter's place."

Cassie was ready to test the depths of Evie's honesty. "Why did you and Dad split up?"

"Oh Cass. It was a long time ago. He is a great guy, but we simply fell out of love."

Cassie was surprised at how easily she responded. "Why did you have to move away?"

Evie paused. She looked at Cassie and took a deep breath before responding. "I decided that I wanted to be closer to family and I wanted to start fresh."

Noting her calculated response, Cassie pressed on. "Didn't you miss Brian?"

"Honestly, Cassandra! Of course I did. He is my baby, my flesh and blood. He really didn't want to move, and I really did. I had to do what I thought was best for everyone. It would not have done any good to drag him along with us and then have him turn around and hate me for it. I tried to think it through." Evie flagged down the waitress and motioned for another drink.

"Why didn't you leave me?" Cassie was feeling brave.

"With Eddie?" Evie paused, as if she was truly confused by the question. "I guess I never thought about it."

"You only thought about what Brian wanted?"

"No. It might not have been fair to ask Eddie to raise you both. He and I thought about our decision carefully," Evie said firmly, noticeably uncomfortable with this topic.

"Why doesn't he ever call me or visit? Did he not want me?" Cassie realized as the words rolled off her lips that this was exactly how she had been feeling. She was finally able to put into words the aching feeling that was in her heart. All this time she felt unwanted. The tears rolled down her cheeks and all at once her vision was blurred with the flood waters.

Evie reached across the table and touched Cassie's hand. "Look girlfriend, maybe it's time for you and me to stop holding onto the past and start spreading our arms to the future. I…we…never meant to hurt you. One day I hope you find the peace that you are looking for. But seriously, you are too young to be held down by all this. You cannot control people's actions, but you can control your reaction."

Through her tears and hurt feelings Cassie did her best to absorb her mother's words. She knew that this was her mother-daughter moment, but it wasn't feeling right. And then she opened her mouth, once more.

"Why did you leave me too? Was it because I don't look like you?" Cassie said, strangled by her sobs.

Tangled Vines of Good Intentions

Evie pulled her hand back slowly. Her face was contorted in a stern, and almost angry expression. She took an audible breath.

"One day when you are old enough to understand… we are here now, together. We need to open our arms to the future." That was all that Evie was able to manage. With that collection of thoughts, she got up and went to the restroom. Cassie was alone, again. A feeling that she should have been very used to by then, but wasn't. The waitress came over and brought Cassie some tissues and a piece of pie. She said that dessert always helped dry her tears. Cassie could feel the pent-up emotion swirling recklessly through her. Knowing that if she didn't force herself to stop crying the faucet would continue to run, Cassie used the tissues and took some deep breaths. Digging into the pie seemed like as good a solution as any, and that's exactly what she did.

She was sad, but as the tears ebbed, she was angry. Cassie was angry for expecting so much from Evie, and always being surprised and hurt when she was let down. She was always let down. When would she learn?

Evie

On Thursday June 2, 2006, she zipped the last of her clothes into a suitcase and looked up at Peter with big honest tears rolling down her face. "I really am sorry, Peter."

"Save it Evie. I should have known better," Peter said as he threw up his hands. Evie had this conversation with him before, but this would be the last time.

"What is that supposed to mean?" Evie tried to sound offended.

"I'm not dumb, or blind. You are a flirt, and a cheat. I should have known better. Just go." His hands flailing wildly.

Evie could think of no reply as she walked out the door. She slammed her car door and put her foot on the gas. Not having a plan, the local motel was the best she could do for the evening. A car full of stuff was all that she had acquired in her 44 years on earth. Evie swore loudly as she pushed, pulled and dragged her giant suitcase, stuffed full of clothes for all seasons, up the stairs to her room on the second floor. The familiar stench of old dirty carpet hit her hard. Dropping her load, she sat on the bed and wept. She wasn't sad over the break-up with Peter. He was right. He should have known, that's how boring he had become. At least Evie was trying to live her life. She didn't intend to hurt him, but then she never intends on hurting anyone, it just happens. It happens to her over and over. In the stagnant air of the room she tried to count the number of people in her life that she hadn't hurt. The carnage was painful to think about.

With a mini bottle of Jack and a can of Coke, she sat in silence trying to figure out how she ended up there in that moment. How had she gotten everything so wrong?

Would it have been easier to stay in a loveless marriage? Would it have been easier to make babies and cart them around to all of their activities for the rest of her young adult life? Was she supposed to follow the cookie cutter norm and do what everyone else wanted her to do? Do what her parents wanted her to do? It never felt like her. For a long time, her life wasn't about what she wanted. Her divorce was her first step to creating a path of her own.

When Eddie asked her parents for their blessing in marriage that was the first time Evie ever sensed that they were proud of her or happy for her. She walked in from shopping with her friends that evening and was greeted with open arms by her mother. Her first thought was that someone had died, but her mother was smiling. She was giddy and couldn't wait to spoil the surprise. Her mother then proceeded to rattle off a list of skills that Evie would need to perfect to be a wife, which included manners, house cleaning, cooking, how to dress, and the list went on and on. Evie knew better than to interrupt her mother. And as she carried on, Evie could feel the rebellion building inside her. Did her mother really want her to quit her job and stay barefoot and pregnant to cook and clean for the rest of her life? She had no greater desires for her only child? And until that evening, Evie had never realized that she might have other desires for herself.

Evie

Evie knew the proposal was coming but didn't know how to prepare herself for it. She didn't know how to make such a permanent decision. She was never the girl who thought about marriage, the big day, the dress, flowers, or venue. It was all very overwhelming, and she was grateful that finals would distract her. With the buzz of their nearing graduation, she had all but forgotten about the impending question until it smacked her right in the face, in front of her whole family, plus a room full of strangers. Under the pressure, the only thing she felt she could do was say "yes"—that was expected of her. Even though she knew the moment was inevitable, she never took a second to figure out what she really wanted. She wasn't ready to be a rigid wife like her mother. So, her plan was to focus on her career.

Evie was stuck in the cycle of trying to make others happy, and her marriage was no exception. That was how she became a nurse, a wife, and how she became a mother. There was a moment there when she felt numb. This was not the story she wanted to write. Divorce was her only option.

She remembered the conversation like it was yesterday. It was a humid evening when they dropped the kids at Carol's and went to have a drink. Unsure if they could manage a conversation, which was a feat not accomplished in years. They sat down at a high-top table at a restaurant in the next town over. It was a neutral location; neither of them had ever been. It was a fairly busy place, split into restaurant on one side and bar on the other. The restaurant was packed with tables covered in crisp white linen with small candles glowing dimly in the center. White Christmas lights strung around support beams added a romantic ambiance to the room. The bar was where they preferred to sit and promptly ordered a drink. They were seated in a corner, with a very perky server. Evie noticed how young and bubbly she was, how her ponytailed bobbed and swayed when she walked away. She was dreading every word of the conversation to come.

Tangled Vines of Good Intentions

Evie ordered a glass of wine, smooth, full and red, while Eddie needed something harder and went for the brown stuff. After the second round, the tears seemed to start without warning for them both, and by the third, it was clear they weren't stopping.

"Maybe I wasn't ready? I just know that I am not happy, and you aren't either. We tried." Evie's tears were real, and her words were honest.

"Did we try hard enough?" Eddie questioned, but Evie knew he was clinging to the vision of the life he wanted.

"I think we did. At some point it isn't trying, it is more like going through the motions."

"Well I never made it to that point. I never stopped trying."

"I know. And I thank you for that. Please know that I never intended this."

"Do you remember that time in college when you wanted to have a fondue party?" Eddie's face lit up at the memory.

"When? Oh, when we had two different Sternos going in the dorm room? Or do you mean the cheese sauce I made that was a bit too thick and slightly lumpy?" The memory made her smile.

"Or that time we went camping and you almost burned down the site trying to make bacon cheeseburgers!" Eddie recalled.

Laughter escaped her. "If you told people that the reason we divorced was because of my cooking, everyone would understand."

In that split second the weight of the evening lifted and fell like a dense thick fog. "What do I tell people, Evie? What do we tell our son? And Cassie? Poor girl."

"Poor girl? Cassandra will be fine. We tell the kids that Mommy and Daddy are living apart for a while. I mean, unless you want to sit down with them and talk divorce?" Evie was unsure.

"Brian is old enough, and Cassandra is almost five. I think we need to be open with them. I want them to learn that in their own lives." Eddie was thoughtful in his response.

Evie

"Suggesting that I am not open? Look, I did my best Ed. I am just not as perfect as you are. And you can call her Cassie or Cass or your daughter. She has been in our lives for over five years." She grabbed her drink to calm her nerves.

"You did the best you could. I get that. But do I think you were open and honest about your feelings, about how to fix things, about when things started to derail? No, I do not. And as for our daughter. I have my own demons to fight when it comes to her. I mean, I just wasn't prepared. I just never imagined…" Eddie trailed off.

"That you would have a child that didn't look like me, or you, or your son?" Evie was stunned at how hurt she was by this realization. "Shame on you!"

"Whoa. No. This has nothing to do with what she looks like, and everything to do with the fact that she has another set of parents out there in the world. I am adjusting to the adoption part, Evie. Honestly, you know me better than that, skin color is not a factor here." Eddie was stern.

"That sounds like white privilege at its best. You just don't see color at all, right?" Evie rolled her eyes.

"Please stop, Evie. Chances are that Cass will have to face some forms of discrimination in her life, but it won't be from me. She is a terrific and beautiful child. And I love her very much, but it feels different then the love I have for Brian, and I honestly don't know why. I am working on it."

It was not a proud moment for either of them.

"Eddie, I am going to move back home, to Connecticut." Evie watched his face pale in color, and she was nervous that he was about to hit the floor.

"Please don't. Don't go, don't do this to me Evie." She could feel his desperation. He was still trying to save this.

"I need to start fresh." She could barely get the words out through her tears.

Evie knew that her husband saw it coming at some point, that he knew he had lost her long ago but didn't have the heart to press her on why. She knew the truth would shatter him, and she was not ready to break him like that. He loved her, loved her enough to want her to be happy, even if that meant she would be happy without him.

Her parents practically disowned her after her divorce from Eddie, which wasn't that bad since she had hated them for as long as she could remember. They were always putting so much pressure on her. She had to do her hair a certain way, she had to sit down in a lady like fashion, she had to maintain a certain GPA, and she couldn't associate with certain people. This kept on for much of her young adult life. Evie could clearly recall screaming matches the three of them would get into over her going to boarding school in 9th grade. Of course, Evie wanted to stay local with her friends, and her parents wouldn't even consider it.

When she moved back to Connecticut with Cassie all those years ago, she never even bothered to try to make it work.

"What are you doing with that little girl? Please explain it to us again." Evie's mother sat at the grand dining table with her handkerchief in hand.

"Mother, no matter how many times I tell you why, you will not get it. You don't understand my decision because you would not have made it yourself!" Evie was doing her best to keep her volume in check, but her anger was getting the best of her.

"So, you spoke to her mother and she didn't want her? Did you follow up with her after the birth? Maybe she would have changed her mind." Sally was struggling.

"Adoption doesn't work like that, Mother. The point is to take a human with another set of DNA and call them your own. I shouldn't expect you to get it. We have the same DNA and you have never treated me like you cared about me at all. Thanks for teaching me how to be a good mother." Evie could feel the heat tingle in her cheeks.

"You are our only child and we loved you the best we could. But it doesn't feel like you have come here to make amends, more like blame us for your bad fortune, or blame me for your bad decisions. You haven't changed a bit. Never taking responsibility for your actions." Sally was serious. "This turn in your life is yours to deal with. Not my problem, Evie."

And with that, Evie left the table, grabbed Cassie and walked out of her childhood home with no intentions of ever returning.

It was time that Evie made her own decisions and let go of her parents' harsh judgments. And yet at, 44 years old, single, no kids in tow, she still had no clue who she was, and she couldn't imagine her parents' judgment being worse than the judging she did to herself. It was time for some soul searching. Time to stop hurting others in an effort to find what she wanted. There had to be a happy medium. There had to be a way to put her life back on track. To become a person that she could stand to be around.

Evie needed a break, a change of scenery. She needed to take a minute to lick her wounds and get back on the horse. And in a moment of clarity, she had an idea that might get her recharged and moving in the right direction. She would go to Florida. Heck, maybe she would even move there. She wasn't keen on moving so far from Brian, but he would be off to college soon anyway and he wouldn't need his mommy anymore. She could set up some interviews and still have lots of free time to think. Still having her job in New York, the job-hunting part would be more for comparison. It was time to lay out her options and make a smart move. The more she thought about it, the more excited she became, and then she realized she needed a companion, a girlfriend, to go with her. That list was short.

Her brain jumped from thought to thought in the hazy fog of her buzz. With another swig of Jack, the tears fell from the realization that her baby boy would be off to college in a few short months. Brian had turned into such a bright young man. He was so much like his father; he was all heart.

Evie was grateful every day that he forgave her for making such a mess of his childhood. She had never wanted to leave him. And truthfully, she wasn't gone that long, but to a kid it must have been confusing. Right after the divorce Evie was away for two years before moving back to New York, only 30 minutes from Brian. She and Joe had an apartment together, and when things ended a few years later, she kept the apartment.

A triumphant grin swept across her face at the memory of her first night in the apartment after Joe left. In fact, it was the first night she had ever spent in a place that was all her own. No one to tell her what to do. She ordered take out and watched movies in her spacious bed until she fell asleep, sprawled out in the middle. She was the driver, and that was a good feeling. She never had that feeling when she was married, or even in her childhood. Eddie always wanted them to be the same. He wanted them to share the same experiences, and then feel the exact same way about them. He wanted a female version of himself. Which she was good at being, until she just couldn't anymore. Until she came face-to-face with a man that represented all of the things Evie believed in. He was sexy, smart, powerful, adored by others, mysterious, bossy, and in control of his destiny.

Out of Jack in the motel room, Evie passed out with the image of Dr. Ron's killer smile dancing in her head.

Hours later, the ringing of the hotel room phone startled her awake. Head throbbing, she felt disoriented and out of balance. She swayed to the bathroom to splash some water on her face in an effort to come back to earth. The noise stopped, and she calmly set to changing her clothes and turning in for the evening. As she tossed and turned, trying to drown out the TV next door and latch back onto the image of the handsome doctor, her thoughts brought her right back to Cassie.

Evie was in way over her head with no clue how to explain this all to Cassie and was terrified that she would never speak to her again, if Evie ever could tell her the truth. Leaving Cassie with Gert was supposed to be temporary, but Evie was just not ready to face her. She wasn't sure how to be a mother to her, and that was the painful truth that everyone else had to swallow. And the fact that Evie never really tried was the painful truth she had to swallow.

Eddie was furious when he heard that she was not planning to bring Cassie to New York with her, but he wasn't offering to raise her himself. They were barely communicating at that time. He wanted nothing to do with Evie and made that clear. She wasn't about to argue with him or try to explain her unforgivable behavior. She was spending time with Brian, and she wasn't going to jeopardize that. Evie lost sleep for months toying with the decision to swoop in and take her little girl back. She would get up enough nerve to pack a bag and jump in the car, but then fear would make her sit there until the tears started, never putting the car in drive.

To Evie, Cassie represented all the bad decisions and missteps that her parents warned her about making. Her effort to do something truly good was a colossal failure. That was the story of Evie's life. And she didn't need a physical reminder of her failures living with her. She tried desperately to shake the association from her innocent child, but just couldn't. As she thought about it, she never looked at Cassie as a daughter. She was always a solution that didn't work. Evie never bonded with her as a baby because she kept waiting for things to change, for Cassie to fix everything. Cassie couldn't fix the mess, and Evie couldn't live in it. It was not one of her finer moments but knowing that she would feel real unconditional love no matter what with Gert gave Evie some comfort.

Tangled Vines of Good Intentions

All at once a big idea broke through her alcohol-numbed state. In that moment, she decided she would try. She would try to start fresh with Cassie and see if they could build a relationship. They would take the trip to Florida together.

Like most of her bright ideas, the trip was a disaster. Evie faced pressure, disappointment, and pain. All the reasons she didn't want to move Cassie in with her. This time it was a concentrated punch to the gut that took her breath away. She had to lie to her, again, over and over. How would she ever be able to build a relationship with her? The only good part of the trip was that Cassie actually wanted to spend time with Evie. As expected, Gert had done a great job. Cassie was polite, honest, smart, and fierce. She was so many things at age 14 that Evie wanted to be but couldn't figure out how to achieve. Evie knew that she could never reach out to her daughter again. Cassie had built a life that was her truth, and Evie would not destroy that.

Feeling low after the return from Florida, she found herself back in her car with nowhere to go. When Evie started seeing Peter, she asked if she could move in with him to avoid a rent increase at her own place. Another bright idea.

That night, Evie ended up at a Chinese restaurant near Eddie's house. She parked between two faded lines of a parking spot and pulled her cell phone from her purse. Knowing full well that she could not crash at his house, she sat pondering her next move. The flickering lights of the neon sign flashed bright in the dim summer evening. She dialed his home number just to hear his voice.

"Hello?" A woman's voice answered after one ring. It was Eddie's new wife, Susan. She was lovely. Very warm, happy, young, beautiful. She was always pleasant to Evie, which made Evie feel shitty from time to time.

"Hi Sue! How are you?"

"Oh hey, Evie! Things are good here. Everyone is excited about summer break. The kids are off to camp next week, and you know Bri-guy is getting ready for college. Exciting times around here! How are you, hun? How's Peter?"

"Well, we split up," Evie admitted.

"I'm sorry. Are you okay?"

"Thanks Sue. Yes, I am exploring some new options. Is Eddie around by any chance? I was in Connecticut recently, and wanted to fill him in."

"Yes, of course. Let me know if you ever need anything Evie," Sue said.

"Hello?"

"Hey Ed." The sound of his voice still relaxed her. She exhaled and eased back in her car seat. They had developed a solid co-parenting relationship. Eddie remarried when Brian was 10 years old and had two little girls back to back. The news was a bit shocking to Evie, since the marriage was less than two years after their divorce, but Evie was truly relieved that he was happy. She was grateful that he could move on and was mindful not to get too close to his new family.

"I wanted to let you know that I just spent a week with Cassie. She hates me. So does your mother." Evie held back her threatening tears.

"Well that was a big step, and if it makes you feel better, my mother isn't too thrilled with me either. Anyway, how was the trip?"

"Cassandra asked me a lot of really hard questions. She thinks I don't love her, and that I abandoned her. I couldn't sit there and tell her the truth. I couldn't really tell her anything, I just…I…it was so hard…" Her voice cracked and she was overcome.

"Let me stop you right there Evie. We made a hard decision not to bring her back to New York. You had your reasons and I had mine. But we also decided that we would live with that decision. Cassie is a great kid. Brian is a great kid. You and I were screwed up, so we had to fix that. I am not going to feel shitty all over again for the Cassie situation. I mean, she's going into high school. It is only a matter of time before she gets the truth and has to make her own decisions about it. We have not ruined her life." Eddie was stern. Evie could tell he was not interested in hearing her pity party.

"You are right. We saw the beach, and I think she enjoyed that." Evie made some small talk for a few minutes more but avoided divulging the specifics of her current predicament.

Her next call should have been her first. Carol met her at the restaurant. They sat at a worn-out booth with a sticky tabletop. Evie had soup while she talked, laughed some, and let her best friend make her feel better. Over the years Carol had always supported Evie in her search for happiness, despite not agreeing with her methods all the time. Evie sensed that her friend admired her spirit, but preferred her own safe life. Carol stayed in her marriage. She never thought about divorcing her husband. It was about keeping it together for the kids. These days she only had one kid left at home, and things were quiet and dull. Carol seemed more than happy to have Evie stay over for a while.

After Evie left Joe in 2001, she begged Carol to go on a girls' vacation with her. They could hop in the car and go, but Carol wouldn't even entertain the idea. She was a loving mother and devoted wife. Her life was PTA and sports, recipe cards, Girl Scouts, and other things that Evie couldn't conform to. So, Evie went on her own. At the time she had a four-door black Toyota Corolla that got great gas mileage. She drove down to Maryland and spent a few days at the beach. She explored all kinds of shops, took in the sights, and was thrilled by the night life. At 39 years old, she was still searching for something. But she wasn't sure that Maryland was it. When she came home, she told her friend all about her trip, and how she was already planning her next one to

Myrtle Beach. Evie loved to explore new places. The thought of starting over where no one knew anything besides what she chose to tell them, was right up her alley. She could erase all of her failures as a daughter, as a wife and as a mother. Evie could reinvent herself, in hopes of getting closer to figuring out the person she really was.

And now in 2006, as Evie sat at Carol's kitchen table buttering her toast, she had an alarming thought; perhaps the wake of destruction she had left behind for all these years might be her biggest clue to figuring out who she was. What kind of person was capable of ripping apart a family, then turning her back on a six-year-old girl, just to keep looking for something else, something that fit? Maybe nothing would ever fit again. Maybe she had to face the fact that she was chasing something she would never be able to obtain. She wanted a life that she was never meant to have. The moments she spent with him in the past were meant to be left in the past.

Evie felt a headache brewing and abandoned her toast. She put her dishes in the dishwasher and tried to leave the kitchen as tidy as she'd found it. Time to retreat to the bedroom for a little afternoon nap. The vibrant turquoise walls were plastered with band posters, and Hollywood heartthrobs, whose pictures had been torn from Tiger Beat magazine. Trinkets lined shelves, and framed pictures of happy memories sat on top of the dresser. Being here threw Evie back to the days when she brought her own daughter to play in this house, in this very room. She latched onto a recent memory of watching her teenage daughter explore the beach and drifted off to sleep.

When Evie woke it was nearing three in the afternoon. Feeling low, she decided to do what she always did, head to the bar. The Bar on East was always her favorite bar. She had only gone a handful of times while she was married, and always enjoyed the low-key atmosphere. She made it a point to pop in from time to time, when she was between relationships. The bar only had a minor facelift in all the years that she knew it. And if you weren't a regular, you probably wouldn't even notice. The glasses had fewer chips, and the cardboard coasters we more regularly rotated, plus there were more beers on tap to appeal to the younger crowd. The menu had doubled its fried options and added a side salad for juxtaposition. But it still was a cozy brown hole-in-the-wall with an unmistakable stench and well-worn bar stools. She had been a regular for about a year now, seeking refuge from her failing relationship. The bartenders knew her by name and could get her the exact drink she needed before she even took a seat. As she stepped into the bar and scanned for a seat that night her eyes locked on the back of a man's head. A familiar head. Her heart started racing and she froze.

"Hey, stranger! Have a seat." The barkeep greeted Evie, pulling her from her trance.

She jerked her head in the direction of the voice and managed a contorted smile. She was still seriously thinking about turning around and walking right back out the door to avoid this man. This man that she had not heard a peep from in over 10 years. This man that turned her down and shut the door in her face when she needed him most. This man that destroyed her marriage and shattered her heart. This man that she never stopped longing for.

She watched as Dr. Ron sat quietly at the far end of the bar. He didn't appear to be with anyone or waiting for anyone. He kept his head down, as if he was lost in thought. Evie had a good view from where she was sitting, but hoped she was well hidden from his line of sight. He was dressed in his usual khaki pants and a button down collared short-sleeved shirt, with expensive chocolate loafers and no socks. A favorite summer look, she remembered, because he could easily wear his casual attire under a white coat at work. The shirt was a deep teal that complimented his skin tone, and Evie could see from her stool that it was a rich material that hugged his shoulders and upper back in just the right way, the way an expensive shirt does. The way she always remembered his shirts doing. She watched his every move. Watched his long fingers clasp the glass. They were strong, but she knew his gentle touch. Watched his deep pink lips receive his drink. Those lips that could cause so much pleasure when perfectly placed. She examined the lines framing his eyes on his rich brown skin, those seemed new. He looked older, more mature, and just as attractive. His hair had new patches of white in all the right places around his face to make him look distinguished.

By the bottom of her third drink, her head was telling her to leave, but the liquid courage was daring her to go over and punch him in the face. Her thoughts floated through time drifting in and out of moments they spent together hiding their love like a game, locking office doors, or popping into dark hallways to steal a kiss. One was never enough. Her cheeks blushed with the vivid memory of his strong hands navigating her body as if she had drawn him a map that he studied for decades. He could make her body feel things that she didn't know were possible. It was welcomed, and needed, and he always left her wanting more.

But just as quickly as the smile hit her face, it was replaced by rage. How could he reject her? He said he loved her. What did he mean by that exactly? I love you, but I am not planning to leave my wife, ever, no matter what, even if you leave your husband?! Who does that? A guy. This guy. That guy sitting a few feet away.

Halfway through the fourth glass, she needed to use the restroom. Time to break the seal. Unfortunately, she had to pass Dr. Ron to get there. Evie needed to stay focused. She pictured waterfalls in her head and moved toward the bathroom. Surprising herself with her stability, she made a smooth transition from sitting to standing and walking. Luckily, she was wearing her trusty sneakers. She hesitated a bit as she passed him and caught his scent. Instantly she saw naked Dr. Ron on top of her so clearly that she could count his abs.

"Oh, shit!" Evie let out those words many times, for many reasons, but this time she really meant to keep them in her head!

Dr. Ron spun in his seat to see what was going on behind him. By the grace of God, the bathroom door swung open and Evie stealthily jumped behind it to let a tall blonde walk out. Unseen, she slipped into the bathroom to catch her breath.

How could this jerk still have such a hold on her? She couldn't answer that, but she knew he still did. Her body was alive with emotions. She could feel them swirling inside of her and building with each sip of alcohol. And still she wouldn't even know what to say to him if she could. Or if she even wanted to. After a lengthy internal debate in the ladies' room, Evie knew she needed to get back to her seat and get out of this bar. Enough was enough. She had more pressing things to worry about.

As she confidently stepped out of the bathroom, she felt a flood of disappointment when she saw that he was gone.

She took one long swig to finish her drink, paid her bill, and left. Evie stepped out into the sunshine and headed left toward her car. Staggering slightly and finding it hard to focus, she decided to walk off some of her frustration, and alcohol. There were some shops nearby, plus it was a warm summer late afternoon and she would still be home in time to help Carol make dinner. She made it halfway to her car before making an abrupt 180 degree turn in the parking lot to head across the street for a stroll. As she turned, she attempted to slip her keys in her pocket, and failed. She paused to retrieve the fumbled keys. She was grateful for the tacky New York key chain that Brian had given her years ago, it always made her keys stand out. Before she could lift her head up her body was being jolted by an opposing force. Something hard shoved her thighs and hip. The driver slammed on his breaks, as Evie hit the gravel. It took her a minute to comprehend that she was just hit by a car backing up.

"Are you okay? I thought you had passed me. I am so sorry!" The driver was apologizing from the second he got out of the car.

But the hand that reached out to help her up was not his. It was not the hand of the driver, but the hand of a doctor. The hand of a person who had reached out to her so many times, and that had touched her in so many places. This hand that she thought would hold hers forever. She let her eyes meet his.

"Are you all right? I was on the phone and saw what happened." Concern was etched in Dr. Ron's face. "Looks like you got some scrapes on your hand, but nothing you can't handle. Do you have any pain?"

A loaded question for sure. Evie took his hand and was helped off the ground. "I, I think I'm good. My hip took the hit."

"I am sure you will have a bruise." Dr. Ron gently grazed his fingers over her hip as he spoke.

His body so close threw Evie into a tizzy. She was enraged by the gesture. Who did he think he was?! After all these years, he thought he could touch her, or even help her for that matter.

"I don't need you!" Her voice was much louder than she expected. "When I did need you, you wanted nothing to do with me. I had to figure things out. Make some tough choices. But I survived, without you, without your help. Too little, too late!" Evie continued with her tirade, a little unsteady, and already sore. Her head began to throb, and she wasn't sure if it was from the accident, the drinking, or the yelling. "But since you are here, let me ask you something. Why? Why did you drop me? Why did you drop her? Was it all an act? Did you ever love me?" By this time, the driver had slipped away, noticing Evie's preoccupation. A small cluster of people who were shopping nearby stopped across the street to witness the spectacle she was now making. Dr. Ron stood there expressionless.

"Say something!" Evie's cheeks were soaked with tears and she could feel herself falling apart. She was losing the battle, without really knowing who she was ever fighting against. She fell to the pavement. On her knees, she put her head in her hands and cried. But just as quickly as she hit the ground, she felt his arms embrace her with a strength that allowed her to be weak.

When the blur in her vision cleared and the flood had calmed to a trickle, she was surprised to find herself in the passenger seat of Dr. Ron's car.

"I cleaned some of the scrapes on your hands. I also got you a bottle of water from inside." Dr. Ron was keeping it business, she noted, as he stood outside the open passenger side door. His car smelled liked well broken in leather and man. That man smell that is a heavenly merriment of cedar and confidence. A tempting concoction.

"Thank you for cleaning me up. But I think it's time I go. Surprised no one called the cops on me." Evie tried to lighten the mood.

"Are you ok to drive? I would be happy to call you a cab, or drop you off at your place?" Dr. Ron offered. Always the gentleman.

"I'll be fine. Thanks. I'm between places right now. Might get a hotel for the evening." Evie was shocked at how natural it was to talk to him, to tell him too much. She stood slowly.

"You shouldn't be alone." Dr. Ron was face to face with her. His calm demeanor was challenging her in every way. This was too much, she felt so overwhelmed. Why did he care? And was he offering to stay with her?

"Let me at least buy you dinner." And there it was, an invitation. Perhaps sensing her hesitation, Dr. Ron clarified that he wanted to be sure there was no further pain from the accident, after the alcohol wore off.

Evie was stunned. This was most definitely not how she envisioned her reunion with Dr. Ron.

"There is a quiet place with good food, only a few minutes from here. I'll drive. Sit." He flashed his killer smirk and Evie was stunned into submission. She remembered all too well the power that this man had over her. He was so charming, and mysterious and exciting. But that was so many years ago. He showed her his true colors. He turned her down. Stayed with his wife and left her and Cassie to clean up his mess. How could she ever forgive him?

They sat and ordered with very little small talk. Evie was still desperately trying to keep her lust and longing at bay. She also wanted to keep her anger at bay, for fear of getting kicked out of the restaurant. Although that would be an almost poetic ending to this bizarre day, she simply didn't have the energy to recover from another melt down. So, quiet seemed to be a solid strategy.

They ate in silence. Glancing up at each other every now and then. One asked for the other to pass the salt, and both commented on the good flavor of their meals. As Dr. Ron got up to pay the bill, Evie let out a sigh of relief. This was probably the best outcome she could have asked for.

Dr. Ron turned the key to his 2007 Lexus IS 350. It was silver, sleek, and attractive. He fit naturally into the driver's seat and coasted toward the Bar on East to drop off Evie.

"Thank you for joining me," he said.

"Thank you for dinner," Evie replied politely, trying not to focus on the way his deep voice seduced her.

"Evie, I want you to know that I am very sorry that I hurt you." Evie felt him searching for the right words. "Please don't hesitate to call the office if you have any pain in the morning."

That was the best he could do. Evie got out and slammed the door. She sat in her car until he drove away, then cried hard, cathartic tears. It was time to let go of the pain that he caused. It was time to let go of Dr. Ron.

As Evie laid in Carol's daughter's bed, staring blankly at the textured ceiling, she let herself have one more dance through the memories of the time she spent with Dr. Ron. The times that she told him she loved him, and he said it back. The times when she laughed her most honest laugh with him and spoke her most truthful words. The mutual love between them was the single most amazing feeling Evie had ever had, short of looking into her baby boy's eyes for the first time. This time though, she let go of it all before the end of their story. She wouldn't carry this wound with her anymore. His love was by far the best she had experienced in her time on this earth and nothing would change that, but it had come and gone.

She woke feeling rejuvenated and with a hopefulness that surprised her. She was up well before her alarm for work. She hobbled into the kitchen to put on a pot of coffee for everyone. Then she went out to her car to grab some paperwork from her Florida trip. Evie pulled out a few phone numbers and started making follow up calls to two of the offices she had interviewed with. Evie was ready to start a new chapter.

Cassandra

"Gram, I got my schedule for school! I need to call the girls and see what classes we have together." Cassie shrieked with excitement. She wasn't surprised by her schedule; it was all the class levels that she signed up for, but she didn't know which of the girls would be in which of her classes. So, on this sticky August afternoon in 2006, she went out to the back porch and set to the task of calling each of her friends. The conversations were all painfully similar. Her friends stopped what they were doing to dash out to the mailbox and pull out the letter. As they each read their classes by day and period, Cassie's heart sank. Only two of her besties shared one class together, and none of them were in the same homeroom. The only time they would see each other was the lunch wave. This was not how Cassie had envisioned starting her high school career.

Being a freshman was eye opening for Cassie, so many consequences. When she decided not to do her first book report of the year, the teacher gave her an F on the assignment. No amount of begging or groveling could get her an extension, or a makeup assignment, or anything besides an F which would need to be explained to Gram. The whole situation led to a rather uncomfortable conversation with Gram about being in control of your own decisions and deciding what type of person you want to be. She had no clue what type of person she wanted to be. However, Cassie was very clear that Gram was not going to go easy on her anymore. No more sick days when she wasn't sick, and no more writing notes to get her out of missing homework assignments. Apparently high school was filled with unwritten rules that Cassie had to learn the hard way.

Perhaps the hardest lesson was not about the schoolwork, but about the work to maintain friendships. Kara, Jane, Gia, Hillary and Cassie saw each other for 25 minutes every day. That time was cherished for the first few weeks.

"Guys!!" Cassie could hear Gia's screech all the way in the back of the lunchroom as she walked in.

"Oh boy. I can only imagine what exciting new band update will be brought to us by Gia today?" Jane said dryly.

Cassie burst out laughing and was glad that she had finished her bagel.

"Hey guys, guess what?" Gia waited a nanosecond before continuing. "They just announced the playlist for the Thanksgiving game, and the trumpet section has a solo! It is going to be awesome. We have to work on choreography and everything!" Gia beamed.

Cassie was admittedly happy that her friend found companionship in her trumpet, but she couldn't seem to relate to her joy. Instruments really didn't appeal to her.

"Jane is bored with your band news G. What else you got?" Leave it to Kara to burst her bubble.

"Dear Jane, smoking causes bad breath, yellow teeth, cancer, detention, oh yeah, and death," Gia said to Jane as she walked off to get something to eat.

"Feisty one you are G. I admire that," Cassie shouted to her, and the group broke into playful giggles.

"Hey, Cass, I'll trade you this delicious tropical fruit cup for one of your hard chocolate chip cookies?" Cassie watched as Hillary moved in on her cookie trio. She knew for sure these were not hard cookies, she could see the grease ring on the bottom of her paper plate.

"My greasy goodness! But…fruit cup for half of this gooey cookie right here?" Cassie was a sucker for a fruit cup, and Hillary jumped at the chance to make the deal. Lunch was by far Cassie's favorite time of day. She needed the security of her friends.

"Let's be friends forever guys. Like grow old and wrinkly together." Cassie had barely finished her warm sentiment when the period bell rang and set the entire room in motion.

"I don't plan on ever getting wrinkles, sorry girl." Kara waved and disappeared into the crowd.

"See you tomorrow!" Gia and Hillary said in unison.

"How is the air up there in the clouds Cass?" Jane gave her a nudge, and that was the end of lunch.

As the year progressed, the girls started splitting their time between the besties and new groups of classmates. Jane was discovering lunch detention for being rude, or late, or a whole variety of other unsavory traits that seemed to blossom overnight. Gia was focused on band, and often came in late, or ate with her band mates in the auditorium. Cassie and Hillary stayed friendly, but she joined the track team and competing schedules kept them apart. Some weekends Cassie and Kara tried to have sleep overs or connect on the computer to chat and catch up with Gia and Hillary, but it was never their whole group. The bonds of friendship were being stretched and twisted and Cassie was not a fan. Their world was full of new, evolving technology that wasn't worth a darn since none of them had the coordinating time to use it. She felt very much like she was losing the only people in her life that actually understood her.

The summer of 2007, just before sophomore year, Cassie decided to embrace her relationship with Kara. She would rather have only one of her besties than none at all. The summer days rolled by as the duo filled each hour swimming at the creek and sunning themselves in Cassie's backyard. They watched movies and caught up on the popular shows they missed during the school season, like Ugly Betty and Project Runway. Gram took them for ice cream, and Kara invited Cassie on her family vacation to the lake.

Cassie had been to New Hampshire a few times with Gram and her cousins. They went for a local fair, and Gram took home a second-place ribbon for her pie. Cassie remembered the smell of the air, thick with sap and pine and nature. It felt like such a rugged state, and she liked it. The lake was a whole new experience. Not only did they stay in a lake front cabin, but Kara's family had a boat up there and kayaks. This was the first year that Kara's older sister decided to skip family vacation, so Kara and her little brother both could bring a friend.

"Stop splashing me Jake," Kara threatened her brother. "Jake, I am not kidding. If you don't stop splashing me right now, I am going to throw your towel in the water!" Even Cassie knew not to mess with Kara. Cassie watched the scene unfold as her little brother got so much joy out of annoying his sister. She never remembered annoying her brother like that or ignoring his threatening tone.

"That's it! You're dead!" Kara was on the move.

Cassie stared in amazement at how Jake was still laughing, like he didn't believe her, like he didn't think she would actually do it. Cassie watched Kara roll off her float and swim full speed at her brother. She put both hands on his shoulders and dunked him under water before swimming to the shore. Her light skin glistening in the sun, Cassie couldn't help but admire how beautiful Kara was. And in the blink of an eye, Jakes towel was in the water. Cassie saw Kara move their towels safely out of his reach, in case of revenge. But all the while Jake just laughed.

"Keep laughing, Jakey!" Kara gracefully dismounted the dock into a cannon ball. Cassie was amazed at the size of her splash, which practically drowned him. And then in an interesting twist, Kara started a splash war with Jake and his friend. The laughter between them was infectious and Cassie couldn't hold it in. But as she giggled, a wave of water hit her face, and hair, and raft. It was time for her to join the fun.

In the evenings, the whole family would sit in folding chairs by the fire.

"Mom, I'm cold," Kara said. The moon had swallowed the sun and the stars sparkled in the black night. Cassie watched as Kara proceeded to move her chair next to her mother, until the arms were touching. She then scooted in and leaned up close to her mother's shoulder, as her mother opened her blanket to let her daughter in. It wasn't jealousy Cassie was feeling, but longing.

When the girls were alone in their room one night, Cassie started the before bed conversation. "Kara, you and your mom are so cute. You look so much alike!"

"What? Ew. She's old. We have the same nose, but that's about it. My sister looks more like her."

Having no clue that being compared to your mother could be an insult, Cassie stumbled over her words. "Uh…sorry. I mean, I can tell she's your mom. That's all."

"Duh!" Kara laughed and slammed a feather pillow into the side of Cassie's head.

"Hey! Don't start a war you can't finish!"

"I will take my chances. You wouldn't hurt a fly." Kara took aim and swung one last time.

Cassie knew she was right, and retreated under her covers, protecting herself.

Kara settled down and continued the conversation. "Do you look like your mom?"

"Nope." There was no further explanation for Cassie to offer.

"Your dad?"

"Nope."

"Well I know your grandmother, and you don't really look like her either. So, who in your family do you resemble?"

"Actually, I don't look like my family at all. They all have very light hair, my mother has green eyes, and I have a much better tan." She tried to make light of the situation.

"That's odd." Kara chewed over the information.

"Gram always says that you never really know what DNA will give you. And then she jokes and says maybe there was a mix-up at the hospital."

"What?! Are you serious! Maybe she isn't kidding?" Kara was about to launch a full-blown inspection.

"No. I mean, I would seriously doubt that." Cassie never thought twice about Gram's comment, and always assumed that she just looked different.

"Or maybe your mom had an affair with the mailman. I bet you look exactly like him!"

"Okay. That's enough conversation about my striking beauty for today." Cassie never asked many questions, and never thought about too many possibilities. She believed what the adults in her life told her. But Kara had a solid theory. She made a mental note to run that one by Gram. But as she thought more about it, if she had a different dad, then Gram wasn't her gram at all. That was not an option she was willing to entertain. She wouldn't lose the one person that she loved the most.

The trip went by much too fast and soon it was time to get ready to go. Kara's mother had a list of chores for the whole family. Cassie and Kara had to strip all the beds and pack the sheets in the car, then they had to vacuum the bedrooms, empty the dishwasher, and pack up the snack food bag for the ride home.

"Dad!" Kara yelled, "the vacuum won't work!"

Her dad ran up the stairs two at a time. "Did you girls plug it in, and hit the on button?" Cassie couldn't help but laugh. He did a further examination of the bag before diagnosing the problem.

"Needs a new bag, Kar. They are in the kitchen under the sink."

"Great. Can you fix it for me?" Kara batted her lashes.

"No. Nice try. Your chore."

"But Dad! We have a long list, and we are trying to get everything done quickly here."

"I've seen Cass run, she is fast. Are you good at stairs, Cass?" Still a little unsure of the routine of bantering with a parent, Cassie shyly shook her head in agreement, before getting a smack from Kara.

"I can go get the bag. But I have never changed one before." Cassie slipped past her dad and headed down the stairs. As she looked back, she saw Kara's dad wrap her up in a big hug.

"Don't mess up my hair!" Kara warned. Cassie paused long enough to see her dad run his fingers through her long strawberry blonde hair. "Really mature, Dad!" Kara giggled.

And when that day came to an end, Cassie found herself smiling at the thought of how normal they all were. How nice a normal life was. With her pajamas on she went in search for Gram. When she found her in the den watching her program, Cassie climbed on the couch beside her and snuggled up close.

"What's up, Love? Everything okay?" Gram asked.

"Yeah, I just missed my family while I was gone," she said with a soft smile lighting her face.

"Well, I missed you too," Gram replied.

Tangled Vines of Good Intentions

"Gram, has Mom called at all?" Cassie asked apprehensively, not sure what answer she wanted to hear.

"I haven't gotten any calls dear. Why do you ask?" Cassie felt Gram snuggle closer.

"Wondering if she decided to move to Florida. For some reason I keep expecting to get a postcard."

"Yes. That would be nice." They both let the conversation end there.

Cassie was effortlessly maintaining her relationship with Kara, and by the time September rolled around they were thick as thieves and ready to be sophomores. The highlight of sophomore year came in spring of 2008 when both Kara and Cassie got picked for the varsity lacrosse team. They practiced together every chance they got. Cassie braided Kara's silky hair on game days, and Kara pulled Cassie's curls into a tight pony, managing her frizz nicely. They further bonded on long bus rides and weekend practices. Kara was a better athlete than Cassie, but Cassie was always the loudest one cheering on the sidelines for her friend and for her teammates.

Cassie thought of her former besties often and tried to keep tabs on them during school. Although they were all fading into different crowds, Cassie had a special place in her heart for each of them. She wasn't ready to believe that they would leave her too.

Gia showed up to as many home games as she could and tried to stop by Cassie's locker for quick chats at the end of the day. Cassie happily invited Gia to go dress shopping for homecoming with her and Kara. They all had a blast trying on all sorts of beaded, printed, and feathered gowns, some that they would never wear in public. They hit several large department stores in the mall to thoroughly explore all their options. Cassie was curvier than Kara, and they were both taller than Gia. If one girl didn't love a style the next girl would try it on, and it would look completely different. Cassie stared at her reflection in an emerald green dress and noted all the ways it looked better on Kara. Kara was a traditional beauty and looked good in almost everything. Cassie admired her slim, strong physique, and her dainty hands which were childlike compared to Cassie's big mitts. She had naturally blush cheeks that complemented her sky-blue eyes and had never had a pimple in her life.

"Let's see Cass!" The girls cackled.

"Nope. Doesn't fit. Next one please." Cassie did like the color but didn't do the dress justice.

"Don't be silly, you look great!" Kara popped in. She lit the entire fitting room with her bright smile, and Cassie was envious. It was just the right amount of lip to teeth ratio. It was stunning. Cassie had a big smile, the kind that took over her whole face and exposed every tooth in her mouth. She was always self-conscious about the way her smile was a bit bigger on one side of her face and felt like the Cheshire cat with a crooked grin. It was hard to let go of these little insecurities. And with perfect Kara in her face, in the fitting room, her issues all seemed very valid.

Two weeks later they all arrived at the school gym for the Homecoming dance—all except Jane. The room was covered in gold stars plastered on the walls, floating in balloon bunches, and decorating the tables that were set up around the perimeter of the room. It was a simple theme, but there was something very glamorous about it in Cassie's mind. Cassie and Kara were joined at the hip and showed off all kinds of moves on the dance floor. Gia and Hillary even broke away from their new friends to dance to Flo Rida's "Get Low" with Kara and Cassie. The dance was a blast. They broke a sweat as Fergie, Taylor Swift, and Katy Perry's "I Kissed a Girl" echoed through the gym and up the halls of the school. And when they couldn't dance another step, they sat at a table and watched the guys.

The guys that were looking significantly different than freshman year. They were taller and hairier, and more intriguing. Cassie had her eye on one in particular, a lacrosse player. A tall and lean player, with defined arms that Cassie drooled over when she watched him play. His long blonde curls were always a beautiful mess around his sharp jawline and often covered his striking gray eyes. She was captivated. However, she didn't have the courage to say more than two words to him at school, and somehow, he always caught her watching him at practice. This particular boy was a hot topic on sleepovers with her and Kara. They checked his MySpace page for his likes and dislikes and to make sure he was still single. Cassie was crushing hard, and she was grateful for Kara always listening and never judging. Although the school year came and went without any progress on the dating front, she remained hopeful.

Cassie was seemingly a well-rounded young lady, with a good head on her shoulders. She didn't hang out with the wrong crowd, like Jane, and she was excelling in her studies and lacrosse. Despite her family baggage, she was doing well.

Feeling older and more confident in her curvier body, Cassie was ready to have some fun in her junior year. She was 16 years old when school started. Her feelings for the lacrosse boy were still raging inside her; she was enrolled in driver's education classes that started in October, and this was the year of their first prom.

Kara and Cassie were solid. They had several of the same classes together and were texting constantly when they were apart. The former besties were settled in their respective friend groups, and although there were times when Cassie missed the big group, she understood that high school was a beast that none of them could anticipate. She rarely spoke to her old friends, and she had to be okay with that.

One fall weekend in September, Cassie and Kara were spending the day at the mall. They had conquered Gap, The Limited, Wet Seal, Macy's, Abercrombie & Fitch, Aldo, and Express— about half of the stores on their list, when they both agreed on a much-needed snack break and headed to Mrs. Fields Cookies. They jumped in line and checked out their options. All of a sudden Cassie noticed her friend giving her a silent message. Her eyes bulged and from what Cassie could figure out, Kara didn't want her to turn around. Naturally, Cassie swung her head around and came face to face with Lacrosse Boy. CJ, aka Lacrosse Boy, was standing behind them in line with his little sister. Cassie was so close she could smell his cologne, and she felt the heat of embarrassment almost instantly. She tried to pick her jaw up off the floor and turn back around, but her movements were jerky, and downright obvious.

"Hey," CJ said.

Unable to move, or look back in his direction, Cassie could do nothing. Her head was trying to remember words, sounds, hand gestures, anything! She could feel the blush creeping in to betray her once again.

"Oh, hi!" Kara said cheerfully. "I know we go to school together, but I'm Kara and this is my girl Cassie."

Cassie took a quick breath in, and with a very pink face, peeked up at him shyly through her thick dark eyelashes. She waved. That was it. Then turned quickly to order their cookies and slushies, grateful to be turned around again.

With food and drink in hand, Kara waved to CJ as the girls shuffled away.

"What the hell, Cass! I just gave you the perfect opening and nothing! You did nothing!" Clearly Kara was shocked at Cassie's missed opportunity.

"I…I…uh, sorry?" Her head still cloudy from the run-in, Cassie was not able to process what just happened.

They sat at a table and Kara began to break it down.

Tangled Vines of Good Intentions

"When a cute guy is in your face, normal girls would say hello. Super-cutie that you have a crush on, well then you jump on him!" Kara made herself giggle with that one. "Shake it off, Cassie. Time to get your head in the game if you want CJ to be your prom date!!"

With that, a whole new wave of excitement came over Cassie. She never imagined that he would want to go with her, or that he would ask her, or that she would even have the courage to accept if he did. Riding the buzz of this new chance at romance, Cassie decided to buy a new outfit for her next run in with CJ.

Gram put an abrupt hold on Cassie's daydreaming when the two had a conversation about SAT testing and college preparation later that month. Gram had fliers, brochures, and booklets. She had lists of websites, some with college ratings, and even more with descriptions and pictures. She had an arsenal of college-choosing weapons and every intention of making Cassie use them.

Honestly, Cassie had not put much thought into college. She was all consumed by the daily drama of high school and wasn't ready to think about what was happening more than a year into the future. Still, she knew Gram was right, and her timing was impeccable. The week after their initial conversation, Cassie was called to meet with her guidance counselor to have the college discussion all over again.

The counselor's office was quiet. Cassie hardly remembered that there were other kids in the building. She felt more comfortable exploring different options there. Cassie told the counselor about her time in Gainesville, all about the tour her mother dragged her on, and how much she loved it. She took the time to describe the shops and the architecture of the town and was honestly surprised at herself for speaking about it with such fondness.

"That sounds great! And does your mom think this school is a good fit for you?" the counselor asked eagerly.

"Uh…well…I'm not sure?" Cassie was honest.

"Now is a great time to have lots of conversations at home with your parents, siblings, grandparents. Leaving home is a big decision."

"Right. My parents aren't at home, but my grandmother is definitely reminding me of what a big decision it is." Cassie couldn't remember the last time she had to try to explain her family situation. Sometimes she forgot that her family included more people than Gram.

"Oh. Interesting. Would you like to talk about that further?" the counselor offered.

Totally thrown by the offer, Cassie was quick to decline. "No, thank you. Me and Gram are the decision-making team on this one."

Cassie's could tell that the counselor picked up on her uneasiness, as she switched the conversation back to college options. When that meeting was over, it seemed like the entire junior class was talking about college. And although Cassie was not ready to make solid plans, she knew she should follow suit. Kara and Cassie signed up for Pre-SAT testing on the same day, at the same site.

On the third Saturday in October, they arrived at the testing site; however, she and Kara were spilt into two groups and ushered away in opposite directions. As Cassie took a look back at Kara, she caught a glimpse of CJ walking behind her friend. She quickly turned, knowing that now was not the time for happy, exciting, handsome distractions like CJ.

Several hours later, Cassie closed her booklet, and handed it to the exam proctor. The test was annoying. Cassie was not completely sure of any of the math answers and had cramps from her writing exercise. Grateful to be done with that round, she bolted out the door, down the hallway, and straight for the parking lot to see if she could spot Kara. Cassie paused at the exit door and looked through the glass to see who had made it through the test alive. Kara was done and chatting outside with a few girls from the team, and CJ. Cassie paused before exiting the building, took a deep breath, and walked over to join the crowd. She snuck in on the opposite side of Kara, linking arms and resting her head on Kara's shoulder.

"Hey, girlie! How did it go?" Kara welcomed her friend into the conversation.

"I hated it. Long and tedious." Cassie kept it brief, but honest. She was staring at CJ's shoes.

"Yeah. None of us liked it, that's for sure," CJ added with a casual confidence. All the girls laughed instantly.

Feeling brave, Cassie lifted her gaze and took in the site of CJ's hotness. His full lips curled into a teasing smile that gave him the slightest impression of dimples. As her cheeks pinked up, Cassie knew this was as good a time as any to start a conversation.

"Do you think the math was easier, or the writing portion?" Cassie said shyly.

"I am better at math, I think," CJ responded without missing a beat.

And in that instant a car horn got the crowd's attention.

"That's my ride. Let's jet Kara. See you guys later," Cassie said to the group. She grabbed Kara's hand and ran to the car without looking back. Once safely inside the closed doors, she exhaled.

"It's like you were locked in your room for your whole life, and have never seen a boy before, Cass!" Kara's voice was thick with disappointment.

"I would assume that comment was not test related?" Gram chimed in. She threw a wave at the crowd before pulling off, and Cassie knew Gram recognized the girls from the team, but not the tall drink of water that was most certainly not on the team.

"Cassie is super awkward in front of CJ. I am pretty sure that makes it even more obvious that you are crushing on him…by the way," Kara continued.

"Well Kara, in her defense, I don't have a lot of young people over the house these days," Gram said with a smile. "Maybe we should hire someone to mow the lawn or clean the pool?" she added, and the car erupted with laughter. They did not have a pool.

November brought test results in the mail, and Cassie's scores were low. Gram was concerned, and Cassie was warned that she would not be allowed to get her driver's license until she retested and had a better score. This was a rite of passage she was fine waiting for. Cassie was almost 17 and had successfully completed her Driver's Ed class, despite not being in the same class as Kara. Having her permit, she was allowed to drive an adult around, and she didn't think having a license would be that big of a deal. Plus, Kara had hers, and they couldn't even ride together for a whole year.

Gram seemed extra focused that year, and Cassie wasn't loving the pressure. Gram was requesting Cassie's homework assignments and test scores; and Cassie was forced to schedule a second Pre SAT exam as soon as she could. It became clear that Gram was not about to let her slide or be distracted. Cassie was reminded over and over that life was too big to be sidetracked by a high school crush. The message went in one ear and out the other, as Cassie had no intention of forgetting about CJ.

It was the day before February break when Cassie and Kara got a personal invite to a party at Jane's house. Well, it felt personal. The party was gossip all over the 11th grade lunch wave. They were intrigued. It was a no-parents, tons-of-people kind of party. It would be Cassie's first. However, the girls needed to create a plan that would get them there. Neither had ever attempted a stunt of this magnitude, but since it was

Jane, and they had been so close at one point, Kara knew they could pull it off, and Cassie trusted her.

By the end of the day Cassie had a solid story to sell to Gram that would get both girls out for the whole night. She told Gram that Jane was having a sleepover party to celebrate Cassie's birthday, plus another one of her friends. Cassie couldn't miss a party in her honor! And naturally Kara would be at her side. She delivered her tale with a confidence she didn't know was in her. It shocked her how easily she could lie to Gram, but she knew the truth simply wasn't an option. Gram did question the friendship between Cassie and Jane, and the fact that she hadn't heard a thing about her in over a year. Cassie was able to think on her feet and called this the reaching-out and rekindling of an old friendship. Gram reluctantly gave her permission, with the promise that Cassie checked in around 10 p.m.

Cassie knew Gram trusted her, mostly because she had never given her a reason not to. Still, Gram always insisted on a 10 p.m. check-in, which Cassie was fairly certain was because Gram was brainwashed by the TV and the news station always running an ad at 10 p.m. asking if people knew where their kids were. Cassie had no other explanation, but it had been a really simple rule to follow. And in this particular moment, she truly appreciated the freedom of the 10 p.m. check-in.

Kara's older sister dropped them off and noted the number of cars in the driveway and on the street. She was attending community college, and most likely could see through the sleep over act. Cassie was amazed when she made sure they both had phones, promised not to get in any cars with anyone, to call her if they needed anything, and to run or hide if they heard cops. With that pep talk, the girls turned toward the house and tried to prepare for the unknown of the evening ahead.

After two mixed drinks, Cassie's head was spinning. The music was thumping through her entire body, and she had lost track of Kara. So many people had crammed into Jane's house. Food and cups and trash covered every surface in every room. Cassie tried to clear her head for a second, when she heard the alarm of her phone. The alarm went through two full cycles before someone pulled the phone from Cassie's backpack, which she was still wearing.

"Are you looking for this?" CJ dangled the buzzing phone in Cassie's face.

She grabbed the phone, turned, and ran to the nearest room. Cassie slammed the door and looked around. She grabbed for the light string that was tickling her face and pulled it on. It was the pantry. Attempting to shut out her fuzziness, she dialed Gram.

"Hey sweetie! Having fun?" Gram answered on the first ring.

"Yes! Lots." Cassie was not sure what she sounded like; she was just trying to make it brief.

"Ok. Thanks for calling." Gram seemed satisfied.

"Nigh, nigh, Nana." And with that odd jumble of words, Cassie hung up.

As she stood in the pantry, she scanned the shelves of canned goods, salad dressing, cereal, and snacks. She spotted a bag of pretzels and decided to take it with her. She opened the door and walked right into CJ.

"Oh, hey, are you done in there?" he giggled. "Pretzels, good choice." He pulled the bag gently from her grip and opened it. Taking a handful for himself.

CJ then turned toward Cassie and moved in close. She backed up into the closed pantry door. He gently pulled her chin up and tilted her head so she was looking him straight in his steel gray eyes. Cassie could hear her heart pounding as his hand touched her chin. She stood stone still as he proceeded to lower his head of blonde hair and beautifully plump lips to meet hers. She held her breath as he kissed her tenderly. When he pulled away, she made no movement, had no expression on her face, and then he went in and kissed her again. This time Cassie woke up and moved her lips back, in a harmonious rhythm with his. This was happening.

High school is a magical time. A girl's world is so small yet feels so important. Cassie was fully immersed in the chaos of school drama. Every bit of good news needed to be celebrated for at least a week and everything that was perceived as a bad thing was truly the end of the world, for at least a week. There was little thought of how big the real world actually was. Even the reality of junior year couldn't slow down the runaway train that was Cassie.

Since her make-out session with CJ over the break, which everyone in the whole school knew about, Cassie had gained even more confidence. However, she was not actually dating CJ. They said "hi" to each other in the halls and at practice, but not much more than that. He watched the girl's lacrosse games when he wasn't playing himself, and Cassie held on to that as a hopeful sign. Her sights were still set on prom, even though it was months away.

During one chilly March day, Cassie initiated a conversation about SATs and college. It was not something that she often thought about, but she and Kara had recently signed up for the real SATs, and she was genuinely curious to know Kara's thoughts. It seemed like all they talked about lately was lacrosse and CJ, with the occasional chatter about the latest episode of Keeping Up with the Kardashians. The girls were recapping Cassie's second Pre-SAT scores during 3rd period, when Kara mentioned that CJ aced his test and was looking to go to a local state college. A little stunned to hear this personal information roll so casually off her tongue, Cassie turned on her shocked face and went into full detective mode.

"How do you know about his scores, or college plans for that matter? You never mentioned that you talk to CJ like that?" She was blunt and direct with Kara.

"Oh Cass, it's no big deal, must have slipped my mind. He was in my Driver's Ed class in the fall." Kara spit out the statement oddly fast and rushed off to her next class, giving Cassie a wave.

She was completely perplexed. She wanted to believe that Kara was trying to protect her from being even more upset about not being in the same Driver's Ed class. That would have been a very logical friend thing to do. Cassie's face was pink and hot as she continued to stew on this new bit of information. She couldn't help but feel like there was more to the story here, like Kara was hiding something. It was the way that she smiled a little when she said CJ. Kara seemed, proud, or excited, like she was bragging. How friendly were they? It ate at her all day. She needed to get to the bottom of this.

"Kara?"

"Oh, hey Cass! What's up?" Cassie called Kara after dinner that night, when she thought she would be calm enough to listen to her best friend.

"Why didn't you tell me about CJ?"

"Uh…tell you what?" Kara stuttered.

Not expecting to have to clarify, Cassie took a deep breath to calm the anger brewing inside of her. "How long have you and CJ been friends? How friendly are you? Why didn't you tell me about Driver's Ed?"

"Oh! Well, you know we see him all the time at practice and what not. So, when he was in Driver's Ed with me, I didn't really think anything of it. Haven't we been stalking this kid for like a year now? I figured you would be mad since you couldn't join the class, too."

"When did he tell you about his college plans? Do you guys talk like that?" Cassie pressed.

"I didn't know it was against the law to be friends with him, Cassie! It should really be you talking to him. I haven't heard any progress with that." Kara was defensive.

Cassie found Kara's twist interesting. She made a point; Cassie had not had much conversation with him at all. "Fine. I'll see you tomorrow then." Cassie was not in the mood to argue.

As prom grew closer and closer, she didn't think it was a good time to hold a grudge against Kara. She needed her support and wanted to do this with her best friend. After a week of less talking, Cassie decided to let it go and get back to good with her bestie.

Easter Break came and went, and before she knew it, the month of May was upon them. She had plans to make. The most important item on the agenda was a prom date, despite the fact that Gram kept stressing SATs. Cassie had a SAT test date at the end of May, and she was happy to put the thought aside until then. She knew that the distraction of prom was real, and it was one week before her test date. Once CJ agreed to go with her, she could switch her focus to SATs. And Cassie was ready to ask CJ, or at least she had been convincing herself that she was ready for a few weeks now.

Kara still seemed a bit off, like she wasn't in complete support of Cassie's decision to ask CJ. Kara said that she was old school and believed that the guy should be asking the girl to prom. They were both in total agreement on a day for dress shopping though. They cleared two school nights and a full weekend to hunt down perfect dresses. They had boutique stores on their list from as far as three towns over. They wanted something unique, something special, and something perfect.

As the days ticked by, closer and closer to prom, Cassie couldn't wait any longer. She needed to make this the day that she made her move. She didn't see Kara at their usual morning rendezvous spot, a bank of floor-to-ceiling windows facing the lacrosse field, and desperately hoped she would catch her for a last-minute confidence boost. Kara was elusive for most of the day. The only way Cassie knew she was even in school was when she passed by one of her classes and peeked in to try to get her to take a bathroom break. Kara never looked up, and Cassie had to keep it moving before the teacher noticed her. This was odd. Cassie wasn't really sure what she did to upset her, and definitely wasn't sure how to fix it. But one thing at a time. She was on a mission.

It was the end of the day, and Cassie boldly strolled over to CJ's bright orange locker as he was packing up. "Hey CJ!"

"Hi. Cass, right?" He continued to pack his bag.

Cassie began to bite her nails in an unconscious move of nervousness. "Cassie, right! Hey, are you going to prom?" Cassie could feel the sweat beading on the small of her back as she spoke with a bit too much excitement.

"Um. Yeah. I'll be there." CJ was getting ready to shut his locker. He was clearly in a rush. This was a now or never moment. As he turned to walk away, Cassie grabbed his arm.

"Great! Would you like to go to prom with me?" It was out. Just hanging there. Motionless.

"Thanks, Cass, but I already asked someone else. But I'm sure I will see you there. Later." And with that, he was gone into the sea of students making a mass exodus. Cassie stood there, in the way, getting bounced around like a ping pong ball, until she hit a locker and slumped to the ground.

"Hey. Hey! Hello?" A voice from above was trying to get her attention, and with a little kick to her thigh, it worked.

Cassie lifted her head slowly. "Jane?" Her eyes were blurry with tears. She couldn't be staring up at Jane, could she?

"That's my name. And this here is my locker. Might you be moving anytime soon?" Jane said, a little snarky, and clearly ignoring Cassie's tears.

"Sorry," Cassie sniffled, and made her way to her feet.

She stood for a minute. Not wanting to leave the warmth of another person. She wasn't sure she wanted to spill her guts to Jane, but she wasn't sure she wanted to spill her guts to Kara either. Cassie dried her eyes with her shirt, leaving black smudge marks down her sleeves.

Jane smirked at the mess. "You can try putting dish soap on that a day or so before you wash it…usually does the trick for me."

Cassie looked at Jane, as if she was looking at her for the first time all year. Jane had on a black fitted t-shirt, a cute black and white plaid skirt with high skull patterned socks, and short dark hair that was pinned up in every direction. Dark purple eye shadow and dark smoky black eye pencil surrounding her bright blue eyes stood out in contrast to her smooth pale peach skin. Cassie was in a bit of a trance. She had forgotten how beautiful her old friend was.

"Your eyes are beautiful." Cassie let out slowly.

"What the hell is wrong with you?" Jane replied sharply. "You are all teary, then you are gazing into my eyes! Are you high?" Jane sounded earnestly curious.

Cassie sat for a minute before trying to act more like herself, despite how she was really feeling. She gave Jane a warm smile. "Do I seem like a girl that would use drugs, Jane?"

"No. You aren't ready yet." Jane returned her smile. "Are you getting picked up? Pretty sure half the busses are gone already."

"Oh shit!" Cassie was back to reality, and reality was that it was Thursday, Gram was at her garden club meeting and Cassie was on her own for a ride. "Nope, no ride, I definitely missed my bus."

"If you promise not to hit on me, or cry, or get your makeup all over my car, I can give you a ride," Jane offered.

"Really?" Cassie was shocked.

"If you break any of those rules I am pulling over and kicking your ass out." Jane was firm.

"How long have you been driving for?" Cassie was not sure how she missed that event.

"Well, I will be 18 in 6 months. I can assure you I didn't get my license yesterday," Jane said casually. "Ready to go?"

"Yeah," Cassie said. "Thanks."

The awkward silence in the car was shattered by the Panic! At the Disco song blaring through the speakers as Jane flipped the radio on. This happened to be one of Cassie's favorite jams at the moment, and she couldn't help but sing out loud. Jane gave her a look, and then laughed it off.

"You haven't changed much, have you?" Jane said.

"What is that supposed to mean?" She asked, surprised by the comment.

"You are still very carefree and careless."

That seemed like an aggressive statement; and although she was not sure she could handle any additional drama, Cassie wondered if this was some pent-up emotion that Jane needed to get off her chest.

"Well, that type of comment deserves an explanation, don't you think?" Cassie said assertively.

Jane turned down the radio. "Cassie, you were crying in the hallway ten minutes ago and now you are singing and laughing like nothing happened. You are carefree and don't seem to hold on to anything negative, but you are so careless, thoughtless. I mean, you never seem to be able to look at things long enough or hard enough to see the whole picture, or maybe you don't want to? I didn't really get that about you, but it makes more sense now. You have been able to stay happily entertained in your little bubble because you never bother to look for the truth."

This was big. Cassie was not really sure what Jane was getting at, or why. I mean, who didn't want to live in a happy bubble? Why would Cassie want to dwell on the negative? "You think I ignore the truth about what?" she asked.

"Just in tough situations. Look at your family life. Where the hell are your parents right now?" Jane was not sugar coating this conversation at all. "I mean, unless they are in jail, or drug dealers, or dead, you should at least know where they are or how to reach them. And if you don't, you should ask why. Same with your brother. It's like he disappeared. And you dropped all of your friends except Kara. But has Kara actually been a good friend to you?"

Jane paused, as if expecting a response. Holding back residual tears, Cassie was letting all this sink in. Jane was not wrong about her screwed up home life. "My parents clearly don't want me in their lives. I can't change that. It was out of my hands. And I wish I still had Brian, but I didn't do anything wrong." Cassie let a tear fall. "And I didn't think that I dropped my friends. I let you go when it seemed like you all wanted to go."

"Yes, your parents suck, but why? Why would they have two babies and only ditch one of them? And why keep them apart? You deserve an explanation. And why didn't you fight for your friendships? Why give up so easily?"

Cassie, still a bit puzzled, was starting to see Jane's point. She had not heard from her mother since the last day of their Florida trip, and she didn't know where she was. Plus, her friends all faded away and she never put up much of a fight, or even tried hard to get them back.

"Why are you bringing all of this up now, Jane?"

"I don't like seeing you hurt. I don't like seeing people take advantage of you, and I don't want you to be an oblivious adult who has no clue when people are screwing them over."

Cassie could sense that Jane was building to something. That even though she might have pointed out a character flaw, there was a reason for why she was bringing all of this up now. "Why are you giving me a ride?" Cassie's voice was strong.

"Excuse me? Would you like to walk? I can stop. Or turn around and bring you back?"

"No, I mean, what are you really trying to say, Jane? Why is all of this coming up right now and what brought all of this on?"

CASSANDRA

"There we have it, folks! When she wants to admit there is something more than meets the eye, then she is very determined. Cassandra, I have some bad news for you. Kara has a boyfriend."

Cassie was struck by the sound of Kara's name coming from Jane's lips. Cassie thought Jane had long since erased both their names from her vocab. How in the world could she possibly know about Kara's love life? How could Jane possibly know more than she did? Cassie was speechless, she didn't see this conversation coming at all. She sat for a minute with a look of utter confusion unconsciously making her eyebrows furrow on her face and her lips frown a bit. She was not sure she had the energy for anymore truth.

"Take a deep breath, this is gonna hurt…Kara is going out with that lacrosse guy." Jane kept her voice calm.

The words sounded muffled. It was like Cassie heard them but didn't know what they meant. She was frozen in time with those words floating in the empty space that was now her head. She was numb. As the minutes melted away, Cassie was hit with another very clear thought—prom. No more prom. Kara was going with CJ. With the car quietly idling in Cassie's driveway, Jane handed her a napkin to help soak up the flood waters cascading down her face.

Jane was so right on. There should have been pretty obvious clues, but Cassie did not see them, and did not try to see them, because she wouldn't have wanted to see them. Cassie found herself ill-prepared to deal with such a deep pain. It was less about Kara being such a shitty friend, and more about Cassie letting her be one. Cassie wasn't sure how to be a stronger person, she didn't know how to not be a door mat. It was a new revelation to her that a doormat was who she had become. The news was crushing. Seventeen years old should be the time of your young adult life. Almost a senior, friends, boys, fun. Cassie was feeling void of all of those, lost inside the shell of a girl she no longer knew, and didn't want to be.

Evie

In July of 2006, Evie stumbled on a job opening at Shands Hospital in Gainesville. She set up a phone interview, and two weeks later was formally offered the position, with the condition that she sit for her state RN certification prior to day one, and that she passes the certification in order to keep employment. Evie was thrilled for the new challenge and set to work ordering books, securing a testing date, and finding an apartment in Florida.

As she packed her car with clothes, and baked goods from Carol, her mind shifted briefly to Cassie. Maybe she would write her a letter and tell her about the move. Maybe Cassie would want to visit? But the reality that Evie knew so well was that she was no good for Cassie. Cassie had been hurt enough. She hit the gas and made one last trip through the town that held so many good and bad memories.

She passed by the park where she'd played with her baby boy. She always made him wear a hat to protect his pale skin from the summer sun. She could picture that hat. It was a

Yankees hat that Eddie passed down when Brian was born. It was a fight to get Eddie out of that hat most nights, but the second Brian got his hands on it, they both knew it was over. It slipped down his face and covered his eyes while he was walking on already wobbly legs, so Evie had to turn it backwards. Where did those days go?

She passed the bakery where she and Carol met for coffee and fresh cinnamon rolls countless times. Evie could smell the sweet aroma wafting through the air as she rode by. It was enough to make her mouth water. She rounded the corner and pulled onto East Street. On her right was the little boutique dress shop where Carol's daughter Jillian found the perfect prom dress. That was a fun day. Evie and Carol and all of her girls went from store to store and sat in endless fitting rooms watching Jillian find flaw in every gown she tried on. All the while Evie was in awe of how beautiful she grew up to be, and picky, like her mother. As she shifted her head to the left, she saw the one place that she was always running from.

The Bar on East had been a friend to her; its walls forever holding her secrets. This was the place where she had her first one-on-one encounter with Dr. Ron. Eddie had a late meeting with his nursing staff and Evie had the day off. She slept in, watched trashy TV programs all morning, and had ice cream out of the container for brunch. It was early afternoon before she was even motivated to get in the shower, and that was mostly due to Eddie calling and waking her from her nap. When she finally left the house, she had no set direction. She was window shopping in the area when she noticed the bar, and a devilish grin curled her lips as she made her way inside. If Eddie could do it, then she could too. She had no clue what she was walking into; no clue that one day would alter her entire future. He was wearing dark pants and a tight fitting tucked in turtleneck. He smelled good, a mixture of rugged, bold cleanliness. She had been attracted to him from the first time they met, but she didn't know it. As she drank in his soft brown eyes and boyish smile, she felt a tingle in places that were very new.

"So, what do you like to do for fun?" Dr. Ron asked.

"Well, today I watched soap operas!" Evie felt relaxed.

"Are you old enough to watch those shows? But what are you into, do you like dancing, or traveling, or drawing?"

"I haven't been asked in a long time, and I guess I haven't had the time to think about it lately. Life has happened very quickly the past few years. I like to listen to music, and sing," she said coyly.

"I bet you have a beautiful voice. If you weren't a nurse would you be a singer?"

"It's not that good!" They both chuckled. "If I wasn't a nurse, I don't know what I would want. Most of my life people told me what to do, and who to be, and I listened. When asked to make a decision on my own, I'm afraid I would crumble under the pressure."

"I don't believe it. You are strong and smart, you may need a minute to explore your options, but I think you would be great at anything you did, honestly."

"How can you be so sure?" Evie batted her lashes as her face pinked with a subtle blush.

"I just have a feeling about you. And usually my feelings are right."

A loud honk from the car behind startled her as she sat at a green light in front of the bar. Evie hit the gas and tried to feel okay with the decision to leave New York, and leave Dr. Ron, again.

There were so many distractions in Florida. Work was super busy, and for the first time, Evie felt truly fulfilled. She was an ER nurse and the rush of each day left her exhausted and energized all at the same time. She loved the thrill and the urgency and the life or death moments that she was a part of. And she was good at it. She had always been good at it, but this was the first time it really felt like she fit her job and made a good choice in her life. This was a strange but welcomed feeling.

She spent long hours at the hospital and enjoyed the pool at her apartment complex on her rare days off. Many times, Evie thought about dialing Gert to check in on Cassie, but she couldn't bring herself to do it. Haunted by Cassie's questions during their trip, she knew that she had truly hurt her.

Evie settled into her new life and did her best to let go of the past. She made friends and started building a life. The days turned to months, seasons changed, Evie was happy for the most part. She kept tabs on her son as best she could. They always spoke on holidays and she tried to call him once a month. Brian was in a serious relationship and doing well in college. He seemed happy that Evie had found a good rhythm in Florida. She invited them down for a visit, but life got too busy for each of them, and time kept rolling on leaving empty promises in its wake.

It was one December afternoon in 2009 when Evie received an unexpected call from Gert. They had a brief chat about Cassie who was now in her senior year of high school. Then Gert hit Evie with the real reason for the call, and all at once, the life Evie had been running from was suffocating her once again.

"I have the letter. And I plan to give it to her on her birthday. I thought it was only fair that you know," Gert said coolly.

Eddie and Evie legally adopted Cassie a few days after she was born. Neither she nor Eddie had much time to figure out how to address the adoption with the baby, or with Brian. Eddie was adamant that he wanted to keep the adoption quiet until Cassie was old enough to understand it. In an effort to appease her husband, Evie wrote a letter to Cassie from the both of them to lay out the scenario as best she could. However, Evie never expected Cassie to get the letter.

Tangled Vines of Good Intentions

The picture in her head the day she'd written it was so far from the reality that they all called life. For starters, Evie fully expected that she would be with Cassie on her 18th birthday, and that they would be a family. The letter was just to make Eddie happy. Evie planned to leave Eddie before Cassie even learned the alphabet. Evie would then reunite Cassie with her biological father and the letter would be pointless. The person that would be adopted into the family would have been Evie, not Cassie. Cassie would be with two loving parents in a warm stable home.

"Hello? Evie, you still there?" Gert shouted on the other end of the phone.

Evie couldn't catch her breath. How could she have forgotten about the letter? "How…did you…where did you…?" was all she could mutter.

"Eddie gave me the letter once it became clear that I would have Cassie permanently. He held on to it after the divorce. It really broke his heart when you two split. I think Cassie was just a reminder of you. It was hard for him to bow out of her life, but he thought it was best for her. I think it was best for him, really. He would never have been able to get over the situation if he had to face Cassie every day. Anyway, you both seemed to want me to tell her when the time was right, but I really didn't feel comfortable making that decision. When he gave me the letter and told me that you guys planned to tell her on her 18th birthday, I just went along with it. But I have no clue how she will react. I wanted to be sure that you knew that I still planned to give her that letter," Gert explained to Evie, who was silently weeping on the other end.

"Yes. Okay. Thank you," Evie said.

"Honey, you both did wrong by this girl. But she is tough and brave, and still has her whole life ahead of her. She could forgive, but she can't until she knows the truth," Gert added, before wishing Evie well and hanging up the phone.

Evie

Evie called in sick that afternoon. She stayed in bed. She was truly disappointed with herself for always choosing to run. And never sticking by Cassie, who was so innocent.

Her first trip back home was planned, just days after the reality check phone call from Gert. She hadn't been back to New York in three-and-a-half years. She finally connected with Brian earlier that year. He brought his girlfriend down for a Spring Break week in Panama City, and Evie drove up to have dinner with them one night. He was so adult like. Brian would be home for Christmas for a few days and Evie was lucky enough to get on his calendar. She was excited, but after her call with Gert, she couldn't help but feel terrified. She had never told Brian the truth, not the whole truth. He would surely hate her; and she was not ready to lose him.

As she stepped off the plane in her old wool sweater that always made her neck itch in the same small spot, Evie was warmly greeted by Carol and her girls. She and Carol had grown even closer after her move. They made time to talk to each other, honest conversations, and genuinely cared about the goings on in each other's lives. Evie knew she wouldn't be able to make it through this life without Carol.

The trip was going well. Evie booked a hotel and rented a car for her second week there. She was toying with the thought of visiting her father. He was in a nursing home, and had outlived her mother by five years, and counting. But she thought better of it. Didn't want to give him a heart attack from the surprise.

Her lunch date with Brian went surprisingly well. Evie decided to tell him the truth, the whole truth—most of it anyway.

"Bri, I have some heavy things to tell you about my life, and my decisions. Most of them were not good decisions.

But I would like the chance to tell you a little more now that you are older." Evie could feel her heartbeat quickening and her temperature creeping up to uncomfortable.

"Ok."

"Ok. I wanted you to know that I asked for the divorce from your father, and it was partially because I was unfaithful to him." When Brian didn't get up and storm out, Evie took it as a sign to continue. "I wanted to start a life with this other man, but it did not work out that way. I was wrong for doing that to your father. So, after the divorce, when I realized that I wasn't going to end up with this other person, I was not sure what to do. I made some selfish choices that hurt you and Cassandra very much. I left you, then I abandoned her. Looking back, I don't know if I would have been a good mom to her or not, but I should have tried. I should have tried the same way that I tried with you, but I just didn't." Evie paused to sip some water.

"Why did you adopt Cassie in the first place?" Brian spoke for the first time in what felt like hours to Evie.

"Let's just say, I was in the right place at the right time. I watched her being born."

"And so you took her?"

"Well, her birth mother decided that she wasn't ready to be a mother, and I thought I was. But I was wrong. And I haven't said that to your sister yet. I am not sure if Cassie will ever understand the events that led to her adoption, but I hope that she will forgive me for not being there for her, you know? In the end my decisions cost you a sister, and I am sorry for that. Cassie really is a great person. And I hope that one day you can forgive me for my mistakes and the pain that they have caused." Evie was desperate for some alcohol, but she was mindful not to order a drink until after the hard-hitting conversation with Brian.

"I do wish that she had come back to New York with you. I don't really understand why you left her," Brian stated.

"It is a little complicated, but I was so upset when things didn't work out between me and the other man, that I couldn't focus." Evie didn't have the heart to tell her son the full truth. As much as she wanted to, all the sorted details were too scandalous.

"Dad told me that she was adopted, and he told me that you cheated. I didn't totally understand, but I was still angry," Brian said honestly.

"I'm sorry," was all she could think of to say.

"Dad left the choice to keep in touch with Cassie up to me. I guess I have to ask for her forgiveness, too. When Dad told me all this stuff, I was so angry with you that I took it out on her. I didn't keep in touch. As time went on, things got better between you and me, but I never tried to fix it with Cassie," Brian explained.

A tear slipped from Evie's eye. She was so proud of the man that he had become, with little help from her. "You were only a kid. We put some adult pressures on you. I'm sure she will understand."

"Time went by so fast. I mean, she drew me pictures and called a few times, but by the time I was in middle school I didn't even think about calling her or writing. When I talked to Grandma on holidays Cassie was never around. And now I'm a college grad; twenty-one years old."

"Look, this is not your fault. You cannot be held responsible for your parent's decisions. For my decisions. In a few weeks Cassandra is going to open a letter that explains that she was adopted at birth. None of us know or can even begin to imagine how she will take the news, but it might be an opening to start anew with her. At the very least it may give us a chance to apologize. We can go see her together if, and when, you are ready to talk to her."

"Holy crap! She doesn't know?" Brian was shocked.

"Your dad and I decided not to tell her until she was older, and we asked your grandmother to respect that. I think she did."

"But she doesn't look like Gram, or any of us."

"But she feels like one of us. I was with her not too long ago, and she really believes that we are her family and that I didn't want her. She may have questioned it over the years, but she never got the truth. So, I am really hoping that we can clear the air and start over."

"Wow, I hope she'll be ok."

"Bri, we are her family. We are the only people she knows. That won't change when she finds out I didn't give birth to her. Her life is still her life, her friends, her relationship with Gram. It's all real. We just need to be a better family; I need to be better."

"I guess you're right. I'm glad you didn't ditch me, Mom." Brian tried to lighten the mood.

"Me too. You are a pretty cool guy. And you let me bring all those orange slices to your soccer games. I felt like the luckiest Mom in the world," Evie grinned. And with that, they fell into easy conversation and left the heavy stuff behind them.

"I need to find a job soon; Lyla is getting sick of me crashing at her place and eating all of her food."

"Yikes! I have heard that before. And she's right," Evie laughed.

They both had a drink, and Evie got the scoop on Brian's plans for the future. She wanted to tell him that life never goes as planned, but instead she was encouraged by his youthful optimism and truly believed that Brian's life would go exactly as he planned. And she felt privileged that she would be around to watch it.

New Year's Eve rolled around and Evie was at Carol's for the evening. She had a small group of their friends over for dinner, games, and laughter. It was a nice evening, but ended early, just after midnight, and Evie decided to take a drive through town before heading to the hotel. She made her way to the Bar on East, for old time's sake. The crowd was thinning, as couples headed home to ring in the New Year with drunken passionate love making. The band was finishing up their set and the atmosphere was still alive with the cheer of the evening. Evie couldn't help but smile. This place always welcomed her; and she understood why Eddie spent so much time here. There was no judgment within the dark paneled walls and the wooden bar stools always felt like recliners after a busy shift at work.

As she was getting to the bottom of her first glass, a familiar face caught her off guard. He was drunk—stumbling drunk—and pulled up a chair right next to her. She wasn't sure what to do at first, but it didn't take her long to realize that she had never seen Dr. Ron this drunk before.

"Where have you been? I've been waiting for you for so long," Dr. Ron slurred.

Evie quietly giggled to herself. She finally had the upper hand. "I was here the whole time," she played along. He flashed that smile that still set her on fire from the inside out. She could feel the blush hit her cheeks and had to look away.

"Can we talk? Are you here with your husband?" Dr. Ron babbled.

"I am not married. What do you want to talk about?" Evie had no clue where this was going. Dr. Ron must have known that she and Eddie had been divorced for over 10 years now.

"Not here. It's private. Come outside to my car, so I can drive you home." Dr. Ron made several attempts to get up off his chair.

"I don't need you to bring me home tonight, but thank you for the offer." She was certain that someone would need to bring *him* home, though. She left a ten on the bar and stood up to face Dr. Ron. He grabbed her arm and pulled her close for support. There were several alarms ringing deafeningly loud inside her head. They stumbled into the cold crisp January air. She buttoned all the buttons on her long coat and steered the drunk doctor toward her car.

"Evie, let's talk. I have to tell you something. I have to tell you…" Dr. Ron was distracted by the open car door in front of him. He sat without hesitation. Evie shut the door and did her best to talk down the voices in her head. She was merely getting him home safely.

"Are you still living off Cherry Drive, Dr. Ron?"

"No. I am not married anymore. I had to move out. I am not married. I have to tell you something…"

"How about we start with your new address?" Dr. Ron obliged, and the GPS rattled off directions.

"Evie," he began, as his hand found hers, "I have to tell you that my heart is broken."

She didn't see that coming. How thoughtful of him to want to tell her the story of some other woman who broke his heart. Playing along would be more like holding her tongue.

"I couldn't stay with my wife. I didn't love her. I treated her like shit. She deserved a better man. I was bad. I was a cheat. I was an ass. I hurt her, I hurt you, I hurt my best friend, and now my heart is broken."

Evie was having a hard time following Dr. Ron but didn't care too much as she rolled up on his condo. The parking lot was quiet. She was grateful that there weren't any small-town gossiping eyes on them at the moment. She still had to get him into the house.

"Here we are, Dr. Ron."

"Come in. I need to tell you something. Something about your daughter."

"No thank you. It's late. You're drunk."

"I am heartbroken. I can't lose you again."

Evie had no clue what to say to this. She was stunned by his rambling, and confused, and pissed that he was so drunk. The alarms were back.

"Good night, Dr. Ron." She decided that he would need to be sober if he had anything real to say to her.

Dr. Ron sat in the passenger seat, holding Evie's hand. She turned to face him. His face had aged. She could see stress etched into the lines in his forehead. But the longer she looked, the deeper she fell into his coffee brown eyes. The space between them grew smaller and smaller. Evie didn't know what was about to happen, but her heart wanted it to, her body needed it to. He leaned in close. The smell of alcohol intoxicated her. It was smooth and familiar as she drank it in. He was so close, she closed her eyes, and in that second, she was 25 years old again and head over heels in love with the doctor who knew her every wicked desire, without her saying a word. His lips met hers, and a lightning bolt of lust electrocuted her senses. She was frozen in time. This was a moment that was happening in the past. She reached her hand up and gently ran it through his hair. She couldn't pull away. She didn't want to. Dr. Ron began to shift toward her in excitement, and as he leaned further his elbow hit her car horn. The harsh tone cut into her beautiful dream and sucked her back to reality.

"I…I…time to go, Dr. Ron." Evie was losing her upper hand.

Dr. Ron got out of the car, adjusted the excitement bulging uncomfortably from his jeans, and stumbled over to the driver's side. Evie let him open her door and she took his waiting hand. They linked arms for stability once again and walked together to his front door.

They didn't say a word to each other; clearly, they didn't need to. They left a trail of clothes through the condo on their way to the bedroom. Evie couldn't keep her lips off of his. The feeling was so familiar and so good. She let him lift her shirt over her head and felt completely vulnerable as he reached behind her to fumble with her bra strap. It didn't take him long. Even in his drunken state he knew his way around a bra. And he knew his way around her body. He touched her, confidently exploring every inch and taking in the full effect of its beauty.

Evie fell into the cloud like down comforter on his bed. In an instant he was at her navel, teasing her midsection with his tongue. Her body was dancing with expectant pleasure. She closed her eyes and let herself feel every touch. Dr. Ron left a trail of kisses radiating upward with his movement. As his hands caressed her in symphony with his tongue, her legs squirmed, and her breathing became erratic. His lips on her neck were soft and passionate, but when he reached her ears Dr. Ron drove her crazy with nibbles and the sound of his rough manly groan.

What she loved most about being with him all those years ago was the ability to drive him as crazy as he could drive her. He wanted her, but she wanted him, too. As he straddled her, Evie was in a dreamlike state. She was wet with pleasure as he pressed his mouth firmly on hers and his tongue fervently massaged hers. He was taking back what was his. This kiss was real, raw, and passionate. Evie was lost. She could do nothing but take in this mind-blowing specimen of a man, and willingly let his body sync with hers creating new levels of desire.

Evie was electrified with each move of his body. She was a woman in need. He turned on a sensation in her that she had given up on. Evie surrendered to the pleasure, lost in the unity, in awe of the connection. And just before she shut her eyes to give herself over to yet another flood of orgasm, Dr. Ron found her ear and whispered, "I love you."

She slowly opened one eye to assess her surroundings. Hoping the evening was a dream, she was bitterly disappointed to find herself in a strange room, alone, in a very comfortable bed. The place was quiet, and Dr. Ron was nowhere in sight. Evie sat up and exhaled. Still in disbelief, she started searching for her clothes. To her surprise they were neatly folded on top of the dresser with a note.

Got a ride to my car, had to head to work for an emergency. Should be home around noon, please stay. R

Evie

The clock looked hauntingly at her as it turned 11:26 a.m. Frantic, Evie threw on her clothes, used the bathroom, and bolted to her car. She found herself in the middle of yet another internal battle over turning the key in the ignition and putting the car in drive. Why would she stay? One night can't erase the pain that he caused. One night…one kiss. And without realizing it, Evie was sitting in her car grinning from ear to ear. That was one amazing night. With some hesitation she turned the car on and drove back to her hotel to pack and prepare for her flight back that evening.

She turned up the hot water in the shower and let her tears blend in with the droplets. It hurt to know that she let her guard down, but the pain was much sharper as she realized she had to put it back up and shut him out of her life. Evie had been trying to find that thing that made her happy, that made her feel her best, that made her want to stay. After that night with Dr. Ron, she realized that it was him. She felt alive when she was with him, she felt herself, and she really wanted to stay.

It was a few minutes before 10 p.m. when she arrived home to Florida. There were several messages from Carol.

"Evie, I got the most random visitor this afternoon… looking for you…call me back!"

"Well, how long does it take to get to Florida anyway?! Call me."

"Seriously? I am in my PJs. Call me."

Evie happily picked up the phone to chat with Carol as she unpacked her suitcase. "Hi! I've only been gone for an afternoon. You missed me that much?"

"Why hello, you naughty girl. Did you leave out some details about your New Year's Eve? I thought we were friends?" Carol opened with a joke.

Evie's mind was churning; she had no clue how Carol knew, or what Carol knew. This would be an interesting conversation. "What did you hear, and more importantly, from who? I will gladly fill in the details…honestly I could really use your help with this one." Evie was going to try the honesty approach, even if she had to be more honest than Carol expected or could even imagine.

"The Good Doctor stopped by this evening. He mentioned that you two met up at the bar last night, and that you left before he could get your contact information. He came to my door Evie! I thought he was the enemy?!" Carol was wound up.

"He is. I think. I mean, he did me dirty for sure. But…"

"But what?! This ought to be good! He ditched his own daughter!"

"But I would like to hear his side of the story one of these days. That's all." The honesty approach was hard.

"So, what happened when you saw him? Have you seen him before? Did you talk?"

"I saw him once, briefly, not quite four years ago. We did have a conversation, nothing important. And last night…he was drunk…I was caught off guard." Evie paused. Carol was silent on the other end, she was gonna get the truth. "And I drove him back to his place and let him have drunken, exciting, familiar, wonderful, passionate sex with me. Then I fell asleep in his fluffy bed with expensive sheets and woke up alone. I left and didn't leave him my number."

After a speechless few moments, Carol finally spoke up. "Well, shit."

"My thoughts exactly." Evie was relieved that her friend wasn't chewing her out. She probably deserved it but was still on a high from her escapades.

"So, what now? Are you interested in him? Can you forgive him?"

"It was only one night. I still need to tell him how much he hurt me. I don't know if I can forgive him…but the more

I think about it, the more I want to." It felt good to Evie, to say that out loud.

"I thought you would say that…so I gave him your number, and address," Carol said casually.

"What?!" Evie didn't know how to feel about that.

"Look, I saw what happened all those years ago. You two were in love. I can't defend his decision to walk away, but I think he deserves the chance to defend himself. You will need to decide if you are tired of blaming him for everything, even things that were not his fault. I think you should hear him out. That's the only way you can move forward, or move on, whichever."

Carol was a good friend. She kept Evie's secret from Eddie, and never rubbed Evie's bad decisions in her face.

"Okay. I do want to hear his side. Why would he turn his back on me, and his daughter?" The thought made Evie a little sad.

"Okay then. Good talk my friend. It is way past my bedtime. Keep me posted."

"Thank you, Carol. I love you."

"You too, Trouble."

In the following weeks, Evie ignored all of Dr. Ron's calls and messages. She was not ready to go back to that time, to face that truth. It was easier for her to run. She hadn't stopped running. Most times she had no clue what she was running from.

But her life caught up with her. On the morning of January 23rd, Evie turned on the shower and set the coffee pot to brew, per usual. She had one foot in the shower when the phone rang. Recoiling, she grabbed the phone, hoping it would be quick.

"Hello?"

"Evie, Gert here. She locked herself in her room and won't come out."

Confused, Evie had to really think about what Gert was trying to tell her. Then she figured it out. "Oh shit!" And as she was spinning from the realization that she might have destroyed Cassie's life, again, the doorbell rang. Naked, she sprinted to the bedroom to grab her robe. "Uh, hang on Gert."

She gave the peep hole a quick glance. And immediately recognized Dr. Ron standing on the other side of her door. "Oh shit!"

Dr. Ron

"Yes, Faruk, I am ready for tonight. I will get out early and we can pre-party at my place." Dr. Ron sat comfortably behind his desk, glancing out the window at the winter sky and bare trees below.

"Okay. No last-minute change of plans now. It isn't every day my big brother gets married."

"Are you trying to make light of the situation? I personally do not believe that an arranged marriage is the same as marriage at all, actually. And you know, God willing, this will not be my only wedding." The two brothers snickered at Dr. Ron's sentiment.

He was set to be married on November 17, 1984, less than one week away. His parents chose a woman of the same nationality from a well-respected family in India. At only 22 years old, she was a good option, a great person, and he was lucky. Still, Dr. Ron did not want to marry her. He was tired of following the beliefs of his family while his personal beliefs were rooted in American culture. He became a citizen when he was in his twenties in order to move to the U.S. permanently and complete his doctorate program. Despite his thick accent, he found small town New York to be a very accepting place. This was the country that he wanted to stay in. However, disappointing his parents and disgracing his family by giving up on his culture was not an option. And so he continued to practice their cultural beliefs.

When Dr. Ron was introduced to Casza in August, three short months before they were set to be wed, he hoped that he would instantly fall in love. He was a romantic at heart. He watched all the great American love stories, from *Gone with the Wind* to *Roman Holiday* and even *The Philadelphia Story*. He wanted to find that one person that gave him a spark. So, he looked for her. Dr. Ron was quite the charmer, and in his profession that charm had many recipients. It seemed like he could have his pick of his staff, the other hospital's staff, and patients if he really wanted. Dr. Ron played the game. He knew before he even got involved if she could be the one. He was on a quest to find something. His reputation reflected his love of the game, but he had very few enemies, or angry customers. He was a ladies' man but was respectful not to mislead anyone. At 30 years old, he was a good boss, and no one would argue that he was a great doctor. Plus, he treated his staff well as far as real tangible benefits like high pay and adequate time-off.

Dr. Ron realized that he would have to come to some sort of agreement with Casza if this marriage thing was going to work out. They had several long, awkward conversations and came up with an agreeable solution. Certainly agreeable to Dr. Ron, but he knew he was twisting his bride-to-be's arm. While he would follow the duties of a husband, he was not required to be faithful to Casza. He could have relations with other women under the condition that he use a condom, always, and got tested twice a year for sexually transmitted diseases.

Dr. Ron

At first, Dr. Ron, tried to fight the testing rule. He used the argument that he worked at the hospital and the employees may be suspicious of the frequent testing activity, but Casza was a smart woman, and stood her ground. He knew she was not willing to run the risk of catching something she couldn't release, nor did he want her to look like a fool. Per the traditional Indian culture, Casza was not permitted to have extra marital affairs, nor was she interested in that. She was looking to be a wife and a mother and make her family proud by starting roots in the U.S.

And so, Dr. Ron and Casza celebrated the traditional multi-day wedding celebration. Day three was the main ceremony held in a beautiful mosque in New York on an icy November afternoon. They were surrounded by over 200 friends and family who had traveled from near and far to witness the event. Dr. Ron's brother joked with him before the ceremony that he started a pool to see who could guess his divorce date the closest.

The newlyweds decided to follow the American tradition of taking a honeymoon. This was a welcome break for Dr. Ron. Work kept him busy, and he always enjoyed a warmer climate for a bit. Sometimes he caught himself laughing at the fact that he ended up in snowy, cold, upstate New York. The two ventured over to Greece. Neither had been for an extended visit, so they booked it for two weeks. They did their best to play along with the honeymoon notion by occasionally holding hands, having meals together, and by trying to spend more time together than apart. The time they did spend together was nice. Dr. Ron was pleasantly surprised by Casza's easy going personality, and found he enjoyed talking with her. He felt good that he would always be able to be honest with his partner, and that made the situation bearable. Dr. Ron tried to seduce his new bride, but Casza was not interested in anything more than heavy petting until those test results were in. He was intrigued by her self-control and thought for a second that they might actually be the perfect pair.

When the newlyweds returned home, it was easy for Dr. Ron to fall back into his pre-marital lifestyle. He went to work, hit the bar, and either left with someone, or went home to eat leftovers that Casza had cooked for dinner hours earlier. This routine was shifted, enhanced really, when Dr. Ron met Eddie.

"Casza, he is great! He is funny and honest, and very American."

"I do think it's adorable that you have a boyfriend!" Her laughter was contagious and they both laughed at her joke.

"Well, get used to this guy. I think I am in love." Dr. Ron gave it right back to her.

Dr. Ron never had a best friend besides his brother Faruk, who was back in India. He missed his brother terribly. The time-zones and their changing schedules made it difficult to even catch up by phone. They were always close growing up. With only two years between them, they experienced much of their lives from the same perspective. Dr. Ron always thought that they would have families near each other and grow old together. But he understood that Faruk preferred life in India. He visited as often as he could, but Dr. Ron had to accept the painful reality that his future in New York would not include his best friend. Eddie filled the void almost instantly. The two clicked. They had similar careers, were close in age, and both were married. The biggest difference was that Eddie was in love. Dr. Ron spared his friend the specifics of his own marriage situation, but he could tell from the way Eddie spoke about his wife that his love was real.

Dr. Ron listened to his friend, and his friend listened to him. They built up the bricks in the foundation of their friendship with laughter and alcohol at the bar. Most nights Dr. Ron would outlast his friend. And he was happy about that because he wanted Eddie to go home and be with his wife. He knew Casza didn't expect to see him after work, but always had a meal prepared in case she did. He really liked that about her, and probably should have told her more often. When Dr. Ron stumbled home from the bar, she was already fast asleep. The king size bed they shared was big enough to fit an ocean between them. And if Dr. Ron was drinking the hard stuff that night, he would hit the pillow and not even move a muscle until the alarm was buzzing the next morning. He regarded his marriage as functional.

In September of 1985, the Giants began their 61st season with a home game against the Philadelphia Eagles. Dr. Ron had plans to have dinner with Eddie, and from there they would head to the bar to watch. As he walked up the central stairway of the older home, Dr. Ron couldn't help but notice the charm in the heavy woodwork of the building. The front door had beautiful original stained-glass work framing the door, and there were intricately carved designs in corners of each dark wood door trim. Before he reached Eddie's door, he could smell the aroma of perfectly cooked meat.

"Hey friend! I brought a six pack, in case we wanted to start early!" Dr. Ron entered the front door and took in the cozy living room before him. The colors were muted and earthy.

"Welcome! Make yourself at home, unless you're a slob," Eddie joked.

"Nice place!" Dr. Ron had made his way to the kitchen and the table that was not quite in its own formal dining area.

"Thanks. We have just enough space. I'll give you a tour in a minute."

Dr. Ron cracked open a beer for himself and his friend, while watching Eddie flip and stir like a professional. "You look good in the kitchen!"

"I wore my best apron to impress you!"

"It worked!" Dr. Ron felt at ease in his friend's space.

Tangled Vines of Good Intentions

Before he had finished his first can, Eddie pulled two thick pork chops out of the oven and set them on the counter to rest.

"Quick tour, then we eat." Dr. Ron followed his friend, eager to return to the kitchen.

As they finished the guest room and started toward the kitchen, Dr. Ron stopped dead in his tracks as he heard the front door open.

"Ed! Smells good. Where are you?" Evie called.

"Buttercup, this is my friend Dr. Ron." Eddie made the introduction.

"Hello. Pleased to meet you," Evie said.

The woman before him was shorter and curvy. She looked like an angel with perfectly rounded features and piercing emerald green eyes. Dr. Ron was lost. In a robotic fashion he held out his hand. But she did not give him a shake, instead she squeaked past them and shut the bathroom door.

"What are you doing here, hun?" Eddie called through the door.

"Forgot a book that I need for class. I'm just picking it up and heading out."

Dr. Ron had moved back to the kitchen and took a seat at the dining room table. He was feeling something for sure, but he was not sure what. In an effort to keep his cool, he clutched his drink and kept his distance. He stared as Evie walked by him and into the bedroom. Moments later she returned with her book, kissed Eddie on the cheek, and was gone.

"Ready to eat?" Eddie asked.

Dr. Ron was not sure what to make of his first interaction with the green-eyed goddess. He knew he was attracted to her, but it wasn't like the other girls. It wasn't primal and animalistic—well, not totally. And it was not the spark that he had always believed love to be. This was more like a car crash of emotions, rendering him useless. He didn't even tell Casza, for fear that his thoughts wouldn't make any sense, and maybe a little afraid that they would. Dr. Ron wanted to be a loyal friend and knew Eddie's wife was dangerous territory.

In October, Dr. Ron decided to test his feelings once again in hopes that time had changed them, despite the fact that he thought about her constantly. He planned a couple's dinner at his house; it would be a first. Casza was instructed to Americanize the meal and be on her best behavior. Dr. Ron picked up three different beers plus a bottle of both red and white wine. He was uncharacteristically nervous. But when Casza questioned him on his behavior, he couldn't quite pinpoint why.

When the doorbell rang, he shot a reassuring glance at Casza and sent her to greet their guests. Eddie came in first and met Dr. Ron in the kitchen. They greeted each other with their usual smile and pat on the back. Casza and Evie entered in behind Eddie. In a moment of déjà vu, Dr. Ron froze, speechless, for just a second too long.

"Uh. Dr. Ron, you remember my wife, Evie?" Eddie filled the pause.

Dr. Ron studied her for a moment before reaching out his hand. He was captivated by the soft rosy glow of her cheeks, her bright beautiful smile, golden wheat locks, and those eyes. The attraction was so strong that he could barely get out a hello. Casza quietly slipped in behind him and gave him a gentle pinch on his side before offering her guests a cold drink. Dr. Ron was saved by Casza rolling through the awkward moment and getting the dinner moving in the right direction by offering them a tour of their home.

He took a moment to gain his composure. Never had he been this off his game. His mental pep talk was stern, this was a big game, with a lot at stake, no time for sloppy plays and rookie mistakes. He could hear Casza rambling on about the furnishings and decorations in the house. To him, she sounded like an actress.

Tangled Vines of Good Intentions

They had a grand foyer with a staircase that flowed down from the second floor. The walls and floors were white, so as not to distract from the lavish, colorful, artwork that Dr. Ron hung proudly from room to room. He had an eye for the extravagant that was perilously close to gaudy. There were several bedrooms, all white except the master. The bathrooms were gold. Gold wallpaper, towels, mirror, handles, gold from top to bottom. From the bottom of the stairs Dr. Ron could hear Casza and the guests laughing over his bathroom choices.

Dr. Ron had a spread of cheese and crackers waiting when they all arrived back in the living room. He was sitting on the oversized white leather couch. It was coupled with some wing chairs done in a colorful paisley pattern. The room centered around a grand fireplace that had figurines on the mantle and two large gold cylindrical decorations that had been a wedding present from Casza's family, displayed on either side. As Evie and Eddie sat, Casza excused herself to the kitchen, and requested her husband's help, which he thought odd. Dr. Ron was happy to oblige, knowing full well that she didn't actual need his help with anything.

"Might I suggest you try to keep your composure in front of her husband, and your wife?" Casza was direct.

Not wanting to fully admit that he was more than curious about Evie, Dr. Ron simply nodded his head and left the room. There was nothing further to discuss. When he returned to his guests, he promptly asked Eddie to follow him to the garage to take a look at his new Porsche. Evie was left alone on the sprawling L-shaped couch.

It was clear that the guys were enjoying their evening together. There was little group conversation during the meal. Dr. Ron focused all of his efforts on Eddie, which was easy and made him feel more relaxed. By essentially ignoring the women, Dr. Ron could successfully avoid another awkward moment. They stuffed themselves with perfectly cooked steak, lobster tails, and baked potatoes, barely leaving room for the homemade chocolate mayonnaise cake that Casza baked. Dr. Ron made a special desert request after hearing all about Eddie's mother the star baker, and her infamous cake. By the end of dessert Evie was practically begging Eddie to say goodnight. Dr. Ron wanted to apologize, offer a do-over, make up for the missed conversation with Evie, but he simply offered Eddie a quick farewell and sent them both off with a wave.

Disappointed with the evening, Dr. Ron joined Casza in the kitchen as she started the dishes.

"Would you like to talk about it?" Casza offered.

"I'm not ready yet. Thank you for dinner," Dr. Ron replied, and they continued silently with the cleaning.

Eddie and Dr. Ron never had much to say to each other about that dinner and continued their friendship with fewer group activities. But Dr. Ron still couldn't shake the feeling Evie gave him, it was unlike any sensation he had ever had. He knew it was in his best interest to focus his energy on finding that somewhere else. The act of cheating is a selfish move, but given the fact that Dr. Ron had never thought of Casza as his wife, he carried little guilt. He loved being wanted, and he wanted the love. And although office romance was not his forte, even he couldn't resist the occasional intern. But all the attention he thought he wanted, quickly turned to the desire to be noticed by just one person. As much as Dr. Ron tried to steer clear of Evie, he would often get lost in the memory of the smell of her perfume, or the sound of her voice, or the spark he felt. He couldn't help but be drawn to her. This was so different; he wanted what he couldn't have.

As the weeks went by, Dr. Ron was better able to handle his feelings. He could hang with Eddie at the bar without asking non-stop questions about his wife, and he resisted the urge to suggest they watch football at Eddie's place. Dr. Ron thought he was ready to follow the rules of friendship, until the day he was tested.

Dr. Ron pulled up his favorite bar stool and started his routine banter with the barkeep. It was a seasonable day in December, and he expected to be alone watching the game that evening. He started with the heavy stuff and moved to beer after downing the last few sips of his scotch. As he glanced toward the front of the bar, he caught a familiar flash of wavy blonde hair. It was up in a ponytail, accentuating the shape of her face. He knew that she saw him. He knew that she was walking toward him. He hoped he could keep his cool this time.

And he did. He bought her a drink and had polite conversation about her day. And as the alcohol flowed through him, he asked her some real questions about herself. He was captivated by her thoughts and lured in by the melodic quality of her voice. Engrossed in conversation, they lost track of time.

"Would it be wrong if I told you how much I am enjoying our conversation?"

"Wrong? Did we do something wrong?" If Evie wasn't going to draw the line, then Dr. Ron assumed he couldn't cross it.

"And if I told you that you are stunningly beautiful?"

"Then I would say, thank you very much."

"Eddie is a very lucky man." Dr. Ron flashed her a smile.

"Yes, he is."

"And you are a lucky woman." He watched her reaction.

"Some days are luckier than others. I don't find doing his laundry very lucky or cleaning the bathroom. But I am very lucky that I don't have to cook; then again, so is he." Dr. Ron adored the way her nose scrunched a little when she laughed.

"How is your marriage, friend?" She kept Dr. Ron on his toes.

"It's dull, honestly. I am searching for something deeper."

"You are married, and still looking?"

Not sure if he was about to offend her, Dr. Ron thought carefully about his next move. "It was an arranged marriage. I always wanted my forever to be with a person who I really enjoyed, someone more like you." The blush on her face made his pants shift with excitement.

"You are trouble. Of that I am sure. Thank you for a lovely evening, but I should really get going." Evie turned to hop off the stool. In a bold move, Dr. Ron placed his hand on her wrist and asked her to stay.

"Just a few more minutes? We have talked about your interests, and your upbringing, I can't help but feel like we have more to say."

"I hope we do. One last drink, and then I have to go," Evie responded.

Dr. Ron knew that he had an opening. He knew there was a weakness in her, but could he betray his best friend? That was a question he did not have to answer in that moment. He walked Evie safely back to her car and hugged her goodbye. He would refrain, for as long as he could.

By March of 1986, Dr. Ron couldn't wait until his next encounter with Evie. The "what if" consumed him. She was the girl he pictured when he closed his eyes and the girl he wanted when he opened them. On a full gut of liquid courage, he decided that he needed to make his move and call her.

Dr. Ron gave his friend a pat on the back and shut the door. He knew that how long it would take Eddie to get home, so he picked up the phone and started the clock.

He was quickly lulled by the softness of Evie's voice, but tried to keep focused on his purpose. He needed to see if she had the same feelings, or even a tiny fraction of the feelings that he did. He didn't make a habit of chasing married women, but he couldn't fight this any longer. He opened with flattery, and when that was well received, he moved on to harmless flirting. Terrified of her rejection, Dr. Ron couldn't summon the courage to tell her that he wanted to see her, that she was constantly on his mind, or that he longed to caress her. Still he knew that this call had opened Pandora's Box.

Tangled Vines of Good Intentions

That evening they talked nonstop for every second of their 15-minute conversation. The conversation was easy, but his heart was pounding. She laughed at his jokes and asked questions that made him feel like she cared. It was different than his talks with Casza. This was less like a best friend and more like a soul mate. He swore he could hear her smile through the phone. And by the time he hung up he was certain that this woman was unlike any other that he had crossed paths with, and his feelings were not going away. He found Casza in the kitchen and began to tell her everything about his conversation with Evie.

Dr. Ron called her as often as he could. They laughed and talked about everything from family to travel to current events. It was like he was a young boy again, totally caught up in the excitement of it all. He hung on her every word. She made life roll by with ease and excitement. And then she showed up. It was an early afternoon in March. She walked right into his office, shut the door, and locked it. Dr. Ron saw the look of determination on her face, that coy smile, the fuck me eyes. This was a face he had seen, a command he had followed, but it all seemed wrong on this angel.

"Evie. Where's Eddie?" Perhaps talking about her husband wasn't the best start, but Dr. Ron was grasping at straws. The sexual tension was filling the room and he could feel the sweat forming on his brow.

"You and I both know that he is driving home, to change, and head to the bar to meet you."

"What are we doing?" Dr. Ron was pleading to himself to keep his dream a dream.

"I don't know. But I can't ignore it anymore. You understand me more than anyone, and I trust you more than I trust myself." Evie had walked around the desk and Dr. Ron was fixated on her teasing hips.

"Then trust me when I say not here, not now." Dr. Ron was doing his best to keep his distance.

"I just need to know if I am…missing out on something."

"I can't let you make a rash decision, I won't. Not here. Not now." He was firm in his words.

Evie leaned forward, grabbed his hand in hers and placed it on her chest. "Can you feel my heart racing? I like that feeling, I love that feeling. That is the only way I know I am still alive. I have never felt that feeling before you." She leaned in and gently bit Dr. Ron's lower lip. His rod stood at full attention. And then she backed off and left the office.

Game on. Dr. Ron was fully aware that he was playing with fire. Maybe he had met his perfect match? He was caught in a wicked game that he knew he would lose, but he couldn't help but play. With the invitation on the table Dr. Ron was quick to confirm his attendance. What started as a fun and flirty affair rolled into so much more. He met her on her way to work, and she met him on his way to the bar. They had lunch in the park, and sex in deserted parking lots. When he was with her, she was the only woman on the planet. She was everything he had searched for; that person that movies were written about. This was not like anything that either had ever felt. It was stronger, more passionate, and achingly real. The months of the calendar ticked on. 1986 came and went and 1987 did the same. But he was happy. These years were not like any others in his life. He was excited to wake up each day and recharged with every phone call, rendezvous, and stolen kiss. The reality of the situation was not in his head. He vowed to keep this from his friend. He knew it would destroy him, and it would destroy their friendship. For the moment, Dr. Ron could have his cake and eat it too, knowing full well that when the time came to choose between Eddie and Evie, it would be her.

It was early on a cold January morning in 1988, and Dr. Ron had just stepped into his office, briefcase in hand, as the phone rang.

"Hello, Dr. Ron here, how can I help you?" But all he heard on the other end of the line was sobbing. He instantly knew it was his angel on the other end, and his heart broke. "Where are you? I am coming."

Dr. Ron met Evie in a public parking garage not far from the hospital. They climbed into her back seat so he could hold her close. The sobbing stained her checks. Her eyes were beginning to puff. Dr. Ron had no clue how to help her. He had never experienced this depth of empathy, and the fierce need to stop her pain. He was at a loss.

"Shhhh. Talk to me. What's the matter, lovely?"

After several minutes, Evie's river of tears narrowed to a trickle. She took a few deep breaths and steadied her breathing. "I'm pregnant."

Terror started coursing through Dr. Ron's veins. He had to ask a question that would destroy him no matter what the answer. "With Eddie's baby?"

"Yes." Evie managed the word as fresh tears sprung to her eyes.

After what seemed like an eternity of silence between them, Dr. Ron knew what needed to be done. "Ok. We end this. You and Eddie need to focus on your marriage and your family. We end this now." He tried to sound confident, but distance was the last thing he wanted. He felt like they had only just begun; they had just found each other.

"I can't do this! Please, no! I can't be a mother," Evie whaled, and buried her head in his chest.

"You will be a great mother. You are caring and smart, and stunningly beautiful." Dr. Ron was comfortable in her grip. "And you two will make beautiful babies."

"No. No. I don't want babies!" Evie was winding up all over again.

"Look Evie, you two created a baby. That is something that you can't hide from. But this is out of my hands. You need to try to make it work and be a family for your child.

I am backing off, because I have to. We both have to do the right thing now." With that, Dr. Ron left the stunned woman to sob alone in the backseat of her car. Before he could shut the door, he heard those magic words. They went straight to his heart and as naturally as breathing he repeated them softly back to her before closing the door and getting back in his car. He pulled out of the lot and couldn't look back. This was painful. This was heartbreaking. A tear ran down his face as he drove away. He could only distract himself with work for a few hours before hitting the bar early, and hard.

And when he finally stumbled home, all he could do was cry. He was not sure what to do. How to let go of the greatest love he had ever experienced and watch on the sidelines as she made a home and raised children with another man. He wanted what he couldn't have. But he did have her, for over a year. That would have to be enough.

A distraction was in order, and oddly enough this one sought him out when he needed it the most. She was beautiful. Ms. Maker had thick dark curls that flowed down her back. He could wrap it twice around his palm. Her eyes were a dark rich mahogany. They were telling, and commanding. She let her pleasure spread across her face and curl her plump pink lips to a pucker. Her skin was youthful, and the tone reminded him of a hot cup of coffee with cream. Her scent was intoxicating and enough to briefly numb the pain. She was sharp and knew how to go after what she wanted. And she wanted Dr. Ron. She was in a four-year program on a lower floor of the hospital. The first time Dr. Ron met Ms. Maker, he knew exactly what she wanted, or so he thought.

She would page him to her floor, only to pull him into a closet and start touching him. In seconds his belt was unbuckled, and she'd dropped to her knees to pleasure him. The first few times that was all it was. He was a broken man, in no mood to have emotionless sex.

Tangled Vines of Good Intentions

He missed Evie. The drinking only made him hear her, made him see her in every blurry face he encountered. When he made time to talk to Casza, it felt empty. He felt empty. As the weeks ticked on, he found it almost unbearable to continue casual conversation with his best friend. Eddie went on about Evie's mood swings, and how he wasn't sure what she was feeling. Dr. Ron couldn't tell him that he knew how she was feeling, or that he was feeling it too. It was all too painful.

It was six weeks after the pregnancy bomb when Dr. Ron broke down and called Evie. "How have you been?"

"I am miserable," Evie replied.

Despite her words, the sound of her voice made him grin from ear-to-ear. Each word electrified his senses. "Is there anything I can do to help you? Would you like me to set you up with an OBGYN or a birthing class?" Dr. Ron would try the friend approach.

"There are lots of things that I would like for you to do, but those two are not on the list," Evie said with a teasing giggle. And they both broke into laughter. The chemistry was still there.

"I think we should just talk for now. You will have to dream about me to get exactly what you want," Dr. Ron offered.

"Done." Evie was quick to respond.

Everything was right in his world once again. All that was lost was now found. She was back, not like before, but back, enough. Afternoon talks became a routine again and were often followed up with quickies with Ms. Maker.

Dr. Ron and Ms. Maker tried nearly ten different supply closets before finding a secluded one with no traffic. She was the physicality that Dr. Ron needed to let out the frustration of not having Evie. She liked it rough, and he was happy to oblige. She was kinky; encouraged hair pulling, and biting.

Dr. Ron

Dr. Ron knew that Evie would never act so desperate. He could feel the difference between being with Ms. Maker and the warm happy place that was Evie.

Ms. Maker found her way to Dr. Ron's office one afternoon, where she waited for him. He walked into Ms. Maker sitting comfortably in his chair and twirling her satin black push up bra in her hands. He was surprised at how brazen she had become in a few short months. They had been having meaningless hook ups for three months now, and Dr. Ron was sure that was all it was, but not clear that Ms. Maker knew that.

"Uh. Hello…not here."

"But why? Right now, baby. Give it to me, I need it!" Ms. Maker whispered seductively as she beckoned him closer.

With some hesitation Dr. Ron obliged. "Bend over." Dr. Ron finished the act, not caring if the release was mutual. As he was pulling his pants back up, he heard a knock at his office door. "Yes? Just a minute," he stuttered, as a heat rushed over him. "Sit and keep quiet!" he instructed Ms. Maker, who looked a bit disheveled.

Dr. Ron slowly opened the door, and instantly regretted it. Evie walked in with a full belly. She looked at his guest, then looked at him.

"Hello, Mrs. Dodd. You are looking well. This is Ms. Maker; she was just leaving." Dr. Ron had no clue what Evie was doing there but was sure she didn't want to include Ms. Maker.

"She's pretty," Evie commented when Ms. Maker was out of earshot.

"She's nothing," Dr. Ron pleaded.

"I understand. Old habits die hard." Evie was throwing daggers. "Look, I came on a friendly basis. Eddie's birthday is coming up, and I was hoping you would help me with a few of the details."

"Party planning? You came to me for party planning?"

Evie exhaled. "And I wanted to see you. Just to talk."

"Well, I would be happy to help, and probably make Casza do whatever I end up agreeing to." They both laughed casually. Dr. Ron put his hand on her shoulder and instantly felt the burn of passion that still existed between them. "I am glad you came. I miss you too. Can we have a party planning lunch?"

"I would like that," Evie agreed.

Dr. Ron loved the deep connection he shared with her. He was genuinely interested in how she was feeling and how her day was going. He could listen to Evie for hours talk about anything from her heartburn to the latest case that came through her clinic. And he could feel that she reciprocated his interest. She cared. The thing they built was mutual. It was everything Dr. Ron could have imagined, and more. She was still so far away, but it would be easier to let her go, if he could still have lunch with her from time to time. The baby was due in four months. Dr. Ron would roll with the punches and do his best to keep his best friend's wife happy at home. Eddie did have her first.

Ms. Maker quietly shut the door to their favorite spot. She looked at him with fire in her eyes and had her clothes off in an instant. As his hands felt the heat of her skin, he closed his eyes and couldn't help but picture his love. He imagined her curves, more dangerous and womanly than Ms. Maker. He imagined the pitch of her moan, more feminine and melodic than Ms. Maker. And he could almost smell the sweetness of her body, much more pure than the flesh before him. Dr. Ron was tiring of this game. He was tired of this woman.

When Dr. Ron got the news of the birth of Evie's baby, the gravity of the situation hit him hard. In all the pictures of his future he never imagined himself as a home wrecker. The thought of betraying his best friend like that kept him up at night. And the reality that he would have to quit Evie kept him in dark closets with Ms. Maker.

Dr. Ron

And then one day he snapped. Consumed with his lack of moral fiber, he decided to take a vacation. He gave Casza a two-day notice that he would be gone, and after an hour of her expressing her anger with shouting, the decision was final. He thought long and hard about going to India but decided against it. There was no way that he could show his face to his family and not be honest with them. Honesty was not an option. If they knew that he was having an affair with a married woman, who was now a mother, he would be a disgrace.

Niagara Falls offered a peaceful place to think about the world; how big it is, how quickly things change, and what should be on the priority list. Dr. Ron spent hours lying in the green Canadian grass and listening to the sound of the falls as a slight breeze carried the mist through the air. Serene. There were moments that were quiet, and soothing followed by hours of drinking and women. The falls were thick with tourists from all walks of life at that time of year. Dr. Ron struck up conversations with strangers about nothing in particular at all. Despite the lazy days and blurry evenings, he could still feel the twist of guilt and agony of his current situation weighing heavily on his conscience. And in a moment of desperation, Dr. Ron turned to his faith. He went to a mosque and he prayed on it. He prayed three times a day for two weeks straight. Dr. Ron believed that the strength and clarity that he was searching for could only be found with help from the Almighty.

Dr. Ron had been gone for a month when the phone rang.

The operator's voice was clear, "Do you accept a collect call from New York, caller's name is Eve?"

His mind went blank. And the operator repeated the question, "Collect call from Eve?"

"Uh, yes. I accept the charge." He waited.

"I miss you. I am exhausted. I have no clue how to be a mom. And I miss you." Evie's voice crackled with stress and exhaustion. It brought a smile to his face.

"Spoken like a first-time parent with a newborn at home. I would be concerned if you felt any other way!" He tried to lighten the mood, but Evie broke into sobs. "Oh, please don't cry, Green Eyes. I promise what you are feeling is normal."

"I have never felt normal, ever in my life. Most times I feel like I am a pinball being shot randomly in every direction to just bounce off the wall and see who is going to hit me next! Like I am bouncing around trying to make everyone else feel good. And now I have this baby. Now I have another person that I will disappoint and let down," she sobbed.

"Hey, come on. Where is your baby now?" Dr. Ron had his work cut out for him.

"He just fell asleep."

"Well that's great. You should really be sleeping now, too. But go to him. Look at him. Then tell me what you feel." He waited as he heard Evie quietly move to the next room. Her breathing steadied.

"I look at him and my heart feels like it could explode with love. He is perfect and he has so much life ahead of him. When I look at him, I feel hopeful. Like maybe I will figure things out before he notices that I don't have my shit together." He felt relief as he heard her let out a soft giggle.

"Why did you leave?" Evie asked innocently.

"Needed to clear my head."

"Because of me? Because of us?"

"Yes. I don't think there should be an 'us'." His words stung his own ears. "I think you should focus on your marriage. It would kill me to know that I broke up such a beautiful young family."

"I was afraid you would feel that way. Getting pregnant was such a shock. The moment I found out I knew in my heart that I had to let you go. But can we still be friends?"

"Evie, hasn't that made things even more difficult?" Dr. Ron rubbed his head to ease the tension.

"I am not ready to let you go. You make me happy. I need to hang on to some happy right now. Besides, you can't just move out of the country."

He could very much understand where she was coming from. "I may never stop loving you…friend."

"I hope you don't," she added, before hanging up.

His 5-weeks away made him realize that this was a problem that he could not run from. Armed with his faith he would try to do better. He took one last look at the waterfall that was his front yard, and knew it was time to go back to his small town and acclimate with his life once again. He felt clear, and strong, for the moment.

Dr. Ron returned home to a very unhappy wife. Casza apparently didn't have as much fun as he thought she would without him.

"I would like to try something different for a while. I would like you to come home and eat with me at least four nights a week. I also want to visit my family, together." Casza was never shy about how she felt.

"Why? Where is this all coming from?" Dr. Ron wanted to do better, but this was not what he expected.

"I want to start living my life, too. You have work, and friends, and women. I have me. And legally, I have you."

"You have this great big house, and you can make all the friends you want!" Dr. Ron felt like this was a well-planned attack.

"You have all these other women, but the one you want is the one you can't have. I think you should try to be satisfied with the person right in front of your face. It's not like you have a ton of options. Unless you plan to divorce me to run off with Evie and your best friend's baby!"

"Casza, be reasonable. The heart wants what the heart wants. No, I am not planning to run off with Evie. No, I will not be here with you every night. Yes, I will do my best to be here more often. That is what I can offer you. And I can apologize that you were forced to marry me." Dr. Ron grabbed his coat and headed out to hit the bar.

He would always be perplexed by the complex nature of womankind. Still, he never quit. He looked at his half-empty third round and wondered how to fix the mess that he created. Perhaps moving away was the right thing to do? Perhaps letting go of Evie was the only thing to do.

Days turned to months and months turned to years. Dr. Ron felt like a shell of a person. Each day he got up, hit the gym, got a coffee and went to work, followed by the bar most evenings, and the occasional dinner with Casza. Life had become stagnant. He was yet another hamster on the wheel. Eddie was meeting him at the bar far less, which was to be expected, and Dr. Ron could only hope that it was because he was enjoying being a family man. He was an honorary uncle to their child. He was there to help his friend when he needed home repairs, or for the occasional family dinner. He and Evie retired their physical relationship in favor of their solid friendship. The sexual tension was apparent whenever they saw each other, so they tried to keep visits short. The only highlight to his days were calls from Evie. They spoke several times a week. They laughed at things the baby did, they laughed at crazy patient stories, they spoke seriously about what they wished life was like. They talked a lot about their feelings, but very little about their relationships. Evie hardly ever mentioned Eddie, and Dr. Ron avoided talking about other woman at all costs. If he couldn't wrap his head around what was going on with Ms. Maker, or why, then he couldn't expect Evie to understand. And even though they didn't talk about it, it was clear that they were both missing something, and still needed each other.

Ms. Maker became another part of the monotony, except for the fact that she was anything but predictable. Dr. Ron never knew when she might want him. She called; she came to his office; she even sent an intern to look for him once. Dr. Ron was at her beck and call, but he couldn't pinpoint why. She was constantly ten steps ahead of him, and he wasn't about to get on her bad side by ending things. Every time she summoned him, he couldn't help but feel like she was after something, but what? She couldn't blackmail him; his wife knew all about her. And that poignant detail eased his mind. He would have to accept the meaningless sex for what it was. He couldn't have Evie the way he wanted, and he didn't want Casza. Ms. Maker offered a release, but she was still no more than another rotation on the wheel.

And before he knew it, it was time for her to go. It was mid-January 1991, and her four years had come and gone in the blink of an eye. Ms. Maker sat before him in the oversized leather chair in his office, clothes on, with big tears streaming down her checks.

"I don't understand. I was a great intern. Why would they not offer me a job? Can't you talk to them? Can't you do anything?"

"I am very sorry. All candidates are looked at very carefully. Not sure I would have much influence on the decision. We don't have any first-hand experience working together." Dr. Ron desperately wanted this conversation to be over.

"But they respect your opinion. All those times I called you, tell them you were consulting. You have to do something!" She flailed her arms in desperation, as Dr. Ron kept his distance. Sensing her tone shift and her irritation start to flare, he knew he had to set this straight. "Look, no one has enjoyed your time here more than me. Still, I am not willing to lie to get you the job. I think it would be best if you explore other options and then apply again in the future when you have other experience under your belt."

"If you let me go, I promise you will regret it." And with that she got up and stormed out of his office.

Tangled Vines of Good Intentions

Dr. Ron followed her to the nurse's desk, watched her storm down the hall, and tap her foot until the elevator came.

"Everything ok boss?" Eddie asked.

"Nothing I can't handle. Thanks buddy." Dr. Ron decided to leave early and drink away the afternoon. Threats were not something he was used to. It was clear now that she was using him to secure a job at the hospital, which was a first. They typically hired 70 percent of their interns; she didn't make the cut. Of course, it was well within his ability to reach out to the hiring board and inquire about her internship, but that was not a path he wanted to go down.

As he sat on the hard-wooden bar stool and tried to offset his drinks with stale peanuts, his head pounded with the events of the day. Could she make good on her threat? Once his brain was completely diluted by the alcohol, he laughed out loud. He was impressed by her brazen words but not scared of Ms. Intern at all. She used him as her toy for the past four years, and that was her bonus. Time for her to walk away quietly.

On her last day, a freezing March 18th, she did go quietly. She did not call him or visit his office. He did not attend her goodbye party. It seemed like a case closed. But that was not this case.

May showers were in full force and Dr. Ron was adjusting well to his new normal. He spent more time with Casza in the evenings. He started to prefer her dinners straight from the oven versus his usual reheated delights. She was a good cook—a great cook—and he told her as often as he could. He was having more sex with Casza, which he truly hoped would make her happy, even though it did not have that effect on him. She never seemed to smile anymore, or maybe it had been going on for a while and he was just now noticing. Dr. Ron wanted to put in a little effort. He was tired of disappointing her.

A new group of interns wandered the halls at work, looking younger and more vibrant than the last; but he was not interested. His afternoon calls with Evie were happening less frequently, which made him cherish every second when she did call. His friendship with Eddie was also fading. Eddie was spending so much of his free time with his son, and Dr. Ron understood. They rarely met at the bar, and work conversations were mostly about sports. Dr. Ron wanted to tell him so much but couldn't. He missed cutting loose with his friend, but given everything, he was happy that they were still on good terms.

This new stable adult thing was significantly less fun than his previous lifestyle, but his heart was committed. He knew that he found all that would make his cup full in this world. He didn't want to keep looking, didn't want pointless trysts—he wanted Evie. And knowing that he was the one who set the boundaries, he had no choice but to find a way to make the best of what he had done.

It was a Wednesday morning, Dr. Ron was working on charts in his office, the door was closed, and his radio was set on low to sports talk radio when his phone rang. He was hoping it was Evie.

"Hello lover, do you miss me?" A woman's voice rang in his ears.

"Hello? Who is this? I think you have the wrong number." Dr. Ron was thrown off at first.

"Meet me in our secret place in ten minutes." The line went dead, but that was all he needed.

He let out several expletives before checking the clock. After running several scenarios through his head, he decided the worst case was that she had a gun, and good aim. This seemed like an acceptable fate. At some point his indiscretions would catch up with him. Plus, he was in a hospital, no better place to get shot. He accepted his fate and called Casza.

"Hey, I only have a minute, if anything happens to me today, I just want you to know that I am sorry that I couldn't love you the way you deserved."

"What? What is going on? Are you ok?" Casza sounded panicked.

"Everything is fine. It's been a strange day, that's all. And I wanted to tell you that." And with that he hung up and headed to the secret spot to meet Ms. Maker.

He knocked softly on the door, and there was a knock from the other side in return. Dr. Ron took a deep breath and opened slowly. He barely had time to assess the scene when Ms. Maker sprung into his arms and planted a deep kiss on his lips. She was half dressed. Her black leather mini skirt was tight around her hips and ass. Her baggy loose knit sweater displayed a bare shoulder that smelled of sweet perfume, and Dr. Ron could see her lacey red bra through her sweater. He tried to push her away, put a little space between them, but she was a woman on a mission. As she dropped to her knees, Dr. Ron forgot what he was supposed to be protesting. He let his anxiety be sucked away and focused on not exploding in her mouth. It was clear that she wanted more. She stood and shoved her tongue into his mouth. Dr. Ron never had the guts to tell her that was a turnoff. But as his hands explored the familiar curves, he felt an unexpected jolt of excitement. As they kissed, his hands made their way to her skirt. Once unzipped he squeezed her panty-less ass playfully. He moved his mouth away from hers and nibbled on her shoulder before removing her shirt. He licked and sucked and soon heard her moan with pleasure. Before he knew it, she had deftly put a condom on him. This was moving faster than he remembered. In a new move, she walked him around the corner and hopped up on a table, spreading her legs to receive him. Dr. Ron obliged. He shuddered as his nerves came alive and the two fell into a fast-paced rhythm. Now that she was facing him it was more difficult to picture Evie. He closed his eyes and let her kiss his neck, but Dr. Ron wasn't enjoying the position. It was too personal.

"Bend over," he whispered.

Dr. Ron

Ms. Maker's eyes flew open giving him a cold stare. "Let's just finish. We can go back to the usual next time."

Dr. Ron did his best not to think about next time. He shut his eyes again and pictured Evie, the last time they made love. The way she bites her lip, the way her eyes smolder with longing. Caught up in the beauty of his thoughts he let himself explode with desire. He stood, inside Ms. Maker, catching his breath. But as he rested, Ms. Maker wiggled out from inside him, and slowly peeled his condom off. She wrapped it in a paper towel and went on the hunt for her clothing.

"Uh…do you want me to take that to the men's room?"

"I got it! You don't have to worry." Ms. Maker flashed him a smile and slipped out the door.

With his pants around his ankles he couldn't help but feel totally confused. Where did she even come from, and where was she going? He felt violated and weak. This was a low point.

Dr. Ron skipped the bar and went home that night. Casza had called his office four times and left him three messages, to which he didn't respond. When he walked in, she was on the phone, and looked startled to see him. He went upstairs to shower and change without exchanging a word.

He turned the heat up as he let the scorching spray envelop him. If only the shower could wash away the actions and not just the evidence. He leaned his head against the tile shower and let the heat hit his back muscles. He tried to quiet his head. He tried to not feel used, he wanted to believe that he never made a woman feel this way, but that was a futile effort.

As he put on his clothes and went downstairs, he could smell the beginnings of a delicious meal. He met Casza in the kitchen and complimented her work.

"What the hell did you call me for today?! You made it sound like there was a bomb in the building, like you were in grave danger. Then you disappeared! I know you are not in love with me, but I deserve a little human decency! I would still care if you were hurt." She stopped to calm herself.

Tangled Vines of Good Intentions

Dr. Ron was in no mood to argue with a usually even-keeled Casza. He did see her point and decided to proceed with caution. "There is this woman..." Dr. Ron started, only to be interrupted.

"I swear, it is always about a woman with you! Why don't you give it up! How do you keep track of them all?!" Casza was clearly unhappy, and practically shouting as she expressed herself with wild jerky hand gestures. Perhaps the honesty was getting to be too much for her?

"Listen. This is an old girl, Ms. Maker. There are no new girls. I swear. Haven't found anyone who excites me." Dr. Ron sighed at the realization that he did have one girl that excited him. "She threatened me when her internship was ending, because she didn't get offered a job, and she wanted me to pull some strings. I didn't. She left. It has been a few months, and she just showed up today. I wasn't sure what to expect. Wasn't sure how crazy she was, still not sure."

"Oh. This is that girl. Why didn't you help her get a job?" Dr. Ron could sense that Casza was noticeably relieved that it wasn't someone new.

"This might be hard to understand, but she was a little controlling. I wasn't having any fun."

Casza laughed out loud. She poured them both a glass of wine and regained her composure. "Sorry. Go on."

"Well, I would like for her to just go away. She was on a mission this afternoon and I didn't even get a chance to ask her where she was working. She mentioned that she might be back, and I didn't even have the courage to tell her not to."

Dr. Ron was grateful when Casza put an empathetic hand on his shoulder as she moved toward the oven to check dinner.

"She makes me feel really shitty about myself. Shitty for all the woman I have treated like crap. Shitty for what I did to Eddie. Shitty for falling in love with Evie. Shitty for marrying you."

"Look, you need to stop lumping me into your pity party. I get that you never had any intention of being a husband to me. I admit, I was hoping the relationship would be different than this, I was hoping you would try. But every time you apologize to me it makes me feel like you have done something awful to me. It wasn't you. Arranged marriage is how we honor our culture. Let it go. I will take responsibility for my own happiness."

"Perhaps that is a lesson that I need." He finished his wine and went for round two, before getting out the dishes to set the table.

"You have made mistakes. We all make mistakes. But what are you going to do about them? How are you going to be better going forward?"

"Have you been reading some self-help books or something? How did you get so introspective and wise, Casza? Plus, you can cook, I am a lucky man." They both broke into laughter and continued their conversation over dinner.

Dr. Ron took Casza's words to heart. He really needed to start taking responsibility for his own happiness. He knew that the easy fix would be to have Evie in his life, but that didn't seem right. So, he set his sights on Casza. Her birthday was rapidly approaching, and this time he would show her the appreciation that she deserved.

On her birthday in June, Dr. Ron took the afternoon off to cook her dinner, complete with dessert. He sent her off shopping and to the nail salon so she wouldn't try to micro-manage the potential mess that he planned to create. He struggled a bit with the homemade strawberry buttercream icing but managed to make her cake look halfway presentable with some edible pearls and fresh strawberries. She returned home moderately happy, and genuinely surprised that he hadn't burned the house down.

The two listened to some Indian instrumental music over a nice dinner of pasta and meatballs. Perhaps not her all-time favorite, but the only meal she would eat if he was doing the cooking. He was careful to pull out the fancy blue china to contrast the everyday white linens on the dining table. He arranged a bouquet of white roses at the far end of the table. He did know how to make an effort, and he knew that she deserved it. And he would not mention to Casza that he got the sauce recipe from Evie, and the cake recipe, too.

He ended the evening with a gift of two round trip tickets to India for one month. This he thought of all on his own. He knew how deeply she missed her real home, and her family. The trip was scheduled for early February of the following year. Despite having to wait another eight months, she was elated, and truly grateful. The gift lifted her spirits to a contagious level. Dr. Ron was riding her high and embraced her in a hug. He held on to her and twirled her around at the base of the living room steps while the music guided their feet to the rhythm.

August rolled around and so did an invite to Brian's third birthday party. It gave Dr. Ron pause. Could he really be three years old already? He picked up his work phone to make a call. "I got the sweetest fire truck birthday party invite in the mail today." He was sure she could hear his smile through the phone.

"Please tell me you are coming; Eddie needs some company at these things," Evie replied.

"I am coming, but not just for Eddie…"

"I am flattered."

"Don't be, I wouldn't miss little man's birthday!"

"Ha. But we are all lucky to have you. You love Bri, you pay Eddie, and you make me laugh without even breaking a sweat. You are a wonder,"

"My life is better with you in it." And with that, Dr. Ron ended his call with Evie.

Dr. Ron

He felt the longing stir deep in his gut. He missed seeing her, he missed touching her and he missed loving her. His thoughts were interrupted by the ring of his phone. "Dr. Ron, here."

"I need to talk to you. Meet me in our spot in five minutes." Before he could protest, Ms. Maker was off the line.

Dr. Ron went from zero to sixty with anger. He was furious that this woman thought she could drop in and demand that he perform. Show was over, and today seemed like a great day for the finale. He was ready to cut this one loose once and for all. He stormed through the storage room door, confident that it would be his last time, not even bothering to do their code knock. He intended to look her right in the eye and tell her to get lost, but the scene was different, eerily different, and he was caught off guard. She was fully clothed and turned away from him, facing a wall of bed pans and medical supplies. She didn't move when he stormed in, she simply stood in silence.

"What the hell is going on?" Dr. Ron tried to sound stern. Ms. Maker turned slowly to face him. Her eyes were red, and he could tell she had been crying. She looked a bit disheveled. Her hair fell sloppily down her shoulders as if she had not bothered to even brush it. The color was gone from her face, leaving an unflattering pale olive complexion. There was no makeup accentuating her big eyes, or coloring her full lips, so her features blended quietly into her face. She was wearing jeans and a baggy t-shirt. This was most definitely not a good look. And he was scared.

"I'm pregnant."

Those words were her weapon. This was the worst-case scenario, she had a gun, and she had excellent aim. Except, Dr. Ron was sure that this would be a fatal shot one way or another. Fighting to regain focus, he shook his head in disbelief.

"Not possible. We were protected every time." Denial seemed very logical to him.

"They aren't 100%, obviously," Ms. Maker retorted.

"Fuck you they aren't! 98% when some crazy bitch isn't tampering with them!" Gloves were off.

"Look, we have been together for about four years now. Why are you so upset?"

"Listen crazy, that is not my seed. I can't help you, unless you are here looking for an abortion!" The sound of her hand across his face was so loud that he was sure it could be heard through the door.

"Listen asshole, I am sure you aren't accusing me of being a whore? That really is your title. I am not the least bit surprised that you are taking the coward's way out. But there is a fee. You give me $150,000 and I won't tell your wife or your boss about how you sexually harassed me and forced me to have relations with you."

Her tears had long since dried up and Dr. Ron could see the trap she had set long ago. "How the fuck do you expect me to trust you?"

"You can trust that if you don't cough up the money, I will have your job."

"Is that all you are good at is threats?"

She took a step closer and ran her hand over the bulge in Dr. Ron's pants. "We both know that's not all I'm good at." The side of her lip curled into a deceitful smile.

"Keep your filthy hands off of me." They stood in a very heavy silence for several minutes while Dr. Ron searched for a way out. "I will give you a third now to keep your loose lips shut. I will give you a third when the baby is born, and you have a DNA test done. Then, if the child is mine, I will give you the rest. Or, I will give you all of it when you abort." Dr. Ron was trying to keep the fear out of his voice.

"I will not abort our child." Ms. Maker had a solid game face. "And once that DNA test proves the baby is yours, I will expect child support."

"It won't. When are you due?" Sweat was prickling the back of his neck.

"End of January, early February."

"You can pick up your check in two weeks at the front desk. I do not want to hear from you or see you until you have DNA results. Not a dime more until I see the results. I hope you are happy." He turned and left the room. Dr. Ron took the stairs to the back exit of the hospital. Chest thumping and pulse racing, he was dizzy and needed some air. The sun nearly blinded him as he stepped outside into the open air. It was all too much for him to take in. He fell to his knees and began to pray.

Dr. Ron kept his distance from pretty much everyone for a few weeks. He kept conversations with Casza short and stopped his chats with Evie. He stayed at work till all hours, and even stopped going to the bar. He was so confused and overwhelmed and couldn't make sense of the situation. When he toyed with the thought of telling the people he cared about, it felt unbearable. Praying gave him moments of solitude. When he had time to examine his life, he wondered how he let it turn into such a mess. Hiding was all he could do.

One afternoon there was a knock on his office door. Hesitantly, he got up and slowly opened it.

"Hey, sorry to bother you Doc, but I wanted to see if everything was all right. You missed Brian's party over the weekend."

"Shit! Eddie, I am so sorry! I can't believe I did that! I picked up an extra shift and it just slipped my mind. What a shitty friend I am! Come in, sit and tell me how Brian is doing." Dr. Ron missed talking to his friend and wished that he could confess everything to him.

"We had a nice time. He had a blast with his friends, cake, candy, pizza, he loved it. Evie and I are going through a tough time. I would like to try therapy."

"Ed, I think that's great. You have a great family; you need to try. I admire your strength." Suddenly Dr. Ron was reminded that he might be part of the reason that his friend was struggling, and the cloud once again began to rain on him.

By the time December hit, Dr. Ron knew it was time to stop hiding. He had to talk to Casza, be honest, and accept his fate. But the conversation was brief. She said nothing, turned and shut herself in the bedroom. She couldn't look him in the eyes for weeks. It was Christmas before they were able to have a civil conversation. They were at the dinner table, which felt excessively large in that moment. It sat ten, although they had never had that many guests over at once. He was pleased that she prepared traditional Indian cuisine that night. The aromatic spices lingered in the air after they had both finished. They were quiet for most of the meal, but he could sense that she wanted to initiate conversation.

"Do you want to talk about this?" He opened the floor.

"I am deeply saddened by this news. What are you going to do if the child is yours?"

"Casza. I do not believe that this is my baby. I mean there is always a chance, I suppose. And honestly, I have no clue what I will do. I'm trying not to think about it." Dr. Ron was pleased that she was speaking to him. He could use some guidance, but knew he deserved to be told off.

"Well, see? That right there is your problem! You never think before you act. Then things get all messed up and you still don't want to think about it. You need to start taking responsibility for your actions, Radesh. This is serious. You may have fathered a child. I will look like a joke, and our marriage will be as good as over in my eyes. Think for a minute. Did you ever have unprotected sex with her?"

Without a pause Dr. Ron was able to answer. "No, never."

"Did the condom ever slip off during intercourse?"

"No, Casza."

"Did you ever use her condoms?" Casza was not backing down.

"Uh…I think a few times."

"Ok. Really think about this next question. The last few times you had intercourse did you use her condoms? Did you let her put the condom on, or take the condom off?"

This was not the line of questioning, or scolding, that he expected. He was feeling uncomfortable. "What difference does it make?"

"All the difference in the world if she was trying to get pregnant." Casza saw the truth, that this in fact could be his child. She stood and stormed away. Leaving the remains of the meal, and Dr. Ron, at the table.

Dr. Ron didn't have the energy to try to win back Casza. She shut herself in her room for the next few weeks. It was like she was a ghost. She did not pack him lunch, or make him dinner, or even say hello when they passed each other in the house. And while he was bothered by the cold atmosphere at home, he was preoccupied with the upcoming birth, and the most important woman in his life that he had not yet shared this news with.

As the New Year arrived, Dr. Ron slipped back into his drinking routine. 1992 could prove to be his most challenging year yet, and the bar was his only therapy. And since Casza didn't want anything to do with him, it got him out of the office, and kept him out of the house. When he was sufficiently trashed, he felt like things might have the slightest chance of not getting worse.

He still hadn't told Evie. They hadn't had a real conversation in several months. He listened to her messages, but her calls went unreturned. He didn't want to tell her until he was absolutely sure. Not talking was killing him but talking might be worse. He only needed to keep his cool for a few more weeks.

Tangled Vines of Good Intentions

Then it happened. The call came that a healthy baby girl was born, and Ms. Maker had already swabbed her for a DNA sample to send off to the lab. Dr. Ron hit the bar early, afraid to go home, afraid to do anything else. Eddie strolled in somewhere between his 4th and 5th round. "Glad you are here, my friend! It's been a rough week." Dr. Ron was surprised to see Eddie out, and happy for the distraction. He pulled up a stool next to him and slid the dish of peanuts toward Eddie.

"It has been a strange day, for sure," Eddie agreed, and they both lifted a glass to that. "Wanna talk about it?"

"Oh, the usual…girl trouble," Dr. Ron said as he threw back a shot of something brown.

"Yikes! That bad?" Eddie pressed.

"Well, let's just say that I am not as good at it as I used to be. I am losing focus. Getting sloppy, and that can only lead to trouble. What brings you down here, pal? Haven't seen you in a while. Fight with Green Eyes?" Dr. Ron was doing his best not to say too much.

"She wants to bring home a baby," Eddie said bluntly.

After a moment of complete numbness, Dr. Ron resisted the urge to grab Eddie and shake some sense into him. "No, fucking way." Dr. Ron didn't understand. What baby? Whose baby? Why? He could feel his stomach churning.

"Yep. I was shocked too," Eddie said.

"No, I mean, don't. Do not take that fucking baby!" Dr. Ron was loud. Panic sneaking its way into his drunken state.

"Why do you give a shit?"

Dr. Ron took a second to compose himself as best he could. His head was fuzzy, and his heart was pounding in his ears. "I just want you to be happy. Is now the best time for another kid? Haven't you and Evie been a little off lately?"

"Thank you for the concern, but I will handle my situation, and I will be happy. Go easy on the sauce my friend." With that, Eddie finished his last sip of beer and left.

Dr. Ron

Dr. Ron was alone with his fear. He sat for a few minutes before heading outside for some air. He stumbled to his car but couldn't get the key in the car door. He fumbled a bit, then dropped his keys. He reached over twice before he successfully retrieved them. On his way back up he got the spins so bad that he stumbled to the rear of his car and vomited. After several minutes of spraying the parking lot with some very expensive liquor, he made his way to the back seat. He passed out for just shy of an hour when the bartender banged on his window.

"Hey buddy, got a cab for ya. You'll freeze out here. It is January 23 for Christ's sake!"

Dr. Ron left the second payment at the desk for Ms. Maker. It was hard to make such sketchy deals at the hospital. Everything about the situation seemed wrong. This woman had manipulated him, and she still had the upper hand, even though she was no longer in his life. And this whole debacle was a painful reminder of how badly he wanted her out of his life. If this was his child, then he could let go of that hope forever.

From the moment Casza shut him out, Dr. Ron wanted her forgiveness. He spent dozens of hours praying on it over the previous few months. Praying and vowing to change his ways, vowing to quit living his selfish life, while praying that the child was not his. His future was in the balance of a simple DNA test. He submitted his, but turnaround time was seven to ten days, and the wait for the results was torture. They used an out of town lab, which could take longer, but anonymity was key.

Casza was painfully quiet at home. Dr. Ron had never noticed how her presence made his big house warm. A chill had settled that winter that couldn't be eased by wood in the fire or extra blankets. Their trip was fast approaching. Their flight was scheduled for the week after the DNA results were due back, February 9th. There was no way he could cancel the trip, no matter what the results said; but part of him wouldn't have been shocked if she asked him not to go. And as if DNA samples and trips out of the country weren't enough for him to worry about, he hadn't spoken to Evie or Eddie to see what was going on with their adoption plans. He tried to approach Eddie at work, but he was clearly avoiding him. One more crumbling relationship that tested Dr. Ron's sanity.

The flakes began to cover the parking lot of Bar on East as Dr. Ron settled his tab. He stepped out into the February chill as Evie pulled into the spot next to his car. He froze, the sight of her stopping him dead in his tracks. Without the results, he still didn't know what to tell her. He didn't know what she already knew. The urge to drop to his knees and beg for her forgiveness was overwhelming. It was all so much to contain, and an overflow was eminent.

Evie stepped out of her car and approached him. Her calm, and almost, happy demeanor struck him.

"We need to talk."

As he stared down at the face of his angel, he felt completely helpless. Yes, he was desperate to talk to her, but terrified that it would be their last. "Get in my car. I have a hunch this is a private kind of conversation." Dr. Ron opened his door for her and brought the engine of his sports car to life. "I'll see if I can warm us up a bit. Listen Evie, some crazy stuff has been going on, I haven't been myself lately," he began, but was cut off.

"Save your excuses. I have your daughter, and I want us to be a family." He watched as a smile spread wide and bright across her face.

Dr. Ron was blown away. She loved him enough to adopt his child to raise as her own. But not with her own husband? What about Brian? This was next level. Dr. Ron had nothing to say. This was beyond anything that he could have imagined, and not in a good way.

He let her joy fade in the silence between them before responding. "I have dreamed of us spending our lives together. But Evie, my dreams didn't include my wife, or your family. We owe it to them to try."

"Try what?! Don't you think I've been trying? Eddie dragged me to therapy! How demoralizing. I am not meeting his needs as a wife, and he is not meeting mine as a husband. What else can I try?" In an instant her eyes filled with tears and the smile fell from her face.

"Brian deserves to have a mom and dad," he said gently.

"He will. And your daughter will too. I have your daughter."

"Evie, that is a whole other situation that I wish you would have stayed out of. What would possess you to take a child like that? Especially when you don't have a stable marriage?"

"Don't lecture me, Dr. Ron. You are the one who got a girl pregnant and left her all alone. She is not just any child. She is your daughter, and I want her to be our daughter." Evie's tone was sharp. Her words stung.

"Look, you don't have the full story."

"I have enough. You created a child, and then walked away. I am giving you the chance to do the right thing, and to do the right thing with me! I thought that's what you wanted. I thought you wanted me!" She was dripping tears to her lap, and the sight was enough to break his heart into a million pieces.

Dr. Ron tried to embrace her, comfort her, but she pushed away. He didn't want to lose Evie, but he wasn't sure he could give her what she wanted under these circumstances. "I love you. But I can't say for sure that the two of us getting a divorce right now would be the right thing."

"I never took you for a coward." She got out and ran to her car before he could stop her. As she pulled away, she hit the gas and let the tires squeal.

He never could have imagined Evie and him raising his baby by another woman, someone as cunning as Ms. Maker. He was reeling from the confirmation; Evie did adopt the baby. The baby that cost him respect, love, and money. Adding a divorce from Casza to the list would for sure get him shunned and kicked out of his family. And no doubt that Eddie would quit on the spot when he caught wind of things. There was so much to consider. So many people who he wanted to protect. He loved Evie, but could they survive these circumstances?

The time had finally come; it was results day. In his last check he left a note for Ms. Maker to call him with the results but for no other reason. Dr. Ron spent as much time in his office as he could that day. He was in an hour earlier than usual, and intentionally cleared his schedule for the entire day. He busied himself finishing charts and cleaning up paperwork. He asked one of his nurses to bring him up lunch but could only push the salad around his plate. As he sat in his oversized leather rolling chair he looked around. He looked at his office and noticed how he didn't even have a picture on his desk, or any personal trinkets. Nothing from his family, not a single photo of his wife. His shelves were full of medical journals, his own published journals and research papers. There was a single large, stark, modern painting hanging that was similar to the pieces he had at home. But there was nothing personal there. Dr. Ron only ever wanted to have his own great love story, but in all that searching he never bothered to create any story at all. Casza was a sidekick, not a main character. And the woman who he wanted in his supporting role, who actually wanted the job, he had to reject over and over. He wanted the perfect story and never left himself open to the option that it wouldn't go as planned. So all he could do was wait, and think, and try to focus on the half-finished crossword that had been in his office for weeks. And as the clock ticked on, he began to lose hope.

The day came, and the day went. No call. Dr. Ron had no way of reaching out to Ms. Maker. So, he left the office late to head home and pack. Dr. Ron was impressed by Casza's thorough preparation. She already started bringing plants over to the neighbor's house, stopped the mail, and made several lists of things to do, and never asked him to do a thing. He knew she wasn't doing it happily though. She was giving him the cold shoulder and didn't even bother to ask about the DNA results when he got home.

The afternoon before their much-anticipated trip back home, the call came. And now that he finally had the answer, he didn't feel any better. The damage was done. The very next morning he and Casza woke at 4 a.m. to head to the airport for their long-awaited family reunion. They were going to see family who they had not seen in years, some not since their wedding. The trip was a gift, and all he wanted to do was give her a little joy to try to make up for all the joy that she gave up on the day that they were married. Dr. Ron knew that he was destroying more people than he ever intended, but maybe he had a shot at redemption with her.

He left without saying goodbye to Evie. It was a weak move. He had not had enough time to figure out what to say, how to say it, and even if it was the right thing to tell her. He needed her to know that he cared for her but wasn't sure that he could do it the way that she wanted. He needed some time to think about his next move. He really wanted to go through all the scenarios in his mind, desperately hoping there was one where she would forgive him.

As he and Casza sat in the comfort of first class, he sipped his hot black coffee and looked out the window into the blue abyss. Casza was tucked under a blanket, but Dr. Ron needed to clear the air. He was desperate to have a friend to help him through this one. After the meal cart came around, it all started to spew out, and he told Casza everything. He told her that Evie had the baby, and that she wanted them to be a family. He told her that he hesitated, and felt like a coward, or worse. He then told Casza that the results came in, and the baby was not his.

Casza took in the information, showing very little emotion. "Radesh, I would like a divorce. I would like you to divorce me, and in return I will not tell your family about what has been going on all this time. I would like you to wait until the end of the year to make it official. That way you can say that you have decided not to move and are putting your career in the U.S. over your wife in India. I will not be returning with you."

By this time, he should have seen it coming. She had to deal with more than she bargained for, much more than was fair. She was a person who he kept like a pet. "I will do that for you. I appreciate you being my friend. I am sorry if I hurt you, Casza."

"I think that she loves you as much as you love her. I think she loves you enough to start a new life, and you love her enough to not want her to give up all that she has. Perhaps you are afraid. Afraid that you will lose Eddie. Afraid that you will gain Evie plus two children. Afraid that you will have to face your past in the eyes of that little girl every day for the rest of your life. You are a coward."

And there it was. Her honesty choked him like a noose. She had nothing left to say, and neither did he.

One month later he returned to New York, alone. As he sat in the very large, very quiet house he couldn't help feeling like he'd never left. The mess that he'd left was still fresh and waiting for him to clean up. But the time away had allowed him to think. He would not break up Evie's marriage. If she wanted to leave Eddie, then she should do it. He didn't want to be part of that decision; he never wanted to be the reason they split. And back at the office there was not one missed call from her—not a note, nothing. He had really hurt her this time.

The spring turned to summer and the summer to fall. Dr. Ron stayed busy at work. He picked up his gym routine again and tried to keep out of the bar. He enjoyed the seasons in New York and took more time to appreciate the little things that surrounded him. He found a new coffee shop by his house where he often spent his Sunday mornings, and he passed a Middle Eastern market on the way there. His new life was a quiet one. As time rolled on, he made good on his promise to Casza. He sent the papers to India and was promptly looked at with disdain from his family. Even his brother stopped calling and taking his calls. This was the reaction he feared the most, but probably deserved. He was alone.

Eddie offered friendly banter when they ran into each other at the job, but nothing more. He received a holiday card from Evie that year. It was a picture of the kids dressed in matching Christmas colors. Included in the envelope were several pictures of the baby. They named her Cassandra. She was very pretty and looked a lot like Ms. Maker. But her skin was deeper, like hot cocoa. Ringlet curls framed her face. Her cheeks were pudgy, and her little body was adorably plump. She looked so different than Brian. Among the pictures was a note.

> *I would like it very much if you were ready to be a father to your daughter. I want to be a family. I want you. I did this for us. I thought that was what you dreamed of. Don't you dream of me anymore? Call me.*

He did still dream of her, and those eyes. He dreamed of happier times when they made love. But his dreams turned to nightmares when he opened his eyes. He wanted to tell Evie the truth, but he just couldn't. She loved the baby who she thought belonged to him; would she love her the same if she knew the truth? That was a risk he would not take. He wouldn't call her, he wouldn't break up her family, he couldn't tell her the truth. Dr. Ron let go of his dreams. He let go of being a part of Evie's life.

Four-and-a-half years went by. It was a hot day in July when Eddie confessed to Dr. Ron that the two were getting a divorce. At the bar, in that place, at that time, Dr. Ron knew it was time for a confession of his own.

"Eddie, I am really sorry to hear that. I always wanted you two to make it work."

"Not more than me," Eddie said, sadly.

"I have a confession…I love Evie. And we slept together when we first met." Dr. Ron didn't have time to react to the fist that was launched at his face. He was falling off the bar stool and everything was going dark.

Cassandra

The summer of 2009 was not what Cassie expected it to be. Gram had her back in an SAT prep course and working at Wegmans grocery store most nights and every weekend. Although Cassie had passed her driver's license exam, she didn't have her own vehicle, nor did she have anywhere pressing to go.

She and Jane had regular visits. They would hang out on the green downtown, or hike through local trails. A few of Jane's other friends came around, and Cassie enjoyed being part of a group again. Jane's friend Amber even invited Cassie to a party at her house one summer night. With the haunting memory of her last party experience in her mind, Cassie was hesitant. But she decided it would be more fun than working and agreed to go.

When they rolled up to the house, she was floored. This was the most people she had seen, outside of school and football games. Luckily, Cassie rode with Jane, otherwise she doubted the two would ever cross paths. Both girls had permission to sleep at Amber's, after omitting several details including the entire agenda for the evening, and especially the fact that Amber's parents were out of town.

This was by far the nicest house she had ever been to. It was huge, and new, with each room a similar shade of trendy gray. She was impressed that Amber did some party prep, as she passed a stairway roped off with caution tape and a "Do Not Enter" sign. There were trash cans in almost every room, and a Costco-sized package of paper towels on the granite kitchen counter. Amber also moved all the breakables to one room that had another "Do Not Enter" sign with some additional instruction, "If you break anything, I will break you. That's a promise". She had chips, pizza rolls, fruit roll ups, and candy accessible at every turn, with music, drinks, and Christmas lights blinking outside on the patio. This was a *party*.

As Cassie took in the scene, she found herself feeling more and more relaxed, ready to let loose and not care. For one second she didn't want to care about how many friends she had, how she didn't have a boyfriend, what college she planned to attend, how many points she needed to increase her SAT scores by, why her family had abandoned her, or if she needed to use paper or plastic. Desperate to turn off her brain, she saw ample opportunities right before her eyes. As they walked through the party looking for the hostess, Cassie made a stop in the kitchen and helped herself to a cold beer.

She fell back in step with Jane, who gave her a look of shock. "Where's mine?" Jane said. Cassie let out a laugh and grinned at Jane before taking a sip. This was going to be a good night. She could feel it.

And feel it she did. After her second beer, she could feel the liquid going down more easily, it was almost tasty. She could feel her voice straining in revolt to her screaming out each song lyric as if she were at a karaoke bar. She could feel her big smile span across her face, and she liked it. And when Jane passed her the joint, she felt fearless. She felt the burning sensation of the thick smoke as it traveled down her throat and filled her lungs. She held it as long as she could and exhaled with the cough of a seasoned pro. She felt the vibrations of the music banging and echoing off the living room walls as she danced. She felt Jane grind with her as they moved to the beat of the rhythm. She felt the strangers around her turn into friends. She felt laughter escaping from deep inside. She felt her head get lighter and lighter. She felt free.

When the morning light disturbed her beautiful dream, she felt a headache.

The first day of senior year was exciting and terrifying at the same time. She was still trying to figure out who she was and what she wanted, and this year would challenge both factors. Her first big writing assignment was to discuss personal growth since freshman year and goals for after graduation. Looking back at her high school career she couldn't help but feel a pang of sadness. Cassie was starting to see the journey as a time of turmoil and loss. She lost friends, lost support, and lost hope. Was she an improved person? Had she made growth? Did she learn any life lessons? All these questions swirled in her head, but she couldn't get them to form sentences to complete her assignment. She spent hours staring at a blank computer screen and wondering what happens next. Taking the something is better than nothing approach, she squeaked out one page with large font the night before it was due.

The journey through this school was nothing like I expected it to be. I would like to think that there was growth made, but am not sure there is a unit of measure small enough to record it. As I think about taking a look back, I can recall areas of personal growth in my home life. Second, there were some gains and losses on the growth at school. Lastly, I would like to share my future growth aspirations.

Tangled Vines of Good Intentions

When I graduated from eighth grade my mother surprised me with a trip to Florida. That was the first time I had ever seen a real beach and palm trees. That is a vision I will never forget. On that trip I learned that there are questions that even adults do not have the answers to. I learned that honesty is the best policy, and that sometimes the only way to find an answer is to ask a question. I have not spoken to my mother since we returned from the trip, but I have stopped wanting to so badly. As I have grown, I have tried to focus on what I have in my life, and not what I am missing. However, that is a daily struggle.

When I think about growth in school, I am not sure that I have completed any giant leaps. I joined the lacrosse team and loved it. I enjoyed playing, but not more than being part of a team. It felt good to win and build my skills year after year. However, there were many challenges in my high school career, and I doubt I will return to the field this spring. I lost a lot of friends, and I let people take advantage of me. I never had a boyfriend, and never found a place where I truly fit in. If there was supposed to be some duckling-to-swan transformation, I clearly missed it. I got crappy scores on my SATs multiple times, even with prep classes. There are things that I haven't figured out yet. I wonder why we weren't told that all this change and growth was a requirement, an assignment, that we would be graded and judged on?

I hope the world has a smooth journey laid out for me. There are a lot of things I want to do. I would like to find a nice, successful, man to marry. Then we can fight over what TV show to watch and if we should have pizza or Chinese food for dinner. Hopefully I will have a good career. I also want to master baking cookies and apple pie, just like my grandmother. In the future I hope to be more like my grandmother. I would like to have a big heart and sage advice for every situation.

In conclusion, I don't have all the answers right now. I don't think I have any more answers than I did as a freshman. Personally, I need to remember to focus on the positives in my life. In my senior year I hope to feel more settled in my own skin. And party more. As for the future, I am heading to community college next year. This exercise has showed me that I have always been dependent on other people. I would like my future self to find that person, place, or thing that makes me feel strong and like I belong exactly where I am. That is my life goal, to belong.

The paper did not go over well with her teacher. Cassie got a C+, and just like her freshman year, she was sure to hide it from Gram. As the holidays came near, Jane and Cassie made plans to see each other over the winter break. They had become closer than they ever were, and Cassie knew that Jane was a true friend. Gram had plans to have the family over for Thanksgiving dinner and this too made Cassie feel warm and fuzzy inside. She had a lot of aunts and uncles and cousins in the area, but she didn't see them very often. Her family was nosy like any other, and they would all grill her on her college plans, but they quit asking about her brother, father and mother long ago. Cassie thought of her mother during the holidays, but the thoughts were fleeting lately. She really wanted to find herself this year. She didn't want to be the girl that wrote that paper. She wanted to be confident and sure of herself. Although she didn't know how, she knew that she could work on it. Think less, live more.

The New Year's Eve party at Jane's house was a way for Cassie to set her goals in action as resolutions. She had more fun than she should have that night. Beer pong was her specialty, and of course Jane was her partner. The girls went undefeated. They laughed and they cried. They smoked and they drank. They tried to make the night last as long as it could, but like every party night, they woke too early the next day and couldn't remember what happened the night before. Jane and Cassie could see the destruction that was left behind from the event, so they knew it must have been a good time. They laughed and hugged each other and agreed that they would try to meet up for New Year's next year. Jane had been accepted into Savannah College of Art and Design in Atlanta, Georgia, and the girls were trying not to think about her departure. Cassie was sure that having moments like this with her best friend would make her more prepared for the future. She was stock piling the memories to use them as a shield against the pain that would come when Jane left. But Jane was not one for emotional moments and made sure to avoid the topic of her departure. Cassie let Jane set her sights on her rapidly approaching 18th birthday.

"What about Tangerine Dreams, or Turquoise Tango?" Cassie looked expectantly at Gram.

"Too fruity. How about something a little more subtle?" She suggested as she perused the walls of nail color in seemingly every shade imaginable.

"Gram, subtlety is not your strong suit. Believe me, there is not a color in this room that you couldn't pull off." Cassie was sure of that. She idolized her grandmother, knew she was unstoppable, and had never known her to be a wallflower.

"I beg to differ!" All three of them broke into laughter as Gram held up a highlighter yellow color that most definitely did not suit her.

The girls were interrupted by the beauty therapist who ushered them to a quiet back room with four oversized leather chairs and tubs of water already at the perfect temperature for their feet. The lights were dim as eucalyptus and mint danced through the air and teased their senses.

Cassie so desperately wanted to hold on to this moment. Seeing Gram relaxed and smiling was one of her favorite sights. They were having so many heavy conversations about life and the future lately, specifically about college majors, that Cassie was glad the conversation topic had shifted to what color nail polish, and if they wanted the massage therapist to touch their feet.

Cassie picked out colors for both Gram and Jane, along with an accent color for their ring fingers. The manicurists were meticulous, and Jane and Cassie were impressed at their flawless nails. Cassie was especially pleased that her Ripe Cherry Red with a gold sparkle accent was a hit with Gram. She stared with pleasure and amazement at her purple fingernails with silver white and black balloons. She could think of no better way to kick off her birthday week.

Their special day continued as the girls headed to Cassie's favorite restaurant for dinner, and dessert. The restaurant was noisy with chatter and laughter rising from the crowd. They were seated in a corner at a table with a fresh white paper table topper and two cups of assorted crayons. She secretly hoped that she would never outgrow her love of coloring, especially coloring on the table during dinner. The waitress ran down the specials for the evening, which included bone-in pork chops, full rack of beef ribs in a sweet and spicy cherry barbeque glaze, and a cedar wood smoked salmon with corn and roasted root vegetables. They all agreed on the fresh guacamole as their appetizer, and Cassie and Jane ordered virgin Pina Coladas to go with their chips. Once Gram got her virgin strawberry margarita, she raised her glass in a toast.

"Cheers to Cass, who is becoming a smart and strong-willed woman. I am often amazed at your strength and tickled by your lighthearted spirit. Not a day goes by that I don't miss my sweet little girl with the bad attitude, but I know she is still in there somewhere. I will never forget meeting you for the first time and getting lost in those beautiful chocolate eyes. I will never forget waving as the bus pulled off on your first day of school. I will never forget tip toeing into your

Tangled Vines of Good Intentions

room and doing everything in my power not to wake you as I slipped a dollar under your pillow. I am truly blessed to have you in my life, and I am excited for all the joys and successes still to come. I believe you are unstoppable my sweet baby girl. Happy birthday." With that, Jane erupted in applause and Cassie rose to her feet to embrace Gram. Gram was extra sappy that birthday. Cassie couldn't help but feel like she was a little bit sad. But there was no time to dwell on it at that moment; Cassie's pulled pork sandwich with three delightful sides appeared and she was ready to make it disappear.

"Cass, do you remember when we would catch fireflies in my backyard?"

"I do. I also remember that time we tried to squish a bunch of guts out to see if they would still glow."

"Ew! You girls are so gross!" Gram added.

"Remember how we would spend hours out in the yard talking, playing tag, or truth or dare with the besties? I feel like it was yesterday, like we were just in seventh grade and having the time of our lives." Jane was lost in thought. "Remember that time Kara, Gia, and Hill decided to make cookies from scratch?" Cassie watched Jane burst out laughing before she could get any more of the story out.

"You mean the garbage pail cookies? Besides the fact that they had eggshells in them, too much cinnamon, not enough sugar, and some were raw while others were burnt to a crisp? I though Gia's mom was gonna throw us out and never let us come back!" Cassie shook her head as if shocked by the disaster all over again. "We did have some great times together."

"You will always have the memories. And they will always bring you back to happier times," Gram added. Cassie quieted, as her thoughts drifted to the friends they once had. "How about we check out the dessert menu? Something that didn't come from Gia's kitchen perhaps?"

And as a perfect ending to her girl's day, Cassie blew out the candle on her desert and opened her present from

Jane. Cassie never took Jane for the sensitive type, but she seemed to have her moments. The birthday card was funny and included a hand-written note. It read, *You are a fearless badass and I am lucky to call you my friend.* In a small box was a charm. Beautiful script in a shiny silver oval that simply said, "Strength". Gram continued the gift giving with her own special card. Inside the card, Gram told Cassie how she was very proud of her for all the struggles that she had overcome in her short life, and she stressed that she has always and will always love her. Cassie wanted to hold on to the excitement of the moment, and for once, not care about the past…or the future.

The days before her birthday were not as carefree as she hoped. She couldn't remember a birthday with this much fuss—not even her 16th. Although she loved every bit of it, she felt like she would wake up on her 18th birthday and everything would be different, like Gram would be gone and she would be on her own. The words in Gram's card kept replaying in her head. The struggles that Gram spoke of didn't feel like struggles. That was just her life. That was the only life she knew. Was there a better life that she could have had?

The day before her birthday Cassie put in her special dinner request with Gram. Pasta with homemade meatballs, garlic bread, Cesar salad, and chocolate mayonnaise cake. She never strayed far from her usual birthday dinner request. In fact, she couldn't remember ever celebrating her birthday without Gram's chocolate mayonnaise cake. The cake was so moist and slathered in a buttery vanilla frosting only to have that be covered up in a coating of chocolate shell. Cassie hated to share this cake, and begged Gram to make it more than once a year, but she refused. This cake was now just for Cassie on her birthday, and as much as she craved the cake throughout the year, she loved so much that she had her own special cake. Gram was oddly quiet that morning but smiled in acknowledgement of her request. As Jane honked her horn outside, she gave Gram a big hug, and made a mental note to ask her what was on her mind.

The last day of being 17 years old felt magical. Although Jane was already 18, and there was absolutely nothing different about her, Cassie was hopeful that she would change. She would feel more like a member of the world, more adult-like. More ready. She walked through the hallways beaming that day. She was excited and made a promise to herself not to worry about Gram until after her birthday.

Evie

"Gert, I'm gonna have to call you back." Evie hung up before saying goodbye. Slowly she opened up the door to face a more pressing issue. "Hello."

"You weren't answering my calls, or returning them, so this was my next move. Seems a bit drastic, but I really need to talk to you," Dr. Ron said.

"I need to talk first," Evie said as she led him in from the outside and escorted him to the living room. "Please sit. I will be right back." She ran into her bedroom to put on something more than a towel. She slipped on a pair of too-short shorts and a tank top. On her way back to him, she shut the shower off, letting go of her plans to get to work on time.

"Can I get you some coffee or juice or something?" This was the first time she had ever felt awkward around him.

"No, thank you. I am okay. Look, I'm sorry to just show up, but…" Evie raised her hand in an effort to quiet him.

"I know you have something to say. I know you want to tell me your side of the story. And I will listen, but I need to start this conversation. I am going to start this conversation, and you are going to listen. You will listen until I tell you I am done. Not a word out of you. You can agree to my terms or you can leave right now and forever hold your peace."

"You start. I will listen. Got it."

"Well, let me start by reminding you that today is your daughter's 18th birthday." Evie shut him down as Dr. Ron opened his mouth at her words. "That was your only chance. One more attempt to speak and we are done here," she said, wagging her finger in his face, "It's her birthday, and her grandmother just called to tell me that she has locked herself in her bedroom because she just found out that she was adopted." Evie took a seat in an oversized chair across from Dr. Ron. Although she didn't want to read the judgment on his face the whole time she was talking, she needed the courage to get through her whole story without the temptation of touching him. She dove into her story, starting with the events leading to this day, eighteen years ago.

It was an average afternoon at the clinic, as Evie called in the next patient. "Ms. Maker? Luciana Cassia Maker?" She led a mostly unpleasant pregnant woman to an exam room and stepped out while she changed into her gown. Evie started a new chart and played with the Halloween decorations while she gave her some time to change.

"Hi, thanks for waiting, I'm Evie, and I'll be your nurse today."

"I'm freezing. Can you speed it up?" Ms. Maker snapped.

"I'm sorry. Let me get you an extra paper blanket and knock the heat up a bit. What brings you in today?" Evie began to take her vitals.

"Isn't it obvious?"

"Yes, you are here for liposuction, right?" Evie looked to Ms. Maker for a reaction. She smiled briefly, and before Evie knew it, she started to cry; and then she wept. As Ms. Maker sat drowning in her own tears, it became obvious to Evie that this was not a textbook, happy-go-lucky, mom-to-be. "I remember when I was pregnant. I was miserable. Everything hurt, and I looked like a blob. It was nothing like I thought it would be." Evie decided to offer up a personal story. "Are you married? Are you driving your husband nuts yet?"

"My boyfriend threatens to leave on a daily basis!" Ms. Maker laughed. "It is different than I expected. It is a lot more work. I was hoping it would be a breeze, but time is moving so slowly, and I keep getting bigger and bigger." Ms. Maker opened up. Evie realized she might be the first person that Ms. Maker could actually talk to about what she was feeling.

"Well your vitals are good. Do you know how far along you are?" Evie asked while continuing her preliminary exam.

"Yes, I believe I am about 6 months. Honestly, this is my first check-up. I started a new job not too long ago, and I needed to wait for coverage to kick in."

"Any family history of high blood pressure, preeclampsia, or diabetes?"

"I…I don't think so. I left home to come out here about 4 years ago. Haven't spoken to my family in years. But I am a PA and have been taking good care of myself."

"Oh! That's great. A physician's assistant here in town?" Evie asked.

"Well, I did my internship at Saint Mercy West, but then they didn't hire me. I finally found a job at a private practice, just outside of town." The disappointment in Ms. Maker's voice was evident to Evie.

"My husband works at that hospital." Evie wasn't sure why she added that fact, chit chatting about her husband was not one of her favorite things to do.

"What is his name, I am sure I know him!"

"Eddie Dodd, he's just a nurse."

"Hmm...the name is so familiar..." Ms. Maker concentrated.

"He works under Dr. Ron." Evie was kicking herself for oversharing that one.

"Yes! I know him, not sure I have ever worked with Eddie. Dr. Ron on the other hand, I think I know him too well."

"I know Dr. Ron very well. He is a good doctor." Evie was curious to know the nature of her relationship with Dr. Ron. Surely Eddie would have mentioned if there were interns on his floor that were cut?

"Let's just say that Dr. Ron is very charming, and can be a little too hands on, if you know what I mean." Evie noted Ms. Maker's soft tone, as if it were a scandalous secret shared between friends.

Evie didn't want to hear anymore. Just the thought of him touching her made her stomach churn. To her relief, the doctor interrupted their water cooler chat and Evie made a polite but hasty exit. This made the day more interesting. She never expected to meet one of his unhappy customers. Making a mental note to joke with him about it, she went about her day as usual.

Eddie had her going to therapy and attempting to work on their relationship, but the two were like ships passing in the night. They would write each other notes, and call on their breaks, but nonetheless Evie was not satisfied. The passion between them had long since died out and her desire to get it back was gone too. Each day she would get up and go through the motions of what had become her life. And each day she became more and more numb. She would often wonder where things all went wrong but could never admit that she knew the answer. She knew she wanted another man, and she knew that man wanted her to try to keep her family together.

The holidays were hectic with Brian. Evie made sure to plan some time that they could all spend together. Usually that meant that Eddie was cooking, and she was with the baby, or

Eddie was with the baby while she was at the store. Still, her little man made life exciting. When his face lit up brighter than the Christmas tree, Evie could feel her heart swell. She adored him and was equally terrified of him. There was so much at stake all the time. Her happiness or his happiness or Eddie's, it was always a choice, always a sacrifice. They reached a point where it was impossible for them all to be happy in the same moment of time.

And when Evie did want to be selfish and tap into her happy place, Dr. Ron was nowhere to be found. She felt a chill from him, which hurt and concerned her. He hadn't returned her calls in weeks, and he seemed to have checked out, again, without notice. Feeling helpless, Evie resigned to letting him have his space. If there was something wrong Eddie would be sure to tell her. All she could do was live the life that she was trapped in.

After the New Year, Evie had another visit from her new friend.

"Evie, I am so glad to see you. I was arguing with my boyfriend, and then all of a sudden I had unbearable pain." Evie could tell that Ms. Maker was genuinely panic stricken, as she latched on to her hand while being wheeled back to a room.

"Ok, sweetie. Try to take full deep breaths. It will help you to relax and calm your body down. Stress can cause lots of problems at this stage of the game." Evie tried to be gentle and kind. She felt bad for her.

"Well my house is all stress right now. Max is driving me crazy. He is such a slob. And you know, he hasn't even thought about marriage! Jerk!" Evie let her vent. "I can't see my future. I just don't know how this is all going to work out." Ms. Maker broke down.

"No one ever really knows what the future will bring. I think we have to do our best and enjoy the little moments. This little baby will give you lots of happiness." Evie was not sure how to comfort her. Her own marriage was in the toilet and she was the last person to be giving family counseling.

Tangled Vines of Good Intentions

"I don't think I can do it alone. I don't want to do it alone. I don't even want to take care of Max. OUCH!" Evie was flooded with empathy as Ms. Maker laid back on the table and cried from her physical and emotional pain.

The doctor came in and received an icy glare, which he always assumed was because he was a man. "Let's check you out and see what all the commotion is about. Try to slow your breathing. When you are relaxed the baby is relaxed," the doctor offered.

Evie stayed, mostly because Ms. Maker wouldn't let go of her hand. And after an hour, Ms. Maker got a clean check up with some normal Braxton Hick's contractions.

"Evie, will you be my nurse during labor?"

"Well, we transfer patients to Saint Mercy West to give birth." She was interrupted before she could say any more.

"What! Oh no, I can't go there!"

"It's ok, they have a great ward over there." Evie was clueless as to why she was reacting like that, or how to put her at ease.

"Promise me you'll be there."

After a little hesitation, Evie could see no way out. "If it just so happens that I am here when you come in, I will take the ride with you. Sure."

And with that Ms. Maker left, leaving Evie to wrap her head around the fact that she didn't want to deliver in the hospital where she spent the past four years. Plus, she didn't mention that her boyfriend would be by her side. This was proving to be Evie's most suspicious case. She had a growing list of questions, a doctor who wouldn't answer her calls, and a husband who she didn't want to ask. Her fingers were crossed that Ms. Maker had her baby and went on with her life without Evie.

Funny how life never goes the way you want it though. When Ms. Maker came back, with a bulging belly ready to split in two, Evie was there.

She was paged to the front desk, but Ms. Maker was wheeled to a room and on an exam table with her legs spread

Evie

before Evie even made it to the front. The triage nurse gave her a warning and sent her back as requested.

By the time Evie found Ms. Maker they were prepping her for transport. "Hi, today is a good day to have a baby!" Evie said cheerfully.

"You have to come with me. I need you! I can't do this alone, I won't!" Evie sensed her distress but was clearly missing some details.

"Where is your boyfriend? I can call him for you?"

"Fuck him. We broke up. And fuck Dr. Ron. I hate them both."

She tried to calm the shouting woman. "Ok, deep breaths. Time to go now." Evie was intrigued, and most definitely going with her. She wanted a little more information on Ms. Maker's connection to Dr. Ron. They could chat more privately in the ambulance. "Why do you hate them both?" she began to pry.

Evie let Ms. Maker hold her hand tight, consumed with pain. "He didn't want to take responsibility. Neither of them did. I didn't make this baby on my own!"

"Who is the father?" Evie was treading carefully.

"Fuck Dr. Ron. He was supposed to be a man and do the right thing! Why is it so easy for men to just walk away?!" Ms. Maker squirmed. Evie braced herself from the blow of the news as the ambulance sped through traffic.

"Does he know? I am sure he would help you."

"He called me a whore. He wanted nothing to do with me."

"Ok, relax, you can do this. You don't need him." She was reeling, and desperate to hide her reaction.

"I don't need them, I don't want them, and I don't want this baby!!" Ms. Maker had reached her pain limit. She was shouting deliriously and couldn't control her breathing. Although Evie had given birth, she had done a good job of shutting out the memory of how very painful it was.

"Ok, here we are. Won't be long now." Evie stayed close as they moved to the maternity ward of Saint Mercy West.

Tangled Vines of Good Intentions

"I want drugs. NOW!"

"We will have to check your dilation. Hang in there, Ms. Maker. You are doing great. Baby will be here soon."

"I don't want this baby. I want drugs!"

They immediately took her to the delivery room. She was 7 cm dilated, and the anesthesiologist was on his way. Evie gave her some time to settle and let the drugs kick in. She went to the waiting room to clear her head. She was so sad that a situation like this could happen to the man who she loved and believed had some decency. Why would he just shut her out? Why was he so good at shutting people out? Maybe this was her way back in. And in a moment of clarity Evie knew what she had to do. She knew that Dr. Ron was not a heartless monster. She knew he would not turn his back on his child. Even more, she knew that he loved Evie. She had a plan, and it made her joyful. A smile lit her face and she was practically giggling with excitement. Time to check the patient and meet her new child.

"How are you feeling?" Evie noted the calm in the room.

"This sucks. I just want it to be done so I can get out of here."

"I know. You are doing great. 8.5 cm dilated. You are almost there. And you can meet your little one." Evie tested the waters.

"I was serious about my decision. I never planned to have a baby on my own, and I won't do it. I do not want to see this baby, don't want to hold it, or name it. I am putting it up for adoption."

That was the end of the small talk between the ladies. Evie did her best to coach Ms. Maker through her delivery and made sure that she took the baby herself to clean her up, give her the APGAR test, put a pink knit cap on her, wrap her tight like a burrito, and walk her to the nursery. There she held her and rocked her and looked at her beautiful dark features. "Happy Birthday 1-2-3. You look like your daddy," Evie whispered. "You and I are going to start a new family. We are going to be happy. You are my only chance, special girl."

Cassandra

And when her body was all out of tears, Cassie lifted her head from her pillow and looked around dazed. Was everything around her a sham? Was her whole life a lie? She stopped herself from falling back into a weeping mess and let one last tear fall from her cheek. She turned toward the hanging mirror to assess the damage. A hot mess on the morning of her birthday. A day that had so much promise.

She sat in silence thinking. It was time to look at the situation. She just found out that the person she called Mom did not give birth to her. But this person hadn't been in her life in years, so it made a lot of sense. And her father, who cut her out of his life to start a new life, was not actually her father. Somehow this news cushioned that blow too. Cassie's mind jumped to Brian; she really truly loved her brother. She wondered if he knew. She missed Brian but couldn't really pin this mess on him. Gram on the other hand…Gram was her world, her rock. Cassie was most devastated that Gram could keep this from her, lie to her, for all these years. Why? And this news meant that Gram was not her Gram.

Cassie flopped back on the bed and curled under the covers. She looked around her room. She looked at the walls that she and Gram had painted together, a new color every summer, because that's what Cassie wanted. She looked at the beautiful painting that Gram gave to Cassie one Christmas. It was of her favorite flower. She looked at the jewelry box that Gram bought for her and thought about the many bracelets and necklaces that Gram helped to fill it with. And when she got to the window, her face muscles betrayed her as her cheeks lifted and a smile curled her lip. That was the yard that she grew up playing in. That was where she ran through the sprinkler, where she played with her friends, where she had summer barbeques, it was where she camped out with her friends, and where she and Gram made snow angels. That was her yard, at her house, and this was her room. Gram was never just her grandmother; she was her mother, father, brother, sister, and friend. She was her everything. And it was Cassie's choice if she wanted this news to take that away from her. It was Cassie's choice.

This life was now in her hands. She was a new person today. She found out that she had other people in the world that might think of her, miss her even. She had people in this world who might look like her. And now she needed to decide what she was going to do about that. She needed to decide how to find them.

Acknowledgements

This has been a long process with many sets of willing and helpful eyes. Kristine, Kerriann and Ashley, thank you for reading the very first version of this creation. I appreciate Matthew for working with me on the first round of edits and reshaping. Thank you, Karen, for helping to clean this up and encouraging me to press on. Finally, I am grateful for Russ who climbed the last summit of the mountain with me, so I could wave my book proudly.

Thank you to my design team at Jetlaunch, and to GoldenLionDesign. Denaye you gave my book a beautiful face. Thank you to Kary and AAE for creating a road map.

And to the person who always encourages me to get moving and stay motivated, TB, I thank you.

About the Author

A true hopeless romantic, Kay Lee has a passion for sharing trysts and dramas from her own creative mind. Looking to capture the heart of readers with her characters and their relatable struggles, her debut novel is sure to strike a chord.

She is a daughter, sister, aunt, niece, and friend. In addition, Kay was adopted at birth and has never located her biological parents. She was raised in a small town in New England and her childhood was nothing short of amazing. Although she is not writing about herself, she relates to, and understands fully the struggles that an adopted person can face. Being different is her normal. Looking to open people's minds and hearts about adoption, Kay presents a fresh look at a twisted situation that shatters the adoption story stereotype.

Kay self-published her childhood collection of poetry in 2017. *The Fantasy of Reality* is available on Amazon now!

CPSIA information can be obtained
at www.ICGtesting.com
Printed in the USA
LVHW081945190220
647493LV00012B/403/J